J. K. Klavans was born in N
raised in her grandmother's
studied at the University o
Bradbury, where she earned an
studies at Denver University s
wrote *God, He Was Good*
She now lives in New York City.

J. K. Klavans

God, He Was Good

Pavanne

published by Pan Books

First published in the United States of America 1984
by William Morrow and Co. Inc. under the title
It's a Little Too Late for a Love Song
First published in Great Britain 1985 by Pan Books Ltd,
Cavaye Place, London SW10 9PG
9 8 7 6 5 4 3 2
© J. K. Klavans 1984
ISBN 0 330 28602 1 (paperback)
ISBN 0 330 28614 5 (hardcover)

Portions of this work were originally published in *Granta* magazine.

Grateful acknowledgment is made for permission to reprint lines from the
following:

"I Can't Stop Loving You" by Don Gibson. © Acuff-Rose Publications,
Inc. 1958. Used by permission of the publisher. All rights reserved.

"In the Ghetto" ("The Vicious Circle") by M. Davis. © Screen Gems-
EMI Music Inc. and Elvis Presley Music Inc. 1969. All rights for the
entire world controlled by Screen Gems-EMI Music Inc., 6920 Sunset
Boulevard, Hollywood, California 90028. Used by permission. All rights
reserved.

Printed and bound in Great Britain by
Richard Clay (The Chaucer Press) Ltd, Bungay, Suffolk

TO
DANIEL JOSEPH KLAVANS
and
HELENE ABRAMSON KLAVANS,
for their love
and for their belief in their children

Many thanks also to

Malcolm Bradbury and The University of East Anglia
Angela Carter
Shirley Yarnall, Charles Larson and The American University
sity
Bill Buford and Granta magazine
The University of Denver, Department of Literature
Elaine, Geri and Raymond
Sonny, Jim and Kristina

1

"I wish I could do it to myself." Dolores stared at the bunged ceiling, sloppily smeared grout the shade of old chewing gum.

Claudine plunged.

"When you love somebody, Claud, are you constantly afraid of losing them?"

"I guess so," Claudine said, poising the needle over Dolores' lip. Dolores flinched, the needle jutting into the thick skin. "That hurt, I know," Claudine said. "Sorry. Gotta be a big girl and take it if we're ever gonna get it right."

"Gotta keep smiling all the time. Right, Claud?" Dolores tightened from the electric shock. "It all hurts like hell."

"Right, babe," Claudine laughed, taking a sip of her Tab, swallowing it quickly, and placing it carefully back on top of the black metal electric box. "Don't let go of the sponge, okay?"

"What happens if I let go?" Dolores joked. "I get electrocuted and die here on the table?"

"You'd like that, wouldn't you?" Claudine placed the needle in the fleshy smile line and pressed the button on the side of the pencil-like holder. "You ain't gonna die. You might kill everyone around you, but you ain't gonna die."

"Thanks," Dolores said, noticing the feet of her stockings were already dirty at eight twenty-five in the morning from walking around the salon barefoot. She rubbed her toes together and made a static noise; particles of dark hair that couldn't be swept from the black speckled linoleum clung to the nylon. "It's just that there ain't a whole lot to talk about before I start talking about him again, you know?" She squeezed the sponge. "Oh, God, Claud. Clauuuuuud."

The needle drew a long dark hair from under the nose area, tender, the skin red, the root in the mouth of the tweezer. "I thought only old ladies were supposed to have hairs like that."

"Well, you got 'em."

"Christ," Dolores said, pulling herself up from the table, "tomorrow we'll practice a little bit on the eyebrows. Okay?"

"You sure you can stand the pain?" Claudine asked. "Maybe we should use Sheila."

"Nah," Dolores laughed, wiping away the black mascara that had collected in the sticky white-out under her eyes. "What've I ever done in my whole life that wasn't painful anyway?"

"You got a five and a half year old who ain't all bad." Claudine straightened out the needle by running her index finger over the edge, a bit of spit on the tip of the finger. "Better shake it this morning," she said, swinging around on her stool to face the pale brunette. "You ain't got it any worse or any better than the rest of us. You remember that."

"How can I forget?" Dolores bent down and combed her bangs into her eyes with her long acrylic nails. "I'm so beautiful," she talked into the mirror. "How come no one wonderful wants to marry me?"

"I guess everyone knows you too well," Claudine answered. She watched her own face in the mirror; smooth, white with just the right touches of color. "Maybe you've given everyone the chance to look too deep. You know? Your life's an open book; you let everyone know everything." She grinned at her own reflection. "If people figure you out, you know, figure out what makes you tick, what's there for them to stick around for? The smart ones won't."

Dolores whispered with the piped-in stereo, closed her

eyes slightly, and ran a long red sculptured nail over the puffy lip area.

"Working here doesn't get you anyplace either, you know. You don't exactly have your pick of men." Claudine examined the whiteness of her hair; maybe just a little too much of a pinky glow. She'd have to tone that down with a rinse. "If only someone interesting would pop up in East Ocean View, you know. But all that lives here is Navy and low-life like ourselves," Claudine joked. "And things don't seem to change here much, do they?" she asked. "You gotta go through a lot of bad and it never gets good; it's just that one day you look back on the bad and it wasn't so bad. You can't worry about it. That's all."

"Claudine," Dolores paused while brushing beige powder over her freckled nose and chin, "we're stuck like Bettina and Cherée and Idella; we're just like those girls hanging on the walls. Just scenery," she said, continuing to cover the swelling redness of her upper lip. "But you're right, least I got Rosie."

"Not a pretty story," Claudine laughed, straightening out her tight black pants, too tight really to stand in all day but she'd manage. "But one that has to be told. Tonight at eleven." Television offered a world of trite sayings that came in handy, she thought.

"I don't know why I talk about it; I just talk about it. I guess, really, I don't care if anyone ever loves me again or not; if he did love me, that is," Dolores sighed. "You check the book?"

"Yeah. I put myself on nails today and you on the machine. I've got a lady coming in in ten minutes. Sorry, babe," Claudine grinned, one corner of her painted lips pulling tightly into a powdered cheek, "you've got to wait for a walk-in."

"Not a pretty story," Dolores offered.

"Right," Claudine said, her red lip liner standing out a little too much from her Brick lip gloss for Dolores' taste, she knew. and she tried to lick it off by inverting her lips in order to appear a closer friend. "But a four-year contract," she puckered into the mirror. "That better?"

2

"Then you'd really be in trouble, Claudine," Dolores said, shaking her head. "You can't walk out on a contract. You've got a following and Caresse won't let you."

"I guess."

They sat in a small group, in a circle, in the back room of the shop. Six of them curled into a daily nine o'clock coffee klatch. Five stood on the floor to show that La Boudoir had opened; the still lifes of Bettina and Cherée and Idella kept the pale green walls warmed with glamour.

"I mean," Dolores said, perching one shoeless foot on a box of Henna Color-Mix, "if we only knew a little bit more, you see. But Claudine and me, one of us *has* to be the girl who runs the parlor cause we don't know the first thing about electrolysis but sticking the probe in and wiggling, and then we just tweeze out the hairs. It's a matter of survival. That's all they taught us in school."

"It's good on white people," Claudine argued, "but you gotta know more to work on blacks. It's different hair. You can't tweeze it out, and the roots are thicker. They made me learn how to do it in beauty college, but every time you pull, the hair root just stays and the hair breaks off. Then they get an ingrown in a couple of weeks and come back complaining. And the way the neighborhood is going black," she shook her head. "The machine works us; we don't work it. It's just another gimmick. You know? And I'm not about to deal with that kind of work on black people. Uh uh," she raised her bleached eyebrows and rolled her pinky tongue into the back of her throat.

"Well, it's different hair for us too," Jude said, taking a drag off her Vantage and flicking the ash on the floor. "Isn't it too early to be eating that?"

"I'm on a diet," Sheila answered between sips of instant chicken broth made from hot tap water and a bouillon cube, her skinny hands gripping the sides of a Styrofoam cup. "Any sin in being on a diet?"

"Well, I don't care," Claudine stood, one hand on a well-rounded hip. "It isn't fair that Caresse makes you sign a four-year agreement before they'll take you into their training program and then they hold you to it no matter what happens to the goddamned shop. I mean, there's money in the nails, but it just ain't enough. And the worst part is that you can't leave, but they can knock you off the payroll any time your following falls apart. The Vocational Center should've warned us before we enrolled in the class too, Dolores," she pointed a long fingernail. "Five years outa high school and you never even done anything else. Least I've had some retail experience."

"And if your following falls apart and they fire you, you'll never get a job in acrylic nails or electrolysis again. Anywhere," Dolores added. "Only hope *is* to get a managering position. Then you're more in control."

"You two shoulda become regular beauticians," Sheila said, "then you wouldn't have to worry about nothing."

"Welllll," Dolores smiled, "the worst thing about it is that I thought I was getting something *really special*, you know? I'm just not qualified *enough*. That's how Caresse keeps us in our place. The Vocational Center doesn't tell you that either when you take the course. They make beauty school sound like God's gift to women and, you know, you just figure that everyone wants to be beautiful and that it'll be fun. How're you sposed to know what you're getting into?" Sheila sipped her soup. "You see," Dolores pointed into the middle of the circle, "beauty costs just like everything else, only there ain't no price tag cause there ain't no such

11

thing. So what if they get ingrowns on their thighs? So then they come back and we take the ingrown out and we charge more. That's all. This is a business."

"Well," Claudine answered while pouring herself a cup of coffee, "I can't see myself going back to work in Himerstein's. I mean, Christ. Those women go in that department store and tear everything off the racks and look down their noses at you, and you've gotta smile and be sweet and hang everything back up for them as if they were little children. Hell, I got two kids of my own to take care of and, you know, they're really more than my share." Claudine's hand disappeared into her white teasing. "I mean I'd lay down and die right here if I had to go back to Himerstein's and deal with department store politics again. I've had it up to here with that." She made a cutting motion against her neck carefully, so as not to rub her makeup. "And besides," she said, "there's always someone giving you orders, and like I told that bitch the day I quit, I don't take no orders from no baby-lady. Hell, she was working in the goddamned baby department in plastic underpanties, and I was supposed to ring out the register on demand," she shook her head. "You know, I still have nightmares about that goddamned baby-lady," she laughed. "I see her standing there with those pale lips and that mousy brown hair, holding those underpanties in her fist and her lips are a-quiverin' and she's saying, 'I'm not going to fire you, Mrs. Downings, but you can go to the office and terminate yourself if you don't ring out that register *now*.' And I'm so stubborn," Claudine gritted her teeth, two perfect rows of yellowed ivory, like old church organ keys, "that I still go walking into that office and tell them off, just go and slam that store locker key on the desk and get myself out of that job, even though I really need it to support the kids and all."

Cigarette smoke escaped from Jude's oversize nostrils. "You see, you two have the advantage," she directed

12

toward Claudine and Dolores. "You two don't have to slip your hands into pomade. You're considered skilled specialists."

"I don't think they even use pomade anymore," one of the girls said.

"We'll see when they start coming in," Jude answered. "And they will. When one walks in that front door, they'll all start to follow. You ever put your hands in that wiry mesh before?" she asked Sheila. "Well, let me clue you, it ain't so hot."

"You got a bad attitude," Sheila said, balancing her empty Styrofoam cup on her lap. "You don't have to hate them. They're just people and they ain't never done anything to you."

"They don't have to do anything to me for me not to like them. Besides," Jude's large nostrils opened wide as she exhaled thick tunnels of smoke, "I don't hate them. I just don't want to stick my hands in pomade, feels like chicken wire coming up to get you. Can you blame me?" She looked around for an answer.

"I can't blame you," Claudine said, "but the neighborhood's going black." She shrugged her shoulders. "Sooner or later we're gonna have to open up and go black too. But maybe," she schemed, "it'll be later. Like, like after we're all dead and gone," she giggled.

"You can't keep them from coming in," Dolores said, "and you wouldn't want to. You work on a percentage, remember? If La Boudoir goes broke, we all go broke."

"Yeah," Jude said, watching Sheila break the sides of her cup between her bony kneecaps. "Virginia freed her slaves," she said, "now how's about keeping her niggers under lock and key?"

"Oh, that's great. That's just great." Dolores bit down on her lower lip. "I'm worried about saving your job for you and all you can think about is how much you can't stand nigger hair. That's just great."

"Who put you in charge?" Jude laughed and looked askance at Claudine. "No one asked you to take over, did they? I didn't see you get no phone call from Caresse."

"Things have gotta change, Jude," Dolores answered. "If we're gonna go on, things have just gotta change." She unwrapped a package of Peanut Butter Nabs she'd been saving in her pants pocket and stuck a whole one in her mouth, the orange of the cracker melting and sticking to the roof of her mouth, making it hard to speak. "Things just can't go on like this," she said, trying hard to swallow. "If we want to stay in business, we gotta act fast."

3

"**H**ow come, after all this time, Claud, I still wake up afraid that I'm going to lose him? I mean, he's already gone. What am I so afraid of?" The medicinal smell of the glassed-in black and red combs in alcohol wafted up into Dolores' face. "God, I hate doing this shit work."

"You want a love song," Claudine answered, "just like you sing. All you want is a little ole love song."

"It's a little too late for a love song, don't you think?" Dolores rinsed off a comb under the tap and placed it in the alcohol.

"I think so, but you must not think so or you wouldn't walk around daydreaming about something that happened so long ago, would you?"

"Guess not." A hard-bristled brush swished its way through the solution. "But I just can't help it. I mean . . ."

"Sure, babe, I know what you mean. Remember who you're talking to." Claudine wiped down the silver top of the brush holder. "It's not easy to go home and look at a kid and not remember where it came from. I mean, it came

14

from your gut. You gotta remember; the kid won't let you forget."

"I know," Dolores said, thinking about the picture of Rosemary she had taken last Easter. She'd taped it on the mirror above her manicurist table, right below the salon photo of the girl labeled Cherée. Rosemary wore a tiny blue dress, clean white patent leather shoes, and was sitting on the stump of a tree with her delicate hands clasped far down in the center of her lap; her long honey-colored hair was clipped up high in a ponytail and tied with a navy silk ribbon cut in sailor points. Cherée wore shining black silk, one shoulder exposed as she leaned into the camera, frosted blonde hair falling over the right eye; she only smiled slightly, her pink lips almost 3-D, alive with a silvery glitter. "I know," Dolores said, "but sometimes where they came from don't seem exactly real."

4

"**W**hat's that smell?" Dolores asked the shaking girl.

"I threw up."

"What do you mean you threw up, Sheila? Are you sick?" Dolores pulled the limp frosted hair out of the girl's hollowed face full of freckles.

"I don't know," Sheila answered. The bottom of her jawline began to shimmy, tears catching in soft hairs and lines about her mouth. "I don't know. Maybe I have the flu or something, but I don't think so. I don't know."

"Come on, you can tell me. Tell me."

"What's wrong?" Claudine asked, walking past them in the back room.

"I don't know," Sheila whined.

15

"Sheila thinks she's pregnant," Dolores said, pulling her lips over her sharp teeth and tightening her throat muscles.

"I don't know," Sheila said, wiping her face with the back of her dried-out hand.

"Is that what the smell is?" Claudine asked. "She puked?"

"Well, don't worry about it," Dolores said, continuing to pull the hair out of Sheila's eyes and place it in back of her ears, "you can still work pregnant. Don't worry. There'll be enough business."

"But I don't want it," Sheila cried. "I don't want it. I don't wanta get fat. I don't wanta get married fat."

"But you *do* want to get married?" Claudine asked. The smell was growing stronger and more revolting. She wondered why Sheila hadn't the decency to spray the pine-scented deodorant cleaner.

"I don't wanta get married fat," Sheila argued, the tears dripping along the hollows of sculptured bones molded out of something like dirtied white putty.

Dolores shrugged. "I don't see what your problem is, Sheila." She looked toward Claudine who stood wincing at the odor. "Have you told Jeff yet?"

"No," the girl cried.

"Well," Dolores said, "if you want to marry Jeff and have a baby, then tell him about it. And if you don't want to marry Jeff, then forget about it and either don't tell him you're having a kid and just have it and shut up about it, or go down to the bank building, on the third floor, with some pee in a bottle and they'll tell you if it's really there and when you can get rid of it."

"Where would I get the money?" Sheila whispered. "I haven't got any money." She cried softly. "I'll have to wait till next month and then it might be too late. You know?" She looked up at Dolores with shoulders that shook loose in their sockets like an old glass doll held together by thin wire clips.

16

"Really, Sheila," Dolores looked toward Claudine who was moving closer, "I'd lend you the money, but I just don't have it either."

"Neither do I," Claudine said, shaking her cotton-candy hair. "We've got kids to support and all."

"He won't let me do it," Sheila said, her eyelashes meeting in points from her tears. "I know it. He won't let me do it. Policemen. They take the morals of the world on their shoulders, you know. He won't let me do it. He'll make me walk down that aisle fat." She cried, wiping her eyes with the back of her bony hands roughened by cheap soaps, shampoos. "And I'll be so embarrassed walking down that aisle fat."

"But if you're going to marry him anyway, Sheila," Claudine said, "then it's just silly to be embarrassed. Besides, as thin as you are you're not gonna show for a while."

"Uh uh," Sheila argued. "I'll be a horrible person either way. Any way, anything I do, I'm going to be a horrible person. But I'd rather sin out of church than stand there and pretend to be blessed by God with a sin right here in my belly." She slapped her hands hard against the hip bones that protruded from her red polyester pants.

"If you need us, let us know," Claudine said, carefully placing her eloquent nails on the girl's shoulder. "We can't help you moneywise, but anything else."

Sheila looked at the flecked tile floor beneath her feet. Her shoes, dark, low heeled lace-ups, looked old and matronly. She wished she were the type who could wear high heels all day and never feel the pain. She wished she were sophisticated like Dolores, or tough like Jude. She wished she were really blonde, not dirty blonde frosted, but real white blonde like Claudine, fresh and seductive with clean white breasts that bubbled from behind cool-looking fabrics. And she couldn't wear the sculptured nails herself; they'd break off because her hands were always in soapy detergent washing other women's heads. And she couldn't walk down the aisle in Saint Pious Catholic Church fat. She just couldn't do it. And she'd seen others she'd a-rather have than Jeff anyway. Jeff. Big deal. A cop with a round belly who swaggered his stuff. Big deal. And he always thought he was so right about everything.

"Isn't she something out of another century?" Dolores smiled; the smile was a kindly smile, the smile of a nurse having administered serum to an already infected child. "You'd think she'd have an inkling of how to take care of herself, wouldn't you?"

"I guess so," Claudine said as she leaned against the bowl, screwed up her face, and flushed.

5

  Claudine diluted shampoos into plastic bottles, the pink liquid meshing inconsistently with water. "Okay. But where is he now?" she asked, shaking the bottle with force. "You know, it was a great wonderful-guy-while-you're-pregnant-routine while it lasted. Not a pretty story."

"Yeah, well, he was really great when he was there. I can't blame him for leaving either," Dolores answered.

"Bull, Dolores. It must have been hell having Rosie alone."

"Yeah, but, while he was there it was wonderful." Dolores studied the Mr. Coffee Maker grains. So dark, so brown, like a handful of seeds just waiting to be planted. She threw them in the garbage, the white paper liner landing on top of the plastic mixer used for permanent waving. "One morning I got up, you know, and I was taking a real long hot soaky bath while he was shaving. I'd just relax and watch him slide the razor over his face. God . . . he was a novice even at that. He'd always nick . . . well," Dolores counted ten Maxwell Houses into the clean paper filter, "I stood up too quickly I guess and I almost fainted. I mean, I just blacked out. I don't know. It was probably the heat or something together with being pregnant. But we didn't know I was pregnant then. I'd just get a sick feeling in my stomach, you know, and I'd walk around feeling like my jeans were riding up my crotch."

"God, hon, I've got that feeling now," Claudine shook. "Too many chocolate cookies before I go to bed. I can't help it. I can't stop." The third plastic container was full and frothing pink.

"Yeah, well, I stood up too fast to dry off and I lost my balance and collapsed half in and half out of the tub. Thank God he was standing right there to catch me. Thank God. God," Dolores smiled, "he was good."

"Uh huh. Sure sounds like it." Claudine finished the fourth container and started screwing on the spurt tops.

"Well, he *was*, Claud. He made me sit on the toilet with my head between my knees and I threw up all over the goddamned place and I didn't even have to clean it up. He did all that for me. I didn't have to touch the stuff. He put me to bed and he cleaned it up."

"I guess I know sort of what you mean," Claudine said as she screwed in the last top. "Like when I was pregnant with Johnnie, I remember Mike and I together. I'd get a sick feeling in the bottom of my stomach like I was gonna throw up whenever he'd start to get up to go to work down at the base, down at Dam Neck. You know, I just had this funny feeling like he was gonna desert me and go back to his ship forever. Well, I was right in a way."

"Yeah, and it was kind of a nice feeling when you think about it now, wasn't it?"

"Dolores," Claudine grinned from the side of her mouth, wiping the necks of the bottles down with a ragged pink and white Handy-Towel, "I'm not crazy, babe. I know it. That was a bad feeling then, and now, when I think of Mike Downings running around out there having himself a good ole time, it's an even worse feeling."

Dolores noticed as Claudine bent to place three of the bottles on the lower shelf that Claud's age was becoming apparent even in the dim light. Twenty-nine was starting to show at the edges of her mouth. There were lines that looked as if they had been cut deep with a metal cookie cutter.

"But you are right in one way," Claudine said, placing her hand in her white teasing. "Sometimes, even now with A. Jacks there, when I'm not sleeping or anything, but just real peaceful and calm in my own bed, I think of Mike and I get that sick feeling I used to get when I was having one of the babies. And it's then, it's then, my friend, that I'm glad I'm not married anymore. No one can play tricks with my emotions anymore. Not anymore. And I can't do it to *myself* anymore. The game is all different once you take that big fall. I'm just not strong enough to play heavy-weight. Not anymore, thank God."

Dolores watched the coffee drip into the pot, just drip, and she felt sorry for Claudine. "You can't tell me you don't want him back. You can't tell me that if Mike Downings walked through that front door right now you wouldn't hold on forever."

"No. I can't tell you that. Specially cause it was all my fault that he left. But I *can* tell you I'm sane now and I like the feeling."

"That's too much of a price to pay for sanity," Dolores said, watching the pot drip. "I think I'd rather dream and be crazy."

"I wish you *were* crazy, babe," Claudine said. "Then they could lock you away and make it all a lot easier for you. As it is," she said, rubbing pink cream into her hands, "don't feel like you've cornered the market in craziness."

6

"He's gonna die," Claudine said. "I'm gonna write a book."

The customer placed three gold rings, one carefully after the other, into a cup full of cleaning solution and rolled up the sleeves of her dark red blouse, silk.

"Pretty," Claudine said sweetly, smiling up from under blue-tinted lashes.

"Thanks," the woman said, looking away, looking away anywhere, while Claudine placed each of her hands lightly onto a clean white towel. "This the little boy?" the woman asked. She couldn't help it. The photograph was epoxied at eye level to the white wall above Claudine's table.

"Uh huh." Claudine chewed her gum with a sucking motion as if trying to extract all the flavor before having to toss it into the bin. She couldn't stand the smell of polish remover to get in her mouth. "He's ten and she's eight, but he only comes up to her hip. Can you believe it? I'm gonna write a book about it. He was supposed to be dead seven years ago." The customer groaned in uncomfortable sympathy, a patient on an operating table. Claudine felt the woman's fingers tighten. Good. "Loosen up," Claudine tugged at the hand, strong healthy bones used to pare apples, slice and dice. "Yeah, can you believe it? Seven years ago and still livin'." The woman smiled and studied Claudine intensely as she swabbed the pinky and removed the leftover Honeysuckle polish. "Yeah, but it's not so bad." The hand was placed limply in a shallow dish of green soapy liquid. Claudine worked on removing the polish from her customer's other hand. "Bad break here," she said. "How'd you do this?"

"Car door," the woman spoke. Words pulled from a silhouette.

"Yeah, like I said," Claudine continued, taking the first hand out of the warm soap and laying it flat on the white towel, folding the other hand into the same dish, "I got to meet John Glenn, you know. You know, the astronaut? He came into the children's hospital one day and waltzed right into Johnnie's room. Yeah," Claudine shook her head in disbelief, "he came right into the room and Johnnie was just laying there like he does and you know, John Glenn, the astronaut, starts to talk to me about Johnnie's ailment and I told him, well, I told him just what I told you . . . that I was gonna write a book about it, specially cause I had met *him*, John Glenn the astronaut, and he was really flattered." Claudine clipped back the acrylic with a metal utensil, the false nails getting lost in heaps of hair across the floor.

"Do you know what's wrong with him?" the customer asked, watching the work closely.

"Nope." Claudine mixed the pink solution in the white powder with a thin paint brush, then tapped it against the side of the plastic carrying box. She looked up into her customer's face and let out a long breath, "Nobody knows. He's just been dying since he was born, you know." She continued painting her lady's hand with acrylic, smooth, white, like dressing paper dolls. "If I'd only realized he was gonna be a dwarf I'd a-never had Michelle, that's all. I mean, he acted real normal when he was a baby and everything," she shrugged.

"That's funny, isn't it?" the woman asked.

"Nope. Don't think so," Claudine said, sucking in both lips. "The doctors say he's smart enough. He just doesn't grow and he can't get used to his body or something. He's a freak, that's all. He's reallllll fucked up."

The metal tips of the shapings cut into the woman's fingers under her own nails. The acrylic, heavy in weight, clung around the bones of the fingertips.

"I'm sorry," the woman said. "I didn't realize things were so bad. I mean, I'd heard your little boy was sick, but I didn't know . . ."

"Oh, that's okay," Claudine smiled. "I just gotta wait until he dies to write the book. Till then we're just gonna have to be poor. I'm hoping they'll make a movie out of it too, you know?"

7

Dolores kept her face turned into the recording list, the titles typed in red ink under the rows of country western, pop, rock'-n'-roll. She placed her palms against the glass trying to feel the vibrations from a remake of an old Frankie Valli single. It just wasn't there anymore. She remembered a time when it had been there for the two of them; she remembered a night when she had watched Phil over a wooden picnic table they had hauled into their East Ocean View living room, and that song had been on the radio. The original. That night had been magic. She tried not to believe in magic anymore.

Dolores let her hands slide across the glass, sweat marks smearing titles, her hips grinding into the metal of the machine. She felt her body moving in small circles to the beat. She couldn't help herself. She moved. Her lips mouthed the words.

"Dance for us, lady," three young sailors behind her yelled. She tried not to look at them, at the crowd. The Blue Garter was always crowded on a Sunday night. The muscle men, the big brawny sailors, the little pipsqueaks who thought they could get ass just because they were shipping off or stuck in port; they always had some sympathetic excuse and, of course, they always wanted to get married afterwards. Only the very young girls fell for it. Usually the young were the ones with the diseases anyway. Only the very young fell. Love substituted for infection. Magic would make the ugliness go away. They were too stupid or scared to know. But Dolores, at twenty-three, wasn't very young anymore.

Dolores looked across the bar, close with smoke and Brut aftershave. The smell was unnerving, the men so clean and shaven looking . . . so young, most of them. She spotted a table where Claud stood talking to a serviceman, not much over eighteen, she thought. He didn't even have a beard to shave yet, probably not a hair on his chest. His Adam's apple stuck out, jutted forward almost into Claudine's large breasts. Claud must be crazy, Dolores thought. Sailors pull in and they pull out, and most of them don't even know in which direction they're headed.

"DANCE." "DANCE." "DANCE." "DANCE." "DANCE." "DANCE."

Sheila's Jeff, out of uniform, walked over and pulled the plug to the jukebox. From Thursday to Monday he worked at The Blue Garter undercover, as if everyone didn't already know him.

The lights flashed off, a Dolly Parton recording of "It's All Wrong But It's All Right" slurred into the rampage for Loretta Sweate and her daughter Louise "Little Feet" Sweate. Loretta ran out first, her spare rolls bouncing. In her right hand she held the lighted battery-operated Olympic torch; her pancaked face glittered as the topless show sold. She swished her large abdomen and prickly thighs covered by a short Danskin skirt, her name a low murmur in the audience. "DANCE." "DANCE." "DANCE." "DANCE." The crowd grew louder and louder, monsters in a movie theater.

Dolores stood against the darkened jukebox, still warm even without color or music, and watched. Jeff, in the background, helped Rod, the manager, bring bright pink and green lights out and attach them to black metal hooks above the bar, the smoke of cigarettes floating. The torch was placed in its special holder at the rear of the circular dance floor, the blue flame flickering into redness in the back wall mirrors. Like pictures in a slide show the people continued to move, colors turned, noises roared onward through the ticking, beating, little timed heart bumps of the dancers. And Dolores watched the young sailor rest his head against Claud's polyestered rear while Claud's boyfriend, A. Jacks, watched all the while. And there was desire. Magic. Loretta Sweate danced to "Bad Girls," loud thumping noises on the wooden floorboards that made the whole scene almost a comedy. The thumping continued, men stomping their feet in perfect rhythm, perfect timing, and the music was turned up louder, and then louder again as Little Feet appeared, her chest flat as a paddle racket, rubbing herself against her mother's large hanging boobs. They stood together, mother and daughter, naked from the waist up, accepting applause.

Dolores watched Claud's A. Jacks clumsily shake hands with the young sailor; A. Jacks' large hands grabbing hold of his opponent's fragile arm; A. Jacks' large form bending toward the boy in a half effort to spar and feint. Loretta and Louise Sweate bent toward hard-backed chairs and challenged each other to lifting dances. Of course, Little Feet didn't have the flab needed. Still, some sailor would take her cunt home and make it worth something. It had only been last year that Loretta had held a private cherry-popping party for Little Feet. Admission had been nine dollars at the door.

8

On Mondays Dolores dressed Rosemary and drove down Ocean View Avenue, along the coastline of the Chesapeake Bay, and turned to the inland body of water off Willoughby Spit. The Spit was only a small stretch of sand, long yet very narrow, and there were always ships anchored close enough to shore so that Dolores could feel safe in their proximity, and in their distance.

As the years had passed, it seemed to take longer and longer to reach the Spit. Dolores' heart pounded excitedly as she looked at the spot. Rosemary, in a yellow gingham dress, sat very still, used to these trips.

"Where again, Mommy?" Rosemary asked, looking out the windshield of the Mustang onto the dark sand. There was no sun. There were no waves rushing onto the beach. Maybe it had all been a dream. Nothing was as Dolores remembered. It had been too long ago. The only proof was her little girl, the child who sat beside her and needed her. But sometimes even the child seemed a figment of her imagination.

"There," she pointed. Rosemary lifted her chin. It was true. The child moved. She was real and honey-colored, with an oversize nose for a five and a half year old, freckled and dappled with large spots over her shoulders. Dolores could look at her and believe in him. It was her love story and, god, she loved the melodramatics of it. All that gushing sincerity when it came to love, she had found the key to keeping it with her even after its death. All the lyrics she had memorized, had sung by the hour while working to make other women beautiful, those lyrics that had helped her pass the time and feel the half-witted emotion she reveled in, they were still there in Rosemary. She turned

26

on the radio and looked at the strip of beach again, backed the car out of the empty gravel parking lot, and drove onto the highway. *"It's a little too late for a love song,"* the radio whirred, *"though I'm lookin' all over the world. It's a little too late for a love song, for this kind of girl."*

9

Claudine sat at her mirrored dressing table carefully applying color-stick to the black circles under her eyes. Then, with her index finger, she drew the blue-whiteness up into the corner of her eye and across the yellowness of her lid. Johnnie stood fingering the edge of a lace hanky anchored by a box of dried rose leaves she kept next to her perfumes. He watched her in the mirror, fascinated, his entire body only reaching Claudine's slender elbow, greased and smelling sweet. A. Jacks sat on the bed, reflected in the mirror, his hands clasped between strong ample thighs, girlishly small hips, fascinated, too.

"Do you have to watch?" Claudine asked A. Jacks. "Isn't there anything else you can do?"

"There *is* nothing else to do but watch," he answered, stretching his thick horse-like neck from shoulder to shoulder, his yellow hair sticking to red pimpled skin.

Claudine ran a small plastic spatula in circles through a bottle of heavy moisturizing cream and placed five dots on her face: each cheek, the nose, the chin, the forehead, and a dot on her neck to keep it from growing old and wrinkled. "Fifty-four nails today," she nodded to A. Jacks in the mirror, "fifty-four. If I do fifty-four nails every day, I'll be doing over three hundred a week."

"Will you get a raise then?" A. Jacks ran large hands through thick curls hanging to his shoulders. He had the arms of a wrestler, wide, large boned, almost too big for

Claudine to think about holding between her own hands. Sometimes, with Mike Downings, it had made her mouth water just to look at his wrists, slender, like he could move gracefully and be cultured like the men on TV who played violins and wore tuxedoes. That was what she wanted. No A. Jacks. A. Jacks was just big . . . a big man who could smother her and her kids and keep them all warm at night.

Johnnie gurgled. "Deeeayeee." No one knew what it meant. "Deeeayeee." Claudine just hoped that he wouldn't follow anyone to the garage down the street and drink gasoline like he'd done when he was five. That guy Frank should have watched him. God, she had been a fool. That goddamned Frank had probably given it to the kid. Claudine spread a brownish tone into the palm of her hand. Had to make it seem like a real suntan. Of course, she didn't really put it past A. Jacks not to give an innocent kid gasoline either, except that A. Jacks was smarter than that, she knew, and A. Jacks wouldn't be able to stand the guilt.

"More tips," she sighed. "Under this contract it's the only way to make a buck. Dolores ain't pulling in anything. She's gone power crazy lately."

"MOM," her name was called from the living room. "MOM, come look at the guys on TV . . . MOM, come quick! MOM!"

"I can't, Michelle," Claudine yelled. "Dolores is bringing Rosie over here at eight-thirty and I'm still putting on my makeup. Call Johnnie for me, will ya?"

Claudine looked straight into the boy's face, his reddish tint making her grimace, the powder in her worry lines caking into permanent features of the evening. "Go to Michelle," she spoke softly. "Michelle wants you."

He looked as if he understood, as if he took it as an insult that she didn't want to allow him to see her go any farther with her makeup. A clown. She watched his arms and legs, the size of doll's appendages, toddle the midsection of a normal-size boy out of her bedroom. He hated to leave the smell of fragrances behind on her vanity table. His nose was perfect, she thought, placed in the center of a peanut face, small and raw with slats of coal blue eyes peering out from underneath slack folds of skin.

"Here, Johnnie," Michelle patted the floor, never taking her eyes away from the set. She had given up looking at him. The television rock group danced in red and black costumes with their faces painted purple. Johnnie toppled uncomfortably, dutifully at her side, his soft skull striking the brown floorboards with a heavy thud. Michelle placed her hand on his underbelly and let it rest there until he calmed.

"It's that funny rock-'n'-roll group from England she likes to watch. You know," Claudine explained to A. Jacks, "Pucker or Kiss or something like that. Don't touch me while I'm putting this on. Okay, A. Jacks? Okay, babe? It makes me nervous. Okay? Allen Jacks, will you behave yourself?" she giggled.

10

Rosemary, stretched upon the dark floor, listened to the electric window fan pour music into the room. Brrrrrrrrrrrr, she played with small brown fingers against her lips. Her hair spread itself in soft webs against the floorboards, cold from the night and even colder now that she had switched on the window fan. Dolores had insisted that the window fan be put away during the winter months, that the window be closed so the heat could be kept inside; but Rosemary had complained, screaming and kicking and biting her mother's hand whenever she reached for the heavy unit. She liked the cold blast of air in the mornings and by threatening to hurt herself on purpose while Dolores was at work, she made Dolores decide to let the fan stay. Once, Rosie had taken a round apple slicer with section cutters and pressed it into her small thigh, making an awful cut that, luckily, had healed. The window fan stayed.

Light from above the fan scattered in all directions, fell in colored bands around Rosemary's body.

The night lingered during the early tickings of the morning, and it was only after Dolores got up and boiled water for her instant coffee that Rosemary turned on the TV to watch Touché Turtle. It was then that Rosemary would begin to sweat under her arms and her hair would stick to places around her face, that she would find it hard to breathe, each minute one tick more frightening than the last. And she would watch the picture wall clock move: the black pieces of wire slowly circle the two children holding hands in a wheat field. Soon she would be dressed and shuffled off to spend the day in Claudine's apartment, and A. Jacks would watch her and Johnnie until Michelle came home from school at two-twenty. And Rosemary could tell by the progression of the cartoons how much time she had left before Dolores had to go to work. Brrrrrrrrrrrrrrr. The floor was growing warmer beneath her as the air grew colder above. She watched the fan and let the drool slide from the corner of her mouth. Time was black wire clipping in circles; soon it would all start again. Brrrrrrrrrrrrrrrrrrrr. Dolores' clock would go off any second.

Face up against the fan, eyelashes splitting into a hundred fragments, she whispered, "Keep her asleep, God. I'll pay you anything, but just keep her asleep." The voice warbled as if the machine were trying to spit it out. "Asleep, God. Keep her asleep."

She stretched her hands to the open window and allowed herself to finger the thin Virginia dust that had gathered on the top and sides of the fan case. Then she ran her hands across her face, smelled the dust, felt it in the back of her throat. Brrrrrrrrrrrrrrrr.

Dolores rolled over and punched the top of her clock, the alarm quickly breaking a peaceful slumber. Her body was cold, the sheets damp in the outline of the space where she slept. "NOOOOOOOOOOOOOOOOOO," she heard Rosie scream from the living room. "NOOOOOOOOOOOOOOOOO, God. NOOOOOOOOOOOOOOOOO."

Dolores felt her stomach tighten, her intestines twist as she bolted toward the scream. "ROSIE," Dolores yelled, her hand touching the side of a cereal box, feeling revulsion at the face of Tony Tiger. *"ROSEMARY."*

The child's lips were close up to the fan, almost touching the cool metal grate, her tears dried in lines pushing back into her soft hairline.

"What's happened?" Dolores asked, standing in front of the child, her hands tightly gripping the small rounded shoulders.

Rosemary clung to the discolored nylon of her mother's gown, the grayish pink caught between her fists and Dolores' back. Dolores looked up to count the time left on the kitchen picture clock. "What's happened, Rosie? I was scared something had happened to you." Dolores demanded an answer.

"Mommy, don't go to work today," Rosemary pleaded. She held on to her mother's gown, hung against her. "Don't leave me. Don't go to work," she pleaded. "Just today, don't go to work. Just today, please."

"Rosemary, stop it," Dolores scolded. She could hardly focus, her eyes were so puffy in the morning. "And don't you ever do this again. You've scared me half out of my wits."

And it was early February cold. Two children stood in a wheat field freezing.

11

The girls giggled, Claud's huge chest shaking within her brassiere. At The Blue Garter there was a chance for something to happen, something to move. Sheila stared at a young, closely clipped boy leaning on one elbow at a table near the men's room. He caught her glimpse and stared back, his eyes widening to a dark black dot.

"Where's Jude tonight?" Dolores asked.

"Stuck in front of the tube. Where else?" Sheila answered.

Dolores followed Sheila's stare. "How old do you think he is?"

"He's gotta be twenty-one to be in here, don't he?" Sheila answered.

"Claudine brought A. Jacks in and he ain't twenty-one, and I don't see a ABC man in here tonight, so I would guess they ain't checking," Dolores said, taking a sip of her beer. "Besides, when you're in the service you can wheedle your way in whenever you want. Maybe he's a friend of a friend of Rod's. Or maybe he's got a good fake I.D. . . . Who knows?"

Sheila studied the boy, her face adjusting like a clay statue in summer heat as she covered the area from his eyebrows to his jawline.

"Christ," Dolores said, "you're almost pornographic studying him like that. You're gonna embarrass him."

"Huh?" Sheila asked.

"Sheila, you were what they call undressing him with your eyes." Dolores laughed, "Don't you think?"

Sheila's stomach pulled at her. She wished the boy would walk over and say something, say anything: Say stop staring at me or love is out of the picture with me, lady, or just take a picture, it lasts longer. She stuck her finger in the foam of her beer. The traffic on Shore Drive made exciting noise, hot rods and motorcycles, big hogs, pulling into the tight parking lot. "Love me, love me not?" Sheila giggled and shrugged, tried not to look in the boy's direction. "I didn't think I was that obvious."

"Why don't you just go over there and introduce yourself, honey?" Dolores asked. "There's nothing *to* introducing yourself. You just walk over there and say 'hi,'" Dolores said, deepening her voice on the "hi." "Pretend you're a movie star or a hooker or something. You know, 'hi, gotta match,' and then look real seductive and let your hair fall over one eye, you know."

Sheila's shoulders wedged up around her neck and she crossed her legs nervously, the swish of nylon heard even above the loud Charlie Daniels on the juke. "Naw, Dolores," she said, "I ain't no slut. I can't do it."

"Then how'd you get Jeff?" Dolores asked, watching Jeff monitor lights from behind the bar.

"I didn't. He got *me*. I mean Claudine's friend, Rod, the manager, he got me for Jeff." Sheila looked toward the men's room. The passage between tables cleared, no young boy alone sipping a beer. The moment was past, lost. Sheila bit the inside of her bottom lip and searched the bar, the dance floor, the entrance to the men's, and then the ladies' room.

"Shoulda grabbed it while you could," Dolores said, pushing her empty beer glass to the middle of their table. "Let it slip away and you don't get a second chance."

"Awwwwww, it don't matter noways," Sheila said, letting the redness of her hand rest against the cold glass of beer, "there'll be other weekends and other weekend leaves. And maybe by then Jeff and I'll be split for sure."

12

Rod leaned across the bar and tackled A. Jacks by the shoulders, his manager's white shirt sleeves rolled up above his elbows. "Listen, Bud," he said, the music roaring loudly from a speaker placed over his head, "a chick like that's not gonna be around forever. Go for it!"

"I dunno," A. Jacks laughed. He placed his beer on the bar top, afraid of spilling it and getting kicked out. It wasn't very often he could even get into a place like The Blue Garter. Usually a guy like Rod would meet him at the front door with a sneer and nod casually into the parking lot. There was no way, no way, he could get into a place like this on his own. It was Claudine that did it for him. It was Claudine who was his ticket into the good life. "I gotta wrestling scholarship and that's pretty special. Not everyone gets a wrestling scholarship," A. Jacks grinned. "I wanta go to college some day. Yeah. I wanta go, and I got this wrestling scholarship, good any time. Maybe next semester."

"C'mon, boy," Rod slapped him on the shoulder, "watch her. Just watch her out there. It's like piranha feeding wherever she turns. If you don't go for it, I might."

"Yeah," A. Jacks watched. "But, you know what I wanta do most of all? Most of all," he said, "and everybody thinks I'm weird, but I wanta paint."

"I mean it," Rod said, pouring a beer from the tap and looking up at A. Jacks over the bar, "that lady's not gonna be free for very long. I'm serious."

"Oooooh, Rod," a redhead at the bar giggled.

"Claud," A. Jacks answered. "She ain't never gonna be tied down. Besides," he said, gulping the last bit of beer from his glass and smiling, "she's got that crazy kid to think about. And I dunno what I wanta do with my life yet."

"That kid?" Rod said. "Isn't that kid dead yet?"

"Hell no," A. Jacks answered, listening to the music, the people shouting, the excitement of the place. "He's gonna outlive us all. That little weirdo. That fuckin' little weirdo," he laughed. "He's gonna outlive us all."

13

"**H**ere, Jude," Claudine yelled across La Boudoir. "The early mail is in and you got a postcard from Dixie Pointer. She says: "HAVING FUN IN PUERTO RICO! WISH EVERYONE WAS HERE! THE SUN IS SHINING AND I AM REALLY BLACK! SHINES EVEN WHEN IT RAINS! BOBBY IS A LIVING DOLL! NO MORE ROOM—MISSING YOU AND LOVING IT! LOVE AND KISSES, DIXIE."

"Let me see it," Jude hollered over her customer's head. "What's the picture on the front look like?" She held her large arm out to snatch the card from Claudine, the flesh of the upper arm shaking with impatience. "And she's gonna get a real brick house when she gets back from her honeymoon," Jude told her customer. "No little ticky-tacky job for this gal. No siding. She's got it made."

Dolores tapped her nails against the glass counter as she stared at the appointment book. She could get by with singing Sinatra early on a Friday morning. All the older customers knew all the words to every Sinatra song there was and, somehow, all the old ones knew that the best work was done on Friday and Saturday mornings before ten. After ten everyone just worked in some sort of blistered haze.

"Think she'll come back?" Claudine asked Jude.

"Ummmmmm," Dolores spoke from the counter. "I bet she will. Ivory towers don't last forever."

Jude razored off the hair on the back of her customer's

neck. "Well, Puerto Rico can't last forever," she said, pulling an aqua roller from the first tier of the carry-all next to her chair. "But it looks like Dixie hit jackpot to me."

Sheila carefully removed the rollers from the gray hair of a customer who was dry and ready to be combed out and placed them back in the carry-all. "What's Bobby do? Sounds like he's got loads of cash." Her eyes flashed large and blue as she waited for the answer.

"Used car salesman," Jude answered.

"Well, that's what I'm gonna marry me then," Sheila smiled.

"What about love?" Claudine asked from her manicurist table. "Doesn't love have anything to do with getting married anymore?"

"We can probably get a good deal on a used car now if we want it. Right, Jude?" Dolores asked while she drew small pencil lines on the book through customers' names who had already shown. "Dixie'll probably have a baby right away, I bet. You know how those used car salesmen are. They're always horny standing on those lots trying to sell their sex appeal all day. Then they come home and give it to their wives."

"Or whoever," Claudine smiled in Dolores' direction. "Remember, he was supposed to have been married when he met her at Sixth National."

"Maybe we should go to Sixth National sometime," Sheila said. "Maybe we could pick ourselves up something that would be worth everything."

Dolores looked at Claudine and rolled her eyes. These customers weren't supposed to know that they hung out at bars, especially the early customers who had been coming to La Boudoir for years. They were the first ones to go when a following began to fall apart. You were taught at the Vocational Center to talk to a customer as if she were a friend, to pretend you did the same things she did, that you drank the same diet cola, wore the same undereye concealer, had the same problems with dropping chin lines, ears that were too long, a nose that had swelled during child birth and never gone down.

Jude noticed that the pores of her lady's scalp seemed to be opening, the hair follicles loose. "Bars are only for the young," she said, wrapping a thin hairnet over her customer's rollers. "I'd rather stay at home and watch the tube, thank you."

Sheila averted her eyes and continued placing the smaller green rollers on the stand. "Well, I'm just gettin' kinda tired of going up to The Blue Garter and seeing Jeff. That's all," she said, her bony thumb slipping against the metal wheel of her cigarette lighter. She inhaled and then paused as she let the smoke escape from her nostrils, her eyes flinching from the sting.

"You can't run away from things, you know, Sheila," Claudine said, wiping her hands across the white towel spread across her table. Jude led her customer to a dryer one of the girls had already set.

"I'm not running away from anything," Sheila said. "I'm just tired of going there."

Jude taped the postcard of Puerto Rico on her mirror and admired the picture of the Baha Hotel set in front of clear blue water and the bright pink flowers in bunches hanging from balcony windows.

"She sure makes it sound appealing, doesn't she?" Jude's next customer smiled.

"Yeah," Jude breathed heavily and stared at the card on the mirror, "but, you know, I really wouldn't want to be in her shoes. I mean," she said, taking another deep breath and exhaling, "she's young. I'm real happy for her. But if I had to start all over again with a man coming home from work every night and settling down on top of me, well, I just couldn't do it now. You know? I just don't have the strength to do it now."

"Maybe if it was the right one," her customer said, another face glaring yellow in the overheads.

"No," Jude breathed and began to unroll, "I thank the Lord for divorce."

The customer smiled anxiously. Dolores saw her glance to the walls, to Bettina and Cherée and Idella. To the pretty pictures. Idella, with her black hair piled high on top of her almond-shaped face in tightly pinched curls, her eyes as dark as a witches' catch, the lashes glimmering with some sort of gold dust; Idella, full face into the camera, nose so straight of a line that a ruler could be held to it for measurement; Idella, skin lightly tanned a burnt orange, large lips to match.

"And sure," Jude continued robustly, "some men settle down. But they're never the ones you go for in the first place. You know, I thought it would stop working after ten or fifteen years, but twenty-five years later he was just rarin' to go and, honestly, I was just plumb tuckered out. Really," she assured her customer, "I didn't have any energy left."

"But," the customer argued, "this man's going to pay this girl Dixie's rent and take her nice places and maybe even give her a little money to pamper herself with. Don't you think that's worth it?"

Claudine thumbed through new magazines looking at the pictures. Pretty ladies. Sitting at the manicurist table all day gave her a stiff neck. It was only those mystery mags and romance thrillers that made the hours slip by when there was no one on the books and no walk-ins. Then she would entertain herself with oodles of thrillers: *My Boyfriend's Animal Fixation, How to Control an Ex-Lover in Bed, The Day I Found My Roommate Murdered in the Tub.*

"Naw," Jude said, bringing the teasing comb around to the woman's left ear and then softly pulling the hair out and upward, "I'm thrilled for her but a trip to Puerto Rico just wouldn't be enough for me. It's just not worth it, you know?"

The woman stared directly at the postcard on the mirror in front of her and pulled her designer jeans snugly over her tummy. "I don't know," she said, crossing her legs.

Jude finished the styling and swung the chair to the right angle placing a hand mirror in front of the woman. The woman asked that the back be combed out more, and then she gave Jude a polite thanks and left to pay the bill up front with Dolores. "Doesn't do much for tips," Jude smiled at Claudine while lowering herself carefully into her pink swivel chair, staring into her mirror and placing a pudgy hand under her billowing chin, "but it sure is a pretty picture."

14

Claudine liked rolling over in bed and finding herself straddled against A. Jacks' overformed body, the muscles bulging from behind his neck, the rippling of his thick arms and legs, and simply the overall of his welterweight excited her in the morning. She would run her fingers over his back and chest with her eyes closed, feeling, touching, sensing the magnificence of the out of proportion one-hundred-and-fifty-five-pound body. A. Jacks would crawl on top of her in half sleep, forcefully spread her limbs apart with one strong foot, and then enter her. A long groan later, like a tremendous shift of pressure, her whole body would stiffen and she would find herself stretching her arms down over his torso, trying to squeeze the solidly tight muscles out of his rear with her sculptured nails. She did it with hatred, with disgust, and partly because A. Jacks was only nineteen years old. What kind of future was in that? She was prepared for him to get up one morning, go over to Old Dominion University, buy his books, and never come back. In fact, she hoped that he would. She prayed that he would so that she could be free. And then he would just leave. Leave. She had been left before and she could be left again. Besides, she had never expected this one to stay any longer than just one night. A pajama party. That was all it had been meant to be.

Somehow, she thought, the people lingered that she didn't love. And those that she had loved had slipped away. Well, she acted foolishly. Frank had lasted a year after Michelle was born, even with the baby crying all through the night and him not being the father. Hell, if only she hadn't lost the ability to speak. But she'd loved him so much she just couldn't talk anymore. Only at work. Only when she went in to talk to the women could she let it all pour out. But, at home with Frank, it had been as if her tongue had grown thick or something. He began to call her stupid. She had just been so much in love. For the first time, she had felt the real magic of love. Not comfort, not trust, not need, or a stipulation because of want, but real desire. Love. And she couldn't move correctly. It was as if Frank's just being there made her overly nervous, as if she wanted everything to look and sound perfect. She had had her hair cut short for the first time, short under her ears in a blonde Pageboy. He hadn't liked it, called her a bitch for changing her looks. She told him it would grow back. But, in the meantime, she began to stumble a lot, knocking things over around the house. One morning she got up early and put away everything that had been breakable. She had hidden the candy dishes from herself, moved the blue bud vase to a closet shelf, carefully placed the flower pots on the back stoop of the apartment. Then she'd made him breakfast in bed. Spilled cornflakes all in the sheets. What a white mess they'd made. And Frank had screamed so loud because of the cold. She had wanted to die. Die. Die. Die. I am going to stay deformed forever, she had thought. Please God, don't let him leave me. I am going to stay deformed and I need him.

Johnnie hadn't been too bad then. Sure, she had known

he was dying, but at two, he'd just stayed in his crib and hadn't bothered a soul. Sometimes she'd even forgotten he was dying. Then, all she had to do was look down at him, grotesque baby monster behind bars. Where had he come from? Frank had wanted to give him to Social Services. They'll know what to do with a freak like that, he'd said. Give him up. He's ruining your life. We can't be normal with him around. Give him up. Give him up. But the children hadn't meant anything to him, she knew. How could they? They hadn't come from his gut. He hadn't felt them feeding off his own flesh. She'd never let them go. Even her precious newborn little girl. Frank would have given her up to Social Services too. He just couldn't realize how much she loved them; she really loved them. It was all beyond Frank. He'd thought her love for them had to do with Mike Downings, and Mike had thought it had to do with . . . well. But it didn't have to do with anyone but herself; when she looked into Johnnie's face she saw someone she knew, someone she had forgotten and, yet, could not forget. She couldn't put him away. Like eating fish brains, she'd told Frank, they make your own brain bigger and smarter. And the desire between them had been so electrifying that understanding each other hadn't mattered. But in the end it had been the lack of understanding that had driven them apart.

"Deeeayeee," Johnnie called. Claudine rolled over. It was too early on a Sunday morning. A. Jacks stretched out against her back, his long blonde hair hanging in his open mouth, the stringy ends stuck against the pinkness of his tongue.

It was as if having one justified loving the other. She felt no loss loving Johnnie. He, in fact, made Michelle all the more beautiful. She had fed them together and bathed them together and brushed their hair together. She had love for both. She had more love for them than she had had for Mike Downings, for Mike Downings' dirty socks and streak-stained jockey shorts, for Mike Downings' drunken stupors and games and bouts of lying, and even stealing the money he'd given her out of her wallet. And when he'd left her, he'd left her in peace with her babies. He had not left her alone. She thanked him for that.

They didn't need a father. She hung their pictures over her manicurist table, always new pictures to show how one had grown and one hadn't. And she was making a good living, a fairly good living. And the babies didn't want much, they didn't eat much, and Michelle always watched over Johnnie and had good commonsense. She was glad Mike left. Glad Frank had left, for sure. Didn't mind where she lived. Robbin Hood was good and cheap at eighty-five dollars a month, and she was only six blocks from the Chesapeake Bay, even if Ocean View Beach was filthy, full of rusty cans and floating newspapers, even if the sand disappeared into the waves more and more each day and in late summer the jellyfish came out and stuck themselves to you, suctioned themselves to your legs and stomach and sucked for blood; you spent the whole damn summer looking for them, waiting for them, afraid to let your children go wading alone. And then there was Dolores living right down the street if ever anything was needed, anything in the world. And she wanted Dolores to be her friend; she admired Dolores. There was something about Dolores that made her stand out from all the other dumb shits that she had ever worked with. And she didn't mind the coloreds and the Navy trash living around her. They were just like everyone else. Why did they have to be any different? They had babies and worked and sweated and slept just like her. Jude was crazy. Or was she? There was no getting away with it. She could pretend to be all liberal and everything, but the truth of the matter was that she didn't like it so much. They sat on their porches and their heads swelled with hurt and anger and she could see the lines coming

42

up even on the little ones' foreheads. They were always worried. And they were always tense. And it was just because she was poor that she had to be in the middle of it all, that she had to look at it, see it, face it. And vitamins didn't help. Writing a book would help; letting the world share her misery would help. But there was never really time for that and there wouldn't be until maybe after Johnnie died.

Frank had screamed, knocking over a plant she had missed putting away, a long flowering red plant given to her by one of her customers for Christmas. "I don't know how you can live this way!" And she had pretended she didn't know what he was talking about. "Here in this shit hole with two whiny kids—one who ain't even a kid. God knows what the hell *that* is." He had opened his hand toward the middle of the floor where Johnnie sprawled on his backside, a three-year-old's body, a newborn's arms, legs, and head. Deformed.

"I love him," she had cried, trying to sweep the dirt from the plant's roots into the broken pieces of ceramic. "If you don't like it, you can just get out. Just get out!" she had screamed.

He'd pulled her face up by the thin pointy chin; strong fingers from another slim wrist.

"What do you want me to do?" she'd spoken softly; his face so close had made her voice change quickly.

"You're picking the freak over me?" he had asked. "Baby," he'd said, getting down on his knees beside her. He'd run his hands over the smooth whiteness of her cheeks.

"I can't kill him, Frank," she'd snivelled. "He's my baby and I love him."

"I'm not telling you to kill it." He was gentle, like the TV violinist, used his greasy mechanic's tools like an artist; she had loved him. "There are places for things like that."

"I know," she had said.

"We'll take him up to Williamsburg and if you don't like the looks of the place you don't have to leave him there. Okay?"

"Okay," she had said. Later, when Frank was leaving, she remembered his fragile outline and the way his own eyes had pleaded wide and teary like a baby's.

"You're a low-class broad, you know that, Claudine?" he had said. "Don't never want to live any better."

"Deeeeayee." She rolled over. She had to remind A. Jacks to call his mother.

15

"*I*n the service?" Dolores asked. She wiped the sand from her eyelashes. Willoughby Spit Beach was elbow to elbow with mothers with their hair tied up in red and white bandanas, babies with sandy thighs squealing at the coldness of the sea-green water against their finger tips, young boys throwing plastic balls of swirled yellow and purple as far as the strength of their arms could propel so that they had an excuse for racing out to sea.

"Nope," he shook his curls like a wet dog, "I'm a do-it-yourself man, you know. But one day I'm gonna go to school and make something outa myself."

His upper lip was too big for his mouth, room left over for it to curl up from the normal lip line almost touching the aquiline nose that beaked forward in three broken steps. He extended one hand, the other holding a black box the size of a small suitcase.

"Phil," he said. He had a lot of teeth. Dolores looked at his feet from where she stretched on her Miller High Life beach towel. He was pigeon-toed to the point of one foot almost looking clubbed. Yet his legs were well developed and covered with thick blonde hairs that curled easily, the color *of* the sand clinging to his ankles. "You look like just the person I've been looking for. Mind if I sit?" he asked.

"Ummmmmm, no," Dolores smiled nervously, pushing up on her elbows and sucking in her stomach so that her position would be flattering. "It's okay," she said, "I guess."

"Really?" Phil asked. "You don't mind?" He held a smile for a long time, like each motion was meant for Dolores to study, to memorize. She could feel the sand under her elbows, the towel rough against the backs of her legs, the sun hot in strips of red against her collarbone.

"No, I don't mind," Dolores said. She touched the top of her head, hot and a metallic orange color from letting a girl from Vocational Beauty School experiment. Well, all the students had to experiment, but she had told the girl that Mandarin wasn't going to look good. Now she had to pretend to be daring.

"Hold on a minute," Phil said, leaving his case balanced on the edge of her beach towel and running across the sand in the direction of the old pink-and-white striped refreshment shack.

"Hey, you can't bring anything down here," Dolores yelled. "It's against the law to bring anything down on the sand."

"Watch the case," he hollered over his shoulder.

He returned walking slowly, holding a can of Coca-Cola in each hand, and a wide smile reaching across his face only dabbled with the color of the sun. Dolores noticed that freckles almost completely covered his face, the bones of his jawline seeming to push their way through the skin. He sat at the foot of her towel, his cut-off jeans darkest blue, like black, damp and sandy, and he placed the red-and-white can against the nakedness of her stomach, the coldness making her sit up instantly with laughter.

"How old are you?" Phil asked.

"Seventeen," Dolores answered, pushing her long spotty orange hair out of her own sun-freckled face. "Why?"

"Jailbait," Phil laughed. "Jailbait."

45

"Then I guess I'm not the person you were looking for after all?" Dolores asked. She smiled, but she felt ugly. It had to have been the hair, or her small breasts, or the pimple on the right side of her nose that she was hoping the sun would clear. It was for these reasons that she preferred Willoughby Spit to the great vast Chesapeake Bay. And it was almost never that she found herself facing the Atlantic from Virginia Beach. Even if the Bay did bring jellyfish by August, even if the waters were darker, full of indiscriminate floating things, she preferred the close darkness to the open course of movement from Virginia Beach to China, and she truly believed that that was where the waters would go, that they would spread themselves around her painted toes and pull her into a strange world with slanty eyes, a strange place with a white-powdered face, a place where she could not function.

"Well, you're welcome for the Coke," Phil nodded as he rose from the towel, smoothed out the legs of his jeans, and reached for his case.

"Wait," Dolores said, swallowing quickly and placing the Coke between her knees. "Do you have to go? I mean, it was kinda nice just talking to someone. You know?" She took a deep breath and looked up at the tall, thin man who continued to block her sun. "Dolores," she said, stretching out her own hand. Phil took it and held to it. She felt the bones of his hand tighten around her own, and she could feel the heat against her shoulders as he slowly bent forward. "What's in the case?" she asked.

"Nothing," he answered smiling, his lips drawing up over so many teeth, all large and white and sparkling. A moment frozen.

"C'mon," Dolores laughed as Phil fell to his knees in the sand. "There's gotta be something in it."

"I sell jewelry," he muttered. She thought he looked like a helpless little boy, his large eyelids closing coyly over greenish-blue eyes. Like the sea. His eyes were like the sea, she thought. *The impenetrable sea.* "Can I see?" Dolores asked, reaching for the black case.

"I don't think so."

"Phil? Phil," she giggled playfully, "C'mon. Lemme see."

"Uh uh," he said, turning to look to the water moving in and out, in and out, "it's just junk. That's all."

"I wanta see," Dolores said, again reaching for the case, knocking her Coke over, the brown liquid staining the granules of gritty sand along the side and beneath her towel.

"Pandora's box," Phil kidded. "Your parents will disown you if you open it."

"My parents have already disowned me," Dolores said, straightening the bra straps of her bikini. "I ran away from home when I was thirteen and when they found me they sent me up here to live with my grandfather. My grandmother's dead. I practically live alone. My grandfather's a crazy old geezer."

Phil ran his tongue over his wide lips. His tone of voice grew very serious and, for a moment, he was no longer like a little boy, but some mystical God who had been in hiding and was now showing himself beneath all his seaweed to only her. He pulled the box around his feet by the handle, making a pattern in the sand, and unlatched the gold clasp. Inside the box was lined with a worn red velveteen, and in each nook lay a ring made out of shiny metal and small delicate half-colored shells. Phil pulled the leather case close to his ribs and held it there carefully.

"They're beautiful," she said.

"Look quickly," he sparkled, delighted by his own cleverness. She stared up into his face and he snapped closed the box. "I could get arrested for this if anyone saw me," he said.

"Open it again," Dolores pleaded. "Only for a second. Please?"

His chest almost touched her shoulder as she fingered the rings. Dolores cocked her head back and squinted. She

47

could feel every inch of her face covered in soft air off the inland bay. Her mouth tasted salty; when she looked at Phil, she could see the mixture of salt and sand gathered in his curls.

"How much are they?" she asked.

"I told you," Phil said, "they're junk. A company in California sends me the settings, and all I do is glue in the shells. You can help me do it some time if you want. I'm staying in an old house converted into boarding rooms down on the east side. How about tonight?"

She smiled slowly and watched him rise from the beach. "Sure," she said. "That is, if you don't still think I'm jail-bait."

"Naw," Phil smiled and pulled the case up under his arm, "I'm only nineteen myself."

"Brat," Dolores laughed, cupping a hand over her eyes and lying back to give a sexier appearance. "Where? I mean, which house? There are lots of boarding houses, you know."

"Meet me at the Wharf," Phil said, walking backward. "At six-thirty?" His smile was never ceasing, she noticed, as if the mouth could not possibly stretch in any other direction. "Dinner," he nodded.

He turned and walked down to the water, and then further down the shoreline silently. It was as if Dolores was completely alone on the beach. She could not hear the mothers yelling to their small children who had floated too far out in the undertow. She could not hear the lifeguard whistle, the babies crying from heat and rash, the girls her own age giggling and smearing suntan lotion over each other's acne-ridden backs. She tried to hide the two empty red-and-white swirled Coke cans, rolling them up in the beer towel and tucking them close by her side.

16

"**C**'mon, Babe, you gotta give in some time," Claudine said, staring up at the picture of Bettina that hung on the pale green wall over the receptionist desk. Bettina stared brightly, big yellow eyes with violet dots in the center stood on either side of a perfect nose air-brushed straight down the middle with a little flip on the end, pugged. Bettina's hair was silver-blonde, cut just below the two perfect earlobes, clean and powdered. And Bettina's lips were alluring in a slight pucker, the pinky-brown of a matte finish giving all the girls the knowledge that Bettina's face was perfection. "You can't go torchin' forever, Dolores."

"Forever," Dolores laughed, playing with the unlighted cigarette. Small ochre-colored splinters of tobacco fell to the glass counter top.

"Forever," Claudine assured her, "is not a pretty story. Take a guy like Rod; Rod's not gonna be around forever."

"Claud, Rod?" Dolores asked.

"C'mon, Dolores," Claudine said, taking her eyes away from the portrait of Bettina. "'Rod's okay . . . and he's real hot for you."

"But Rod?" Dolores shook her head. "I can't see it."

"Dolores, you've got a kid. Face it," Claudine said, "there aren't too many men out there who are looking for a girl with a kid . . . no matter how adorable you think your kid is. Okay?"

"Okay," Dolores smiled. She looked to the large black appointment book, placed the cigarette in her mouth, and lighted it with a pack of La Boudoir's matches, pink paper jacket with the name of the store in quasi-French aqua lettering.

"We need them books for customers, Dolores," Claudine reprimanded, her nails knocking the counter. "Don't use 'em. Caresse wouldn't like it."

"Who's telling them?" Dolores asked, running a pencil down the side of the list of customers' names who had made appointments for Fridays. She had to make sure all the standings were placed properly and given sufficient time. "I do more than my share anyway. Wouldn't you agree?"

"Look, Dolores. Why don't you just give the guy a chance? You know, you're not the only one who gets lonely once in a while. This guy Rod is *real* nice, and he gets lonely a lot too. I know."

Dolores ran her tongue over her back teeth. The grittiness was awful. She was glad she never bought a pack of cigarettes with her own money. "Claud, look," she said, "people don't have different love affairs. It's just one continuous thing with different partners, and it's either good or it's bad. That's all. And mine are always rotten."

"How would you know?" Claudine lightly struck her fist against the glass counter top. Tobacco spillings stuck to the dampness of her hand, the pink-and-white tins of hair spray rattling in the case. "You never give anyone a goddamned chance." Then she snorted.

"Leave me alone, Claud," Dolores said, catching sight of her reflection in the mirror hanging at the end of the desk. It was distorted glass, and it was frightening to watch her cheeks slowly begin to sag around her lower lip. "I'm just being objective. That's all. Just being truthful." Rotten. They had all been rotten. Sure, there had been some nice ones after Phil. There had been some unbelievable ones. God, they had been good. But, in the end, they had all been rotten to her, or she had been rotten to them. "I'm too old," she said, shaking her head. "But I done my share." She smoked and ran a sweaty palm over her face.

"You'll get zits if you keep doin' that," Claudine said,

leaning on one newly greased elbow. Rubbing lotion into her elbows had become a habit once she read in a woman's magazine that rough elbows were a telltale sign of age.

"Forget it. Just forget it," Dolores answered, still watching herself in the mirror. "I just don't even have the desire to begin again."

Claudine tapped her nails on the counter and slipped her foot out of one purple sling-back high heel. "All I know is that last Monday I watched Donahue and he had on these people whose husbands and wives had died, you know? Well, these people were just itchin' to get married again because it had been so wonderful the first time around." She noticed that her elbow had left a smudge on the glass, and she licked her fingers to try to erase the grease with saliva.

"You know, Claud, they look for those kinds of people to put on television. Makes America feel better about itself."

"Noooo. I'll tell you," Claudine said, looking up at the poster of Bettina, "those girls on Donahue really *loved* their husbands, you know. They weren't playing at it. You could see it the way their eyes watered a little bit around the edges and their voices warbled. Really."

"Well . . ."

"No, Dolores." She watched Dolores take a puff off her cigarette and blow. "You know," Claudine added, "that smoke just tears up your skin." Claudine began again, "Dolores, I wanta tell you, they really did miss their husbands, and they had gotten over it and they were ready to go out there and plug away again, find somebody and go into it all again. You know?"

"I know I really should get back out there," Dolores said, looking at her watch. "But it wasn't like I was ever married to Phil to begin with, you know? I mean, it's silly what I do to myself. I know that. But . . . I can't help it. You know, I've built so much up around it that I can't just give it up.

I can't. And I like for Rosie to believe that what she comes from really meant a lot to me. You know?"

"Yeah," Claudine sighed. "Not a pretty story."

"And if I give it up, if I give up Phil, then I'm giving up what belongs to Rosie. Understand?"

"Well, that's like a marriage."

"No. That's like an umbilical cord. We didn't have *real* love," Dolores said. "I mean . . . well, grown-up love." She swallowed hard and pulled her dark brown hair in a ponytail at the back of her neck. "We had love, sure. But it was irresponsible love. You know?" Dolores paused. "If we'd been responsible, Rosemary would have a father right now, and, if he died, I'd be ready to try again too. But I never had it to begin with."

"Face it, Dolores," Claudine said, watching her dab her cigarette into a pink plastic ashtray, "there's no such thing as Mr. Right, and, even if there was, he'd be Mr. Wrong anyway."

Jude slid a Styrofoam cup of hot black coffee on the counter in front of Dolores and nodded like an old tug pulling a helpless battleship into port. The coffee felt warm and good between Dolores' hands. "A woman makes love with her heart in her mouth, honey," Jude said. "You can't tell me that when you go out to these bars, Dolores, that when you meet a guy your heart doesn't race just thinkin' about what might happen. But you never know what's gonna happen, do you?" Jude asked, her heavy black brows knitted together, her scent too much of rose water. Dolores wondered why there were no photographs of loved ones glued to Jude's mirror, only the postcard landscape of Puerto Rico from Dixie Pointer. Jude had a way of taking a person to her breast, smothering to the point of idiocy. Claudine stared at the portrait of Bettina. "It's like walking a tightrope or something," Jude continued. "The feeling goes right from your pussy to your heart to your head."

52

"Jude!" Dolores laughed.

"No, really," Jude assured, "a man makes love with a stranger in his pants. It don't matter who he does it with. A hard dick has no conscience. But a woman, she gives over her dreams when she gives over the rest of her. That's why," she paused, "I'd rather stay home and watch the tube."

Dolores stood there holding her coffee and looking at her appointment book, and it maddened her to know that Jude was right. Why did she have to go back out into it? Strangers in their pants. Strangers in their beds. You woke up in the morning and you knew exactly where you were, exactly what you had done; but when you rolled over to look at the guy you'd done it with, you couldn't remember his name. All you could remember was his face as he came, and the way he had leaned up against the wooden headboard afterward and said "I'm the best you've ever had, aren't I?" They talked about nuclear energy and they drank, and they drank and they drank, until they almost made a little sense. They were children, free to do whatever they wanted. Their babies flooded the ocean floors. They all wanted to be kings; Charlie Manson. They all wanted to cut off tits and hang them in the refrigerator during a flight of fancy. Trophies of the night before. Tits out in the evening trash; old tits much worse than stale bread and sour milk. "My old girlfriend could make the best cheesecake out of sour milk." Who cared? Go get yourself a fresh pair of tits! Like something out of those magazines Claudine read: "HOW I CUT MY GIRLFRIEND UP INTO TWENTY-THOUSAND PIECES WITH A HATCHET AND THEN ATE HER." Something out of raunchy magazines, cheap magazines, magazines whose subscriptions cost the buck nonetheless. And what did she really care? She stood on the floor all day and looked forward to a pack of Nabs and a Coke. Peanut Butter Nabs. And then Claudine would tell her that she was going to ruin her figure. To hell with it.

It was all a cheap bottom line. And she wasn't happy. How could she ever have expected to compete with the vulgarity of the world? Phil had told her that she wasn't going to be happy, but she hadn't believed him. You can *make* yourself happy, she had said. Only if you keep moving, Phil had answered. You can't let yourself slow down, he had said. To hell with it. She didn't even care about slowing down, or slipping backward for that matter. There wasn't time to notice. Time had fallen apart. And all she cared about was her own unhappiness.

17

"*But darlin', you know best, you know how to love me,*" Dolores sang along with Jenny Rae on the juke. Red lights flashed throughout The Blue Garter, and they made the unfinished brown wood walls seem warm and cozy. Somehow, the day and Rosemary were going away. Three vodka tonics and she was just beginning. "*And when you're right next to me, you know when to hug me,*" she sang. "*But darlin', any old way, you know best how to love me. You know best how to hug me. You know best how to kiss me. You know best how to miss me. But darlin', any old way, you know best how to love me.*"

"Dolores!" she heard someone from across the room yell, but she ignored it. The night was so nice. Don't spoil it for me, she thought. Let me alone. Let me watch Loretta Sweate and enjoy her for a change.

Slowly Loretta moved inside her black panties, her fleshy thighs undulating with the soft music. "*You know best how to love me,*" the recording continued. The young servicemen pulled their chairs up around Loretta's small circle of mirrored dance floor. "*You know best how to love me. And when you're right next to me,*" Loretta mouthed the

54

words, her red lips outlining "love" with a sticky pink tongue that seemed to slide down the sides of her mouth like a liquid snail trail. The men sank down in their hard-backed chairs. *"You know best how to love me."*

"Dance, bitch," a sailor from the back yelled, his snap shirt opened down the front exposing a large ship, half sunk.

Slowly, Loretta edged her legs apart with long sculptured nails Claudine had placed little red heart decals on for Valentine's Day eve. There was an "AWWWWW" from her audience and Loretta leaned backward, running her hands through her shagged hair.

The smoky air surrounded Dolores at the box. Rosemary would probably be sitting up at Claudine's waiting for her to come and get her. And then she would want to crawl in bed with her the second she pulled the covers up. Not tonight. Dolores cherished the nights she could take Rosemary over to Claudine's and tell Michelle, say, "Honey, do me a favor, will you tonight, and let Rosie sleep in the bed with you?" And Michelle would always do it. Michelle was a good kid. It was a shame the other one was a freak. Just a freeloader. Everyone should come in for *some* good. That kid would never be any good to anybody. Especially Claudine. She wished she'd thought to tell Rosie that she might not pick her up tonight.

"That's against the law. That's against the law," Rod spoke over the loudspeaker. "Just put the money on the floor or the railing and she'll pick it up. DO NOT TOUCH THE LADY OR HER LINGERIE. AGAINST VIRGINIA STATE LAW."

Dolores could hear a young boy sitting at a table in front of her, fingering the foam of his beer to keep it from running over, saying, "I remember once when I was in here I had a silver dollar and I heated it up, you know, like right here in the middle with my lighter," he played with a silver coin between his fingers, "until I could only touch it on the rim. And then I rolled it up there on her dance floor and she tried to pick it up with her snatch. GOD!" the boy giggled in a high pitch. Even in the darkness you could see his Adam's apple wiggle. "The dumb bitch! She squats down and spreads it and tries to snatch it up with her pussy!" He rolled the coin on the tabletop and it fell to the floor. He let it roll over the tile and shrugged. "Only money," his friends laughed. The boy snickered, still watching Loretta's heavy body twitch intently.

"GET OFF THE LADY!" Rod yelled over the intercom. The music grew louder and louder. "GET OFF THE LADY! FAIR WARNING. VIRGINIA STATE LAW. NO TOUCHING THE DANCER. GET OFF THE LADY."

A young sailor, his hair cut close enough for the scalp to show, jumped the rail behind Loretta Sweate, unzipped his pants on stage, and stood directly behind her. As much as Loretta tried to ignore him and continue with her routine, the boy grew more and more exited, getting harder and bigger, and the audience yelled for more. Dolores turned to watch Rod smile from his announcing platform behind the bar. He wasn't going to do a damn thing but play on the boy. The louder he could get his audience, the more excited, the more money they would spend. They'd buy beer, then they'd go to the toilets and spend quarter after quarter on naked plastic women hanging from key chain bobs or ribbed prophylactics with drawings on the sides, like children's balloons.

"GET OFF THE LADY!" Rod yelled. "DO NOT TOUCH THE DANCER. VIRGINIA STATE LAW."

"Go for it, boy," they were yelling from the crowd, the men in the front row around the stage yelping like chickens getting their throats sliced on barbed wire. "Go to it! Go on! Do it!" they yelled, sliding backward and forward in their chairs with their hands in their laps.

The boy wagged his penis in the air with his eyes closed, his mouth only in a slight smile, like pain, as he stood close behind Loretta, bending back when she bent back and bending forward when she teased the roaring audience. The boy was so drunk he could hardly hold his penis without his hand sliding, and then he began to masturbate all over Loretta Sweate's feet, her thighs, her knees. He aimed low but still managed to spurt the stuff out all over the dancer and she continued, looking toward Rod helplessly. Then the sailor tried to control Loretta Sweate by gripping her right ankle. He pulled her bare foot up into his groin and grabbed her around the waist with his arm so that she couldn't move as much as she struggled to kick and keep her balance. Then the boy was on Loretta's back, riding her as if she were some sort of rodeo animal, and he the showman.

"I REPEAT," Rod yelled over the speaker system, "GET OFF THE DANCER. VIRGINIA STATE LAW."

The crowd grew hysterical, their laughter heard all the way out to Shore Drive. Dolores stood back, nudged in between the jukebox and the unfinished walls. They didn't feel warm anymore. They felt oozy, dirty, as if the ejaculation had not been rubbed into only Loretta Sweate's skin, but into the walls of The Blue Garter as well.

The young sailor began to cry, his hands giving way from Loretta's foot and waist and finding his own eyes. He shook, and his entire face turned a raw shade of pink, like he had exposed not only what part of him hid behind clothing, but what he had kept deep inside, what had known warm comfort and pleasure. Now his whole being was on display. Storefront. Sheila's Jeff grabbed the boy by the white shirt collar and pulled him off the stage. "WUSS." "WUSS," the men yelled.

Sheila's Jeff held his hand up to the crowd to signal that everything was under control, and Rod continued on the loudspeaker, "AND NOW THE LADY WILL DANCE FROM THE REAR, GENTLEMEN," he announced.

Jeff was angling the boy toward the back door when Dolores caught the out-of-uniform arm. "Leave him here, Jeff," she said, putting her arm around the sailor's shoulders. "I'll make sure he doesn't get into any more trouble."

"You sure?" Jeff asked, trying to stifle a belch.

"Sure," she answered. "This kid doesn't need any more trouble. I think he's been through enough for one night."

"Okay," Jeff said, releasing the sailor in Dolores' custody. "I guess if you want this piece of slime it won't make no difference if he leaves with you or without you."

"Guess not," Dolores said.

On their way out the back door Dolores asked the boy if he felt better and he nodded yes. She watched his shiny black lace-up shoes and the way his ankles wobbled from side to side, his knees thin and buckling. She wondered if underneath it all he really couldn't be a wonderful guy, if there wasn't something inside him that made him ache enough to stand in front of a crowd and strip away everything that wasn't human, wipe away his face, and throw his desire in everyone else's.

She made him sit on the back stoop of The Blue Garter, let him hang his head between his knees and breathe deeply. She counted to three and made him breathe, counted to three and made him breathe, kept her arm around his shoulders so that he would not catch cold. She warned him that even though he felt warm, he was really cold. She knew that drunk feeling, she said, and she told him about the time she had gotten stupored right after Rosie had been born and she had gone to a party, barged her way in, and thrown her bra in the fireplace yelling "I'm a liberated mother," even though she really wasn't. She told him she wished that she could experience that drunk feeling all the time, that staying sober was really much safer though cause the cold was good, you had to feel the cold to know where you really stood, to really be alive. Then, she'd said, she'd been really sorry she'd burned her bra because she'd never been able to find another with that much padding, and he had laughed, standing up and throwing his shoulders back to the chilling wind, his chin strong and his eyes alive with glitter. He'd reached for Dolores' hand and she'd given it to him, the excitement in her chest a pounding that vibrated between her ears like a toy buzz gun, the frost against her face invigorating. The night was as black as a child left in the dark, Dolores succumbing to the way the boy had turned to man in front of her eyes, his arms not clinging but warm and his chest not exposed but permitting. And once again, she went for the magic.

"I'm glad I drove my own car last night," she whispered later in bed, turning to look at him, his lips wide apart, eyes half closed. "Aren't you?" she asked, running an acrylic nail across his slender rib cage. "Aren't you, Waverly?" she asked, thinking about the silkiness of her own skin, the breakfast she would get up extra early and prepare, how much toilet paper was in the bathroom, and if she trusted this new man enough to give him a key. She studied his face a second longer. She'd have to wait. To give yourself totally over to the magic of a find, that wasn't smart. She'd seen too many men in half sleep, too many men. It wasn't smart to give in too quickly. Like Claudine, she thought, she could get stuck with a whim. "Aren't you, Waverly," she asked again, "glad that I drove my own car?"

"I couldn't care less," he muttered.

She wondered if the man she had slept with had been all illusion.

18

"FOR YOUR CONVENIENCE," Dolores read, "WE NOW HAVE A BLACK OPERATOR." She placed the cardboard sign in the front window behind the dead fern.

"Bitch," Jude said as she walked out the front door of

La Boudoir to go next door to 7-11 for a Boss Coke. Then she bounced back to the front door, leaned her chubby round face in the shop, and yelled, "What am I complaining for? They can't read anyway."

"So the black chick'll be coming to work tomorrow, Dolores?" Claudine asked, as she painted a customer's nails Tropique.

"Uh huh," Dolores answered, spreading a white towel on her own manicurist table in back of Claudine. She looked up to the picture of Cherée smiling down so pleasantly. "It's a beautiful day," she announced to the picture.

"Sure is," Claudine answered. "Not a pretty story," she joked with her customer. "You ever dated a black man?" she asked.

The woman shook her head in amazement. "Neither have I," said Claudine. "I can't see why anyone would even want to?"

"I have," Sheila said, walking by with a wet towel in her hand. "I dated a black man once."

"You did?" the customer asked.

Claudine rolled her eyes at Sheila and kept painting.

"You mean you went out with a black man as a friend or something, don't you, Sheila?" Dolores answered for her from her table.

"No," Sheila said, walking into the back room with the wet towels she had collected in a lump under her arm. "I mean, I dated a black man. There wasn't anything to it, you know. I don't know what the big deal is about dating a black man."

Claudine looked up from her customer's hand and stared at Sheila. "If I were you, little one," she said, "I'd get a move on and start dumping those towels in the hamper in the back. Then you can sweep."

19

Sheila took two chocolate graham crackers from the refrigerator and waited, then looked into the rattan-framed mirror hanging next to the doorway to see that her makeup was perfect. Nine-fifteen. Why not call Jeff and just tell him that she had another date? Why not just blow him off all at once, get rid of him and his thick hands. She could have her baby alone. Dolores had done it. She went to the stereo and slipped the black plastic disc on the metal turnstyle.

Nine twenty-five. The music played on. Sheila felt hungry as she sat on the floor trying to look funky. Funky was her baby-fine streaked hair falling across her freckled face, an imitation of something off TV. . . . Girls in tight silver glittery pants. She was as thin as they were.

She heard a noise in the hall, but it wasn't her date. Maybe he'd gotten mixed up, or forgotten which apartment she had said. She'd told him she'd leave the door open for him. Maybe that had sounded too forward. Maybe just friendly. She hoped just friendly. She went to the window to look for someone who might be lost. There was only blackness. Dark February blackness, and the air smelled damp.

Nine-forty. The record repeated itself. Sheila went to the refrigerator and got herself a beer. Miller . . . the only kind Jeff would drink. Cigarettes or a joint?

Ten-ten. Sheila closed the heavy green door and locked it. She looked at herself in her bathroom mirror. It was a shame to have to remove a face full of makeup that had taken her an hour to apply. Who had she been dressing for? These dates meant nothing. Halfway through the evening she found herself bored. All she wanted to do was go home, take off her clothes, and have someone hold her body. She liked to feel close, like someone was glad she was alive. It was the only time when she could do everything exactly right. Exactly right. "Soon you'll be big and fat," she joked with her reflection. The music continued, the arm going back to the beginning of the album again. She unbuttoned her shirt, moved slowly from the waist. She ran both hands down inside her jeans. "Take it off," she whispered to herself, "take it all off." An old aftershave commercial; Farrah Fawcett. She twisted her neck and tossed her hair into the air. The baby curls fell in a mass of tangles. Funky.

Ten-fifteen. Sheila took off her watch and placed it on the side of the sink, ran the water to warm, and stepped in the shower, the sides of which she had pasted up with pictures cut from her high-school yearbook. The shower massage pulsated, the music blared, her feet pressed against the sides of the tub. And there was love.

The knock was very soft. She could barely hear it pulsating in her brain as the rest of her body rocked. She was glad she had decided to lock the green door. And the music played on. Played on. She stroked her stomach and tried to look inside her flat belly button. If she stretched wide enough, there was no belly button at all, the flaps of skin unfolded and revealed the perfect unborn person. Was anyone in there? "So happy to make your acquaintance," she played.

20

Dolores listened. She watched the keyhole. Dolores peered over her enlarged stomach, and waited. She cried, huge lumps of black mascara smearing under her eyes making stains on the pink-flowered pillowcases she had taken from her grandfather's in Willoughby. "Good," she cried, "I want Phil to see me this way when he walks through the door. I want him to see me this way."

The pain was everywhere: in the off-white walls, the head-board found at Goodwill, the tightly hung throat muscles. Pain throbbed between her legs, her belly, her breasts. The baby would be born out of pain.

"Dolores, I love you," Phil repeated over and over until she couldn't stand it anymore. She could see him smiling, those oversize white teeth like ivory tusks. He could smile his evil grin, his clever, cunning grin. He wasn't going through the pain, the hunger. He didn't crave bananas all day. He didn't need to suck his thumb just so he'd have something in his mouth. And every night he made her go down on him. Well, she was pitiful. They'd tried to have normal sex, but she'd spotted blood and screamed, "See, you're gonna kill it, damn you. You're gonna kill it," and Phil wouldn't enter her that way anymore. But he hadn't really cared, she knew. He'd just gone to sleep that night and then, the next night, it was as if nothing had happened. He had forgotten all about the damage. What did he care? He'd just said, "I love you. How about making me feel good?" and she knew what he meant. What did he care if he'd jammed his prick into an innocent kid's skull?

"Wouldn't it be nice to have a baby together?" he had whispered in her ear.

"I don't think so," she had giggled. "I'm just getting used to everything. A new apartment and a boyfriend and all. Besides, you'd probably make me get rid of it, wouldn't you?"

"Never," he had smiled. "I'm too much in love with you." He'd sat up on his knees, erect. "C'mon. Let's have one." He had reached for her newly frosted hair and said, "I love you."

"Can't you think of anything else to say," Dolores had answered. "I get sick and tired of hearing the same thing over and over and over. Like a broken record or something."

"Dolores?" he'd questioned. "I don't understand."

"This love shit's for the birds," she'd said. But her heart had felt full, and she had felt happy. She couldn't figure out why she was saying the things she was saying.

"C'mon, sweetheart," he had said, moving closer into her, "don't put in your diaphragm tonight. Let's see what it feels like without it."

"No," she had said, settling back on her pink-flowered pillowcase with him on top of her. "It's stupid, and it's not even a romantic gesture now. You know," she'd said, "if you just rushed in here and swept me off my feet and screwed me . . . then it would be romantic. But now . . ."

"C'mon. . . ."

"Uh uh," she'd said. "I really could get pregnant, you know. I am a girl."

"A woman," Phil had answered, "and a beautiful one."

She had used the diaphram, though, damn it. She couldn't be called irresponsible. She hadn't been some romantic idiot. She'd taken care of herself. She'd said no and she'd stood up and slipped the damn thing in. A girl couldn't stay a virgin until she got married. Not in East Ocean View anyway. Willoughby, West, and Central were bad enough: old dilapidated buildings, rubbish flooding the cracked streets pulled this way and that by the hard winters, the startling cold winds that whipped around ticky-tacky houses and over stumps of trees that one unimaginable day had somehow been able to survive whole, picket fences, beaten and weathered to dark grayness, lifted from the soggy ground flying toward a passer's heart. East Ocean View was just full of temptation. God, how was she supposed to know what to do? She did what she thought was right. Phil had seemed right. Phil had seemed transient, yes. But then, living in a service town he had seemed less transient than most. At least she hadn't had to plan her life around the raising and lowering of the American flag. Those little rosewood crates with flags carefully folded and positioned for safekeeping; baby coffins. No,

Phil had had no roots, but no roots were better than beaten down stumps.

She had gone downtown to the public health clinic and been fitted along with the girls from her vocation beauty class. Jesus. And she'd checked it for holes every day . . . even the days when Phil hadn't come around and she hadn't been able to find him, just to make sure it didn't dry out or something . . . and she'd kept it coated with baking soda. Damn it. She wasn't dumb. They just never told her that you couldn't take a hot bath afterward. All she had done was take a bath. What was she supposed to do? Let it slide down her legs. It dried and stuck to her thighs and it was dirty. She wanted it out of her. Who would have thought they'd live long enough to make it to the bathtub anyway? Jesus Jones. Rosemary had. Damn Rosemary. Damn fucking Rosemary. Why did Rosemary have to be so strong?

21

"I'm glad I'm not married anymore," Jude said, reaching over to pat Sheila's stomach. "I like my freedom. I like knowing I can pick up and leave anytime I damn well want."

"I don't see you going any place so special," Sheila said. She shook her head in quick little motions, the veins along her temple line showing through the translucent skin behind the freckles. "You keep that postcard taped up on your mirror, but I don't see you getting up off your can and going anywheres yourself."

"Truthfully," Jude said, lighting a Vantage and taking a long pull, "you ever fucked a nigger?"

Sheila's cheeks flushed and she slumped at the shoulders, her waist a little pudgier than before under a breastbone that stuck out like the edges of a corselet. The breastbone stuck out of everything the girl wore, her neck always twisted as if the sharp vein and bone points were directed inside as well as out. "I had a black boyfriend once," she said, "when I was in high school."

"I bet you thought you were real cool," Jude added. The dislike Jude felt for Sheila was apparent, but everytime she needed anyone it was always Sheila she called.

Sheila answered, "I was real quiet and he sat next to me in history class. We helped each other, and we fell in love."

"Hah!" Jude laughed.

"We did," Sheila began to shake and her eyes grew wide. "We fell in love. But they made us break up. We was afraid to see each other around school or anything, so we ended up breaking it off. You know, all the kids would yell things at us, and some white boys wrote Nigger Go Home on his locker, and they called me slut and everything. And one day these black girls they get me in the bathroom and they try to pull my hair out of my head saying I had stolen one of their men. I don't know," she said, "me and Raymond was better off, I guess, not bein' together. But . . ."

"But what," Jude asked, blowing smoke in the air.

"I just never fell in love with anybody the way I fell in love with Raymond. Never," she said, shrugging her shoulders. "No one makes my knees weak like he used to," she smiled, her chipped tooth exposed.

"Why don't you find him now?" Jude asked. "It's never too late."

"It's too late," Sheila said, rubbing her tummy. "Besides, Raymond got married right outa high school. I think I'd feel he was inferior if we got together now, you know?"

"Not really," Jude answered. "But I guess it don't matter anyway with you gettin' married now and all. Right?"

"Oh, yeah," Sheila said, pulling her frosted hair out of her eyes, "I almost forgot about that for a second."

22

"*H*as anybody ever told you they loved you as much as I tell you I love you?" Phil smiled and again, it was held a long time for her to memorize.

"No," Dolores laughed, sitting on the edge of the bed. She sat with her knees up, feet balanced on a white stool in front of her vanity mirror. Her grandfather had called her a whore and told her to get all of her profitless possessions out of his home. Raising you has been futile practice, he had said, there's no tinkering with the devil. "And I don't care," Dolores said, offering Phil a slice of pepperoni pizza from the cardboard box on her lap.

"Say it back," Phil said.

"Honestly," Dolores said, biting down on the pizza. It was too hot and she could feel a blister ballooning on the roof of her mouth right away, "I wish you would quit bugging me about it. I'll say it when I'm ready to say it."

"Put the pizza down and tell me that you love me," Phil ordered. Still, he was grinning and she didn't think that he would be hurt if she said no. Playing was half the fun. Without play there was no game, no intrigue, no thrill, emotion.

"Uh uh." She tried to breathe the sea air. "I won't either." But it wasn't there. The window was open, but there was no musty salt of the sea drifting off the bay.

"You will too," he cuffed her wrist. "I'm telling you now. You better say it."

"Quit," she giggled and pulled her arm away, dropping her slice of pizza to wooden floorboards. "Now see what you've done? There's all kinds of hair in puffballs down there and everything and you've made me drop my pizza in it."

"You're my woman," Phil played, "and you're gonna tell me you love me."

"Okay," Dolores said. It was late and the room was damp and stuffy, and things weren't right. "Okay. Okay. I love you," she said.

"I don't like your tone of voice," Phil said, grabbing her wrist again and wrenching it this time, the small bone under the circle of his fingers feeling like it would snap any minute. His greenish-blue eyes sparkled and they made her smile even though she hurt. She couldn't help it. Even when he hurt her, he charmed her. It was magic. And it was all painfully funny.

"Okay, I love you, I love you, I love you," Dolores said, letting the entire box of pizza fall to the floor, "God, honest, I do, I love you."

23

"**Y**ou a friend of the new girl's, Barbita's?" Sheila asked, washing a black woman's head.

"Uh huh."

"Does she have a big following or anything? Do you know?"

"She's pretty good," the woman said. "I followed her from the beauty school."

"Oh," Sheila said, "you know, they promised me the next chair that opened up." She scrubbed the woman's scalp hard with her thin fingers. "They promised me that last year when I got outa beauty school. Now they got me doin' their shit work and that's the end of the line."

"That's too bad." The woman smiled as the girl massaged her head. Sheila looked down into the sink at the black woman's face, so serene, so pleasant, as if someone had just handed her a whole plateful of chocolate candy and said, "lick it up."

"You see the story of Miss Jane Pittman on TV?" Sheila

asked. And she began to feel nervous. She hadn't felt nervous when Barbita had shown up for work in the morning with her spike heels and tight pants. That hadn't bothered her. Blacks were just like whites as far as she was concerned.

"Yes. I saw it." The woman spoke distinctly. Almost too distinctly

"She sure was an ugly woman," Sheila said. She squeezed the pink liquid and watched it ooze into the wiry mesh of the woman's hair. She let a dot of the shampoo lay across the darkness of the forehead. "I mean, not because of her origins or anything, you know, that's not what I mean. I mean, ugly comes in all colors." The woman's eyes were closed, and her jaw jutted forward. "You know," Sheila said, trying to ease out of her one-sided conversation, "I'm gonna have a baby."

"Oh, really?" the woman smiled and opened her eyes slightly. "I couldn't even tell you was pregnant. How long has it been?"

"Four months," Sheila said, straightening up and cupping her hand over her belly.

"Married?"

Sheila was glad she was wearing rubber gloves. She could feel the sickness rising through her chest and she could taste it in the back of her throat. She looked across the store for Jude. Jude, she thought, if I ever needed a friend, it's now. Sheila watched Dolores making small talk with the new girl. Dolores with her assuredness, and Claudine with her makeup and her fingernails and her pretty face. And now there was Barbita with her long dark legs and tight jeans.

"Married?" the woman repeated. "I bet the father is soooo proud."

Sheila looked down. The sink was porcelain and white, the black hair frizzing in the bowl only a second after the water had hit it. She bent over and vomited. It came. It just came and came and came. The vomit poured from her lips and dribbled from her nose, and her thin hair fell over her face and tangled itself in the goo.

The black woman screamed, screamed so loud that the whole store turned to watch, and then there was a clickety-clickety-clickety and Dolores was behind Sheila pulling her up from the waist and running a smooth hand over one ear.

"OH, GOD! OH, GOD! OH, GOD!" Claudine yelled. "WE'RE TERRIBLY SORRY. REALLLY! OH, GOD! GET HER CLEANED UP. JESUS CHRIST. AND GET SHEILA OUTA HERE!"

24

Sheila unbuttoned her shirt and examined herself in the bathroom at the back of the shop. She'd make more money if she were a dancer in The Blue Garter. Claudine could get Rod to give her a job. She was thin. She wouldn't show for at least another month or so. Knowing Rod, he would probably get off on seeing a pregnant woman do a strip dance. Yeah. That would be a class act. Why not try?

Because Jeff would be there. Jeff would be there watching every move she made on stage, every bump, every hip movement, with disapproval. And she could never show herself in church again. She would be even more of a sinner than she already was. Making money was one thing. Keeping yourself clean was another. Just step into the shower, she thought. There's love in the shower. There's rest in the shower. There's peace of mind in the shower.

"Hello, Jeff?" she spoke into the receiver of the extension phone she had brought into the bathroom. "Jeff," she cried, "I can't, I can't talk about it now. Yes, I'm still in the shop but they want me to leave. Jeff, are you there? I threw up all over this woman. Why? I don't know why. I guess it's cause I've still got my mind set on having the baby and all. I'm a good Catholic. Jeff? Can you come pick me up? Jeff," she cried looking at herself in the small bathroom, "I'll marry you now."

"Jesus," Sheila cried into Jeff's arms when the patrol car pulled up in the rear of the beauty shop, "I can't get a fair deal from anybody. You know, they even hired a black girl to take my place before I left. Yeah," she whimpered. "They said it was because the neighborhood was going black, but," she cried harder, "I know it was because they saw my work that day they let me style that woman who came in and wanted to look like Loretta Lynn, and that was it."

"I know, baby," Jeff said, holding her against his blue uniform. She felt safe. He would make a good father. "I know. Everything's gonna be all right. You'll see, baby. Everything's gonna be all right."

"Jesus," Sheila cried, "too rotten to be true. Too rotten to be true. I just wanna go home and take a shower. I love you."

25

"I'll tell you something, Jeff," Rod whispered behind the bar, "someday that Dolores and me," he motioned by clasping his hands together. He was such a pretty boy. He had a style of his own; he had a kind of Frankie Avalon virtuosity. He stood with his head cocked, always, waiting for the right moment, waiting for the kill; he was the kind who simply assumed women would fall in love with him because he didn't really want them back. He'd had a good track record in the past. It was just that things had slowed down lately. He was nearing forty, and he had become unglued. Still, he had all of his hair and didn't intend to lose it. Every night he spent alone he smothered his head in mayonnaise before he hit the sack. No, he didn't intend to lose it.

"You really think you two could make a go of it?" Jeff asked.

"Yeah," Rod nodded, "when I'm ready. Sure. When *I'm* ready though."

"I don't know," Jeff said, leaning his head under the tap and taking a large swig of beer in his mouth, gargling like it was mouthwash, and then gulping. "You know," he said, wiping his thick lips with the back of his hand, "you've had your problems, and she's had her problems and, well, hell," he laughed, "do you think two people with so many problems really oughta get together? I mean, take me and Sheila for instance . . ."

"You create your own problems," Rod smirked.

"Yeah, like, neither one of us had anything to worry about before and," he grinned foolishly, his chin dimpling, and whispered, "look at us now . . . happy as two pigs in slop. Try to get one like Sheila, Rod. You gotta make problems together."

"Thanks, buddy," Rod said, patting Jeff on the shoulder. "I'll keep that in mind."

26

"I love you more," Phil played. Then he cracked his jaw by placing one hand on either side of his mouth and pushing hard to the left.

"No, you used to," Dolores sobbed. "But I ruined that when I got pregnant."

"Now, honestly," he said. "You did it on purpose, didn't you?"

"No, I swear it, Phil. Really, I didn't want this. Really," she tried to catch her breath. "I hate this."

"I love you more," he said, rolling over on top of her and catching her red highlighted hair in his fist.

"I love you more," Dolores said.

Phil nuzzled his face in her hair and sucked in air of dyes and peroxides. She breathed heavily, watching him bury his face in the pretty colored web from the corner of her eye.

"You're going to get rid of it, aren't you?" Phil asked. He moved within her hair, his nose craning toward the side of her neck. She could feel the tip of the gigantic beak lightly tickling the hairs that she had made sure were bleached blonde there.

"I don't think so," Dolores answered. "I don't want to anyway."

He took one hand and pulled the hair that hung softly around her face to the back of her head. "I can't stay," he said. "You always knew that. I told you that."

"Phil," she said, "you can get your FCC license here. They run classes here."

His eyes widened, and Dolores felt as if she were looking into the total density of the bay. He was empty, a confusion; she had thought that she knew the type of fish that swam in the bay, every piece of seaweed tangling her legs, and here she was looking into strange depths not of a bay, but of a human ocean beyond recognition.

"I can't," Phil said. "I told you I wasn't going to get tied down here."

"But I want you to stay with me," Dolores cried. "It's us. It's our baby."

"Right," Phil moaned. "You want it. Now, I'm telling you something, Dolores, and you better be listening to me real good. You can't have it. You can't have it and travel with me, and I know you wouldn't want to have it alone. That's all there is to it. That's it."

"Fine," she said. "Only, don't give me this love bullshit,

this crap lingo when you don't mean it." She cried, "I love this apartment. I know it's not a whole lot, but I love this place. It's mine. And you're mine. And this baby is mine. And I'm gonna keep what I have. And what I have happens to be East Ocean View."

"You see," Phil said, rolling over on his side and smiling that neverending smile, that wide grin that couldn't be penetrated. He made up his own religion as he went along. The religion of Phil. Phil. "I love you more."

"Don't be stupid," Dolores screamed. "More than what?"

"Just more," Phil answered.

There was nothing she could do but nod her head in agreement. More. More of nothing was still nothing, she guessed.

"I won't find myself supporting the devil's child," her grandfather said. And she had been satisfied. Lord knows, sometimes, she wasn't sure of the child herself.

27

"**D**olores?" Sheila cried over the phone, her cheeks suctioned, "I can't do it anymore. I just can't do it anymore."

"C'mon, honey," Dolores answered. Rosemary sat on the floor in flannel pajamas, her light brown hair newly washed and set in tiny pincurls, darker because of the wetness. "I know it's different, but it's not *that* big of a deal, really, is it?"

"It smells funny, Dolores," Sheila whimpered. "I'm sorry. But it feels funny, and it smells funny, and I can't do it anymore, that's all. I know I'm just gonna throw up every time I have to wash one of their heads. I was so sick today, Dolores. Really, I felt like I was gonna die. I don't know why this is happening to me."

"I know," Dolores said, raising her eyebrows and turning from Rosemary to the television set that roared with three straight after-dinner *I Love Lucy* shows. She pictured Sheila, shoulders slumped, pale and washed-out looking, her hair a mousy shade of light brown, even after the girls lightened and lightened it. But the results were always the same. "Not a pretty story," Dolores said.

"I mean, with the baby coming and all . . ." Sheila whined. "Well, you know about stuff like that. You know, every day it just aches a little more and a little more. I mean, I just don't feel like I can make it anymore, and Jeff says that it's all right, you know?"

"Sure. Fine," Dolores answered. "Well, I hope this is what you want." Rosemary played with a package of cotton ear wads Dolores had brought home from the beauty parlor. Dolores cupped her hand over the receiver, "Rosie," she said, "don't get those things dirty. They go behind your ears," she smiled.

Sheila continued to speak. "I know everybody depends on me there and everything, but I just feel like this is the best thing, you know? I feel like it's what I should do. For right now anyway. I ain't got much of a choice."

"Fine," Dolores answered, watching Rosemary stuff the cotton wads behind her tiny ears. She was glad Rosemary had been so strong. Hot water. Hot water could scald, punish so many people, change the color of the skin, cause the strong muscles of a man's arm to weaken like wax in the sun.

"So," Sheila said, "I love Jeff, I guess."

"Okay. Fine," Dolores said. Conversation ended. "I'll call the beauty school tomorrow and find a fill-in for you."

"Find a replacement."

"Okay," Dolores answered.

28

"MUD FIGHT!" a sailor from the back of the bar yelled. "MUD FIGHT!" The stage was set: dark Virginia mud on plastic, wall to wall across the platformed stage. The Blue Garter smelled, Dolores burying her nose in the arm of a long red-and-white striped sweater. The air carried an odor of manure, the grotesqueness of animals bringing everyone into focus.

"I like the smell of shit," Jude said as she slouched in her chair, her long heavy arms and legs hanging from the sides like monstrous weights. "When I was a girl on the farm I always smelled of shit."

"I can believe that," Claudine smiled.

Sheila excused herself and went to the girl's room. She was starting to show. It was every ten minutes and a trip to the girl's room. Every ten minutes and Jeff was always by her side, undercover. It was ridiculous, always being watched by a cop. What if she wanted to leave? Take herself and her baby and get on the next Greyhound. What then? He'd be sure to kill someone. She had learned when she first started dating Jeff that he had a bad temper. Have you had your distemper shots yet? she had asked him after he had found her flirting with a guy that looked like her older brother. Jeff had taken a swing for no good reason, broken the kid's nose with a pool cue. Of course, a cop could always call it self-defense. She had called it police brutality. He had called her an innocent of the Sixties. What the hell do I know about the Sixties, she had asked in rage; I was only born in sixty-four. Exactly, he had answered, you don't know a damn thing about police brutality and that kind of hippie talk but what went on when you was a kid playing Peace-Talk in your mother's vegetable garden. And he had been right, and she had thought then that she would drop him, but there had been something too strong about him, and I love you had come easily. It had all been easy. Why did she have to be the only girl in the world that went to a bar looking for a good time and ended up walking away with the undercover cop?

The mud fight started. Loretta Sweate came out topless, her large flabby breasts hanging down to her waist, her face still dopy, dull, and chubby, her eyelids too heavy to be held wide even by the aquamarine color with which she crayoned them, and yet her mouth was still alive, bright, alert . . . wide and fascinated by the crowd. The smile fractured the dullness of the fleshy jawline, arrows of pleasantness spreading from the reddy lip edges to the chin, from the reddy lip edges to the bottoms of the nostrils. Her opponent was a larger woman from a bar in Portsmouth, The Catch-As-Catch-Can, surprisingly flat chested for her size. The girl from The Catch seemed all muscle. And the bets began.

"MUD FIGHT! MUD FIGHT! MUD FIGHT!" they stomped. Dolores developed a headache quickly and sat with her head held between her hands at the table. Sheila swallowed vomit. It was too much of a trip to go back and forth to the bathroom every ten minutes. And Jeff was watching. Jude applied her lipstick, holding a small hand mirror in front of her face.

"You're just like a little pussycat," Claudine said.

"Look, Claudine," Jude said, holding the mirror out at an angle, "with this little gadget I get a full view of the whole place without drawing attention to myself. It's just like watching television or somethin'." Jude hunched forward and placed the mirror on the table. Her skin looked clear and almost smooth in the dark light. "I think shit smells lovely. Don't you?"

"My mother took in a foster girl once who actually saved her shit in bottles," Sheila said. "I don't know. She had some kinda disease or somethin' where she had to wear a baggy round her waist. I don't know. It was gross. Anyway, I kept smellin' somethin', and smellin' somethin', and there was nothin' bad in the refrigerator, you know. But I opened the windows of our bedroom wide one day and there were all these string bean jars of shit on the ledge. Can you believe it? She had to save them for her doctor, she said, and my mother wouldn't even let me laugh at her. You know, that's a case of a girl actually thinking her own shit don't stink."

"That's something," Dolores said, still holding her head in her hands, getting used to the smell while trying to hold her breath. "Still, maybe you shouldn't be so cruel. You know, the girl was probably real embarrassed about it."

"Are my roots showing?" Claudine took her hands and parted her hair from the center of the teasing.

"Black as they come," Dolores answered. "Too bad you're not still working, Sheila," she said. "You could do it for her tomorrow. I'm not too hot on streaking."

"You're all right," Sheila said. "You ought not try to get me back in the store. You know, I made up my mind when that woman, Barbita, walked in that door. I was promised that spot, you know. If you weren't my friends, I probably wouldn't even be talkin' to you."

Claudine glared at Sheila. "You sure picked a hell of a time to leave."

"MUD FIGHT." The feet began to stomp.

"Oh, there aren't that many," Jude said, inspecting Dolores' split ends.

"You're lucky you didn't see all the little pickaninnies peeking in the windows today," Claudine said, lighting a cigarette. "Want one?" she offered. "Putting that sign in the window's like drawing flies to honey."

"Well, I didn't quit 'cause of prejudice," Sheila said, watching the muddy floor and the women exercising against the metal pull bar. "I quit 'cause I'm pregnant." She took a cigarette and waited for it to be lighted. "I want that understood."

"MUD FIGHT."

"I wouldn't touch Sweate's opponent with a ten-foot pole," Claudine said, curiously watching Sheila hold her cigarette to one side and spit into a tissue. "Why don't you go to the bathroom?" she asked, disgusted.

A. Jacks stood close to the stage. He wanted a good view, wanted to see if it was legal wrestling or not. Claudine excused herself from the table and made her way across the hot, crowded floor. She called his name and he held out his hand for her to grab, then pulled her the rest of the way toward him. She could smell the drip from her armpits, but it didn't matter. There were so many smells, you simply had to pretend the zoo was an enjoyment, an adventure too exciting to miss.

The bell rang. "Get her, Loretta!" the crowd yelled. There was music in the background, always music, some loud country song with the word BULLSHIT hollered in conjunction with stomping feet, hard-heeled, hard-kicking shoes against battered wood. Loretta was done. The other woman had Loretta's face smack dab in the mud. Dolores looked back over the bar to Rod. Couldn't he find some other way to make a go of this place? She wondered. He was the kind of man who lived on the edges of morality. In a way, that was very appealing. In a way, he made her blood surge, like she was the innocent school teacher and he, the demon outlaw, come to rape her in the night.

Loretta lifted her head. "Get up, Loretta!" the sailors screamed until the sound reverberated down the cavities of missing fillings of their rotted teeth and into their brains. "Get up, you slut!" Loretta lifted herself up on her knees and was slapped down by heavy arms. Her face was dark, caked in soil, her belly covered in the black ooze. Quickly, she reached up in time to pull at the woman's panties with her heart-decaled sculptured nails. There was a kick at Loretta's left shoulder, the The Catch-As-Catch-Can woman's muscular leg heaving itself with brutal force against the slumped shoulder of the dancer. Louise Little Feet watched from the blackened back room behind the bar. Her tongue hung between her teeth as her mother was rolled over and over again in the dirt, black mud dribbling from her mouth, her screams shrieks above the voices of servicemen, the whole thing another colored circus act.

Again, Loretta was kicked in the belly as she tried to stand. *"Stay down,"* A. Jacks screamed above the crowd of wild men and tickled women.

"Get the fuck outa here," some men in the front row yelled at him. Someone threw a beer, and it hit Claudine's hair, the cotton-candy whiteness turning a putrid shade of yellow.

"Look what they've done to me!" she cried as she tried to wipe the sticky stuff from her hairline, the beer dripping into her eyelashes, the dark blue mascara seeping into the caked blush of deep purple. "I'm ruined."

"Stay down, Loretta," A. Jacks yelled, his fist in the air. "Stay down."

Loretta looked over the metal bar that protected the audience from flingings of mud by a cellophane wrap. Her face was beaten; blood ran from her flattened nose and the sides of her mouth.

"FIGHT TO THE FINISH, LADIES," Rod echoed from his loudspeaker. "WE'RE ALL COUNTING ON YOU HERE AT THE BLUE GARTER, LORETTA. LET HER HAVE IT. THAT'S BIG SAL FROM THE CATCH-AS-CATCH-CAN IN PORTSMOUTH, LADIES AND GENTS. THE CATCH IN PORTSMOUTH, 2255 HIGH STREET. DOWN BY THE WATER. LET BIG SAL HAVE IT, LORETTA!"

"Jeff," A. Jacks said, grabbing the out-of-uniform cop by the arm, "Jeff. You've gotta stop this fight."

"Outa the way, long hair," a sailor smiled, pushing his way through.

"Biggest night we've had all year," Jeff smiled at A. Jacks and slapped him on the back. "A cop could get himself in a mess of trouble if he wasn't real careful," he said. "Understand?"

"STAY DOWN!" A. Jacks yelled, pulling himself closer to the metal bar. "STAY DOWN. SOMETHING'S NOT RIGHT HERE!" Perspiration poured down his face as his eyes darted from one woman to the other. "SOMETHING'S NOT RIGHT HERE!" A. Jacks yelled.

Claudine pulled him back from the crowd, the men encircling the stage, shoving and spitting obscene remarks like blood from crows' mouths. They loved the gore. Loretta's breasts were covered with muck, her daughter hiding in the back doorway, a look of horrified laughter on her face. "Mother," Louise called. Rod just faced Little Feet and gave her a pitying look. "You should know better," he said. There was nowhere for her to go. Soon she would be the one to waddle in the dirt. *"Mother."*

"Rod," A. Jacks yelled, pushing his way to the rear of the bar. "This fight is wrong. I want it stopped, you hear?"

"Listen, Buddy," Rod patted him on the back, "we're old friends. Right?"

"Look . . ." A. Jacks shook his head.

"A beer on the house. And one for your lady," Rod said, clenching his jaw and giving Claudine a dirty look. She turned away from his eyes and held A. Jacks' thick arm. "Two for your lady," he said.

"Now, you look here, Rod," A. Jacks answered, "this is damn illegal and I want it stopped. *NOW!*"

"Throw him out," Rod said to Jeff. "I want him out."

"OUT? Jesus Christ, Rod. You can't do this. Jeff," A. Jacks pleaded, his thick shoulders twitching through the crowd of bodies, smells, and hair, like an animal baited into a metal

81

trap by only a flash of fluorescent color. Claudine stood behind him and watched, helpless, wet, embarrassed because of her sticky face . . . embarrassed because of Rod.

"You're underage, A. Jacks," Jeff said, placing a hand on the boy's shoulder. "You're too young to be seeing this anyway," he winked.

"What about *her?*" he asked, pointing toward Louise Little Feet. "You can't tell me she's twenty-one years old."

"Out," Rod said calmly. "I want you out."

Loretta still struggled in the mud with her opponent. The arms, the legs, the thighs filled with mud and blood and secretion from parts of the body the men were amazed still existed. "Give it all you got, honey," a man in a T-shirt exhibiting a picture of Raggedy Ann fucking Raggedy Andy yelled. Just then Loretta reached up for the woman's panties again, this time yanking with all of her might, her long acrylic nails popping off five at a blow. She might have lost the battle of strength, but she still had her own panties. There were some things that counted more than others. Cunt was one. Let them see your cunt filled with mud, she thought. That's worse. That's worse. I might be dead, but my cunt will be filled with roses. Yours will be a hairy pile of dirt. She pulled. The black bikini bottoms stuck snugly to the woman's ass, the firmness of her buttocks holding the Danskin tight, the muscles of the ass flexing with the movement of Loretta's hand.

"I want him out *now*," Rod said nodding his head. He was the boss. It was his operation. "OUT."

The black panties slipped. "YEEEEEEHAWWWWWWW," the squids yelled. The girls were stilled in their chairs, their eyes wide as they studied the mud covering the opponent's waist, Loretta's left hand still groomed with cracked acrylic nails filled with a sticky substance making them claw against the tough-looking skin.

Claudine hurriedly followed A. Jacks out the back door. There was no argument. There was only hate in A. Jacks' face for men like Rod and Jeff; men who were so close-minded that they saw nothing, knew nothing that would cost them a buck.

The black bikini pants drew down in slow motion, the opponent from The Catch roaring back and kicking Loretta hard in the head, the blood spurting out and blending with the mud, the audience half in hysterics, half in uproar. The penis fell from the woman's body over the bloody gore of Loretta Sweate. The muscles above and below the instrument flexed proudly. "GET THAT GODDAMNED FAGGOT OUT OF HERE!" a sailor yelled, jumping to the stage. A whore was a whore, but she was still a woman. Loretta had saved her pride. If the men could have touched her, they would have helped her to her feet, but the law was still the law.

Behind the bar Louise Little Feet gasped and stared in horror as her mother lay still on the stage floor, the crowd moving around her. "Jeff," she lurched forward, "is she all right?" There were yells, and there were lulls in the yells, as if the noise had never had a beginning, and would never end.

Sheila tried to make it to the bathroom, but threw up three times in the crowd getting there. There was no smell apparent. It mixed with the beer, and the blood, and the mud that had somehow gotten over the plastic lining and metal bar and spewed itself across The Blue Garter.

"Go home," Rod told Little Feet. "There's gonna be a bust. Jeff'll take you."

"But," she argued, searching for her mother in the crowd.

"Go home," Rod said, "I'll take care of Loretta."

"Okay," Louise said, glad that she didn't have to perform after all. Her knees shook as Jeff put his arms around her and helped her into the car, kissing her on the mouth, his soft lips fleshy against her gums.

29

"I could never love you," Dolores said, holding Rod's hand as they walked along the sand dunes in the darkness of Central Ocean View. "I'm still too much in love with Phil. You know that," she said. "Everybody knows that," she said, looking at him in amazement.

"But that was over six years ago," Rod answered. "Dolores, this is now. I make good money," he stretched out his arms and smiled. Behind him stood the remnants of the old Ocean View Amusement Park, torn down in an effort to clean up the area. The old roller coaster that had loomed monstrous in its trellis work, white sticks that had stood high on dark nights and were responsible for the death of a sailor dressed as Santa Claus who had foolishly taken a fatal ho-ho-ho bow at the very top, remained a still, crumbled picture in a B-film for television. *Death of Amusement* it had been called. Of course, the locals had been used for extras, but Hollywood had brought in its own sparkling, dazzling, perfected stars.

"I don't care all that much about money," Dolores laughed. "You don't seem to understand. It's not money I'm after."

"C'mon, everybody cares about money," Rod glared.

"No," she giggled, "I don't care that much about money. Really."

"I know your kind. You care about love," he said, holding her hand tightly. Thank God, he still had his hair.

"No," she answered, pulling her hand away from his. "I don't believe in love. That love shit's for the birds. I believe," she paused and looked at Rod in the dark. He was so very baby pretty. She *could* let herself fall in love. It would be delicious. Spring would come again. And her hair felt right. She looked more like Natalie Wood, young, than anyone else, the girls all said. And the dark Ebony eyeliner pencil inside the bottom of her lid really had made her eyes look seductive. She could fall in love with Rod. Rosemary could stay nights with Michelle until things became settled, until they really declared their love. The moon was even full. Kiss me, she thought. But, of course, at the moment she thought that, he didn't. He just stared at her, moonstruck, she thought, like a silly curly dog in heat. And he was old. She didn't have the strength for oldness, for seriousness. Her eyeliner would just have to go to waste. "Fuck you," she laughed and turned away. "It's none of your fucking business what I believe."

The moon looked as if it would go up in flames if struck by a match, and the once Hollywood amusement park of Central lay still, ancient white wood available for spontaneous combustion.

30

"It was even before, but now that she's hired Barbita and taking care of the books Caresse is going to start treating her like a manager. It's not fair." Claudine beat her fist into the pillow. "She didn't even give me a chance to get in there and compete. She just took over and I didn't even catch on to what she was doing. A. Jacks, how could I be so stupid?"

"Don't worry about it," he soothed her. "You're still making more money than she is. You've still got a steady income. Don't worry." He ran a thick hand down her slender neck. "Were you embarrassed tonight?" he asked.

"When the beer hit me?" she asked, sniffling.

"No," he groaned and lighted a cigarette. "When I was thrown out."

"No. I just followed you, didn't I? I wasn't embarrassed." She turned to him and hugged him tightly. "No," she laughed, "I was just upset 'cause I looked like a total wreck."

"Yeah," he laughed. "You were a funny sight."

She felt old. Glad it was dark. Could he see that her stomach was beginning to paunch out? Getting old. "Not *that* funny-looking, I hope?"

"Naw," A. Jacks said, kissing her. "You're my babycakes. You'd never be funny-looking to me. With or without your makeup in place."

"Really?" she asked, rubbing her cold runny nose across his developed chest.

"Sure," A. Jacks answered.

"I don't believe you," she grinned. "Really?"

"Really," he answered. "You're as beautiful to me in the morning as you are at night. Always."

"Always?" she cuddled.

"Always."

Claudine was glad the lights were off and the night was over, that the children were asleep and that in the morning she could get up before Allen Jacks and wash her face real good with cold water and pat moisturizer into her skin. Without her beauty routine she would hate to think of life. No man in his right mind would want her the way she really looked in the morning. And after the moisturizer, she'd blend in a little color gel to give herself a fresh and dewy glow. To look just like Bettina, that was her goal. To know that her face was perfect enough to be hanging on the wall in a beauty parlor. To know that every woman who walked into the salon would look up at the picture of you and think she'd like to have your face.

"Goodnight, darlin'," she said. "Thanks for being here."

"Now, none of that silliness," he sighed. "I'll always be here with you."

"Um," she said, turning her face into his shoulder. "I think the answer to everything," she said, just before nodding off, "is falling in love again. I've gotta get Dolores," she sighed, "to just fall in love again."

31

"You've got to see this, Dolores," Claudine laughed. "Quick, c'mere. You've got to see this!"

A. Jacks helped Dolores up the steps and into Claudine's living room. The night had been loud and long, and Loretta and Louise had danced more than their six routines apiece. The men had grabbed and Dolores had giggled with them all, hoping that one of them, just one of them once, would amount to some kind of happiness. Why did they all have to be jerks looking for a lay? Once, around eleven-thirty, she thought she'd bumped into someone who could have been nice. He was close-shaven but he had a slightly devious grin and one dimple. She'd accidentally knocked into him when someone had pushed her from behind. She hadn't seen who did it, but it didn't really matter cause when she looked up from her half drunk stupor, there had been Mr. Wonderful. And she had felt so safe for an instant. He'd grinned at her, run his big soft hand over the top of her head, just as if she'd been a little girl who'd been playing out in the snow and had come inside to sit by the fire with wet flakes still in her hair. That hand over the top of her head. She had melted. She'd just stared up at him dumbly. But it didn't matter because that hand over her head had just been another kind, yet meaningless, motion. And she had to learn that. She had to beat it into her thick skull that every motion didn't have some deep meaning, that every man who placed his hand on top of her head wasn't making some holier than holy gesture assuring her that the rest of her life she was going to be taken care of. It just wasn't so. The close-shaven man with one dimple had walked right by her, had not even looked directly into her face, and had gotten lost in a whole group of close-shaven men. And she had cursed the United States government for offering men the security of a home and food, of friends and decent work, when women with children clawing at their rayon slips combed the sands of the earth during the night, hiding their faces and their embarrassment in the dark, looking for hidden treasures ejaculated into the seas and washed up on the shores. Women were left the scavengers of life, and not by any fault of the men. Men, she was sure, were just as embarrassed by their fish women, by their mother immaculates providing purification and deodorization by way of creams and polishes, waxes and varnishes, mouth gargles and glycerine. And she was sorry, she was sorry, but looking into the crowd of men watching Loretta Sweate turn and show things that were sluttish, she knew, she was sure, that half of these men were goddamned butt-fuckers.

"She's got the pink and I've got the red. It's all right, isn't it, Mom?" Rosemary asked from where she and Michelle sat on the floor painting Johnnie's fingernails. "It's all right, isn't it?" she asked again.

"Sure, sure, it's all right," Claudine giggled and turned to Dolores. "Isn't that just the cutest thing you've ever seen?"

Dolores' head swam. She couldn't manage walking the block home in the dark of East Ocean View with Rosemary. All the niggers out there. All the Navy. It was all her fault, she knew. It was all her fault that she wasn't with Phil. She should have clung to his shirttails and let him drag her like a used prophylactic through the dirt. She was strong; she could have managed. He wasn't any fucking butt-fucker. The way he had written to her so gently. The way he had been so beautifully sexy in his letters. They had made her cry. Each one had made her cry, and she had pressed each one carefully back into its envelope and placed it into her bottom dresser drawer with her lingerie until he had written that one letter that had said, "I hope you're not saving these letters." Then she had known. Then he'd gone and proven her doubts right. He'd gone and fallen in love with someone else, just like everyone said she should do. He had his life to live and she had hers. The letters were just paper, words printed in a chicken-scratched hand for a kick and then forgotten. *I hope you're not saving these letters.* She knew she should just go out and find someone who could make her life happy, someone who wouldn't mind if she said she just wasn't going to work anymore, someone who would kiss her between her toes upon request in the middle of the night and make all of her dreams pleasant. But that was a fantasy, too. There wasn't anyone who could soothe all her hurts, make all of her pains go away. There was only Phil. Only Phil and Rosemary. They were all that was real, and they were all that was make-believe. Because she was sure, after that letter, that Phil had found somebody else. *I hope you're not saving these letters.* But, still, Dolores couldn't imagine, really, that anyone could be to Phil what she had been to Phil. She felt sick.

Johnnie sat smiling, his pink and gray face like Silly-Putty gone bad from too many comic strip copyings. Tiny little fingernails. He steadily held them out for everyone to see. So proud underneath it all. So strange that he was really so proud. It was hard to imagine how he could really think, act, have feelings. "Poor little guy," Dolores thought, "disgusting, grotesque thing. How could Michelle and Rosie even stand to touch him?"

The radio played from the kitchen, *"It's a little too late for a love song, though I'm lookin' all over the world. It's a little too late for a love song, for this kind of girl."*

"I'll walk you two home," A. Jacks volunteered.

"It's been a long crazed road of passion, a story too fine for my eyes. It's been a second too hard forgotten, it's been some nights of lonely lies."

"But Johnnie's nails aren't dry yet," Rosemary argued. "I don't want to go home yet."

"Rosie," Dolores spoke, "it's close to three in the morning. C'mon now. You're not even supposed to be up this late. You should be keeling over like Mommy."

"Have a cup of coffee or somethin'," Claudine offered, wiping underneath her eyes to make sure no mascara had collected there from the evening. "It'll sober you up."

"No," Dolores said, feeling the sickness in her chest. She had to get home and get to bed. She wanted to look at that letter again. Just that one letter. She had taken all the rest of them out of her drawer and thrown them away. She'd dumped them into the kitchen wastebasket and thought good riddance, but then, when she was taking the trash out to the dumpster, she'd had second thoughts, and she'd dug her hands deep into the brown paper bag that she used as a liner, through the old spinach Rosemary had refused to eat and the old cereal and coffee grounds and Lord knows what else, and she had still been unable to come up with the letters. They had disappeared and she had been panic-stricken that Rosie had found them and taken them over to Michelle to read for her. That would have been the end of everything. Rosie would have found out that Phil wasn't a storybook character, that Phil wasn't some shining Prince with a silken voice, but that her father was just another guy with a hard-on who had once stretched across her mother's bed and said "you're the best thing that's ever happened to me," and that her mother just couldn't let that glory-filled moment go, that all the moments she and Phil had spent together were just sparkling bubbles that go pop in the air, and that any *love*

Rosemary had been born out of had been as empty as the ozone level.

"Yeah, Dolores. Stay!" Michelle said, jumping up and down balancing a Dixie Cup on her head.

"It's a little too late for a love song, though I'm lookin' all over the world . . ."

"That's hard to do," Rosie laughed, trying to balance her own paper cup on her light brown hair. There was a ring of pineapple juice left in the bottom of the cup, and a bit dribbled down the side of Rosemary's face.

"Don't copy me," Michelle whined. "Mommy, make her stop copying me."

"I'm not."

"You are, too."

"It's a little too late for a love song, for this kind of girl."

"Am I copying, Mom?" Rosie asked.

"Rosemary, we've gotta go," Dolores said, taking the cup off the child's head. "It's late, Claud," she said, "and I've gotta get home and get her to bed. See, she's already acting cranky from being overtired."

"Okay," Claudine said, closing the polish that had been left open on the arm of the green plaid couch. "Hey," she motioned to Dolores with her head as A. Jacks angled toward the door. "What happened with the sailor from the other night? You know, Wonderful Waverly, the one who did it on stage?"

"What?" Dolores pretended not to understand.

"You know," Claudine smiled, "what was the deal with scoring tonight? I saw him there."

Michelle and Rosie giggled as they bent over Johnnie's fingers to blow them dry. The nails were soft and small and the blowing seemed to tickle the boy. His face screwed itself into a million wrinkles of pleasure, his eyes shining brightly through the flaps of reddy skin.

"I don't think he even recognized me," Dolores said,

pulling Rosie toward the door by the hand, "and I sure didn't make a move to recognize him. And, hey," she said standing in the cold hallway, "tell your friend Rod to call off his watchdogs. He's really giving me the creeps. Yuck!" Dolores laughed.

32

"Sheila," Dolores said, looking out the front glass of the store from the receptionist desk, the sun beaming down in a walkway of white against the cement pedestrian path, troubled victims of the neighborhood hauling brown sacks of Twinkies and Vanilla Fudge Ripple from the 7-11, broken yellow plastic woven baskets of faded laundry under muscle-bound tired arms. If only the sun could break completely through the cold, if the dark worried faces could feel warmth in the creases of broken skin lines, if East Ocean View were a brightly colored portrait of stripey-suited people. But that was not real life; that was a museum piece. Balloons don't fly forever, and certainly not in thunderstorms. "You've got to stop calling on the telephone. I love talking to you, but it's cutting off business, you know? People might be trying to make appointments, okay? You understand, Sheila?"

Claudine rolled her large blue eyes, blue mascaraed lashes, at Dolores, and Dolores placed her hand over the receiver. "How can I be any more blunt than that?" she asked. Claudine shrugged and walked away.

"Look, Sheila, you know, I don't know what to say. Why don't you just marry the guy? There's not that much out there, you know. And you like him, don't you?" Dolores counted the number of bottles of polish she had ordered for the month and compared that to the number she had ordered the month before while Sheila continued to babble. Caresse would be proud. She was putting La Boudoir back on its feet. They might even renew her contract, this time *officially* as manager. Then she'd be proud to say that she didn't *work* in a beauty parlor, but that she *ran* a beauty parlor. Not that she wasn't proud now. Her grandfather had looked down his nose at her and her little girl, but she had been proud enough. She enjoyed the work. She liked talking to the women. It was better than being a secretary, or, like Claudine said, a salesgirl. It was as if, in the salon, she was protected from everything that was not beautiful. She was beautiful. She and Cherée. "Sheila," Dolores said, holding the phone under her chin as she checked the amount of conditioner she had ordered on the books, "Rosemary is the best thing that ever happened to me. I love being a mother. There's nothing better. Really," she crooned in her beauty parlor face, the face she wore that was perfectly covered in creams, then base, then three different blushes for contour and color, then eye color and liner and mascara, then lip liner and matte—stick and regular color—before gloss, "don't be silly. It's the most beautiful experience a woman can have. Sure, you're fat for a while, but, when your belly bursts, you're given the gift of watching a dream become real."

"Right out of *Modern Mother*," Claudine laughed as she walked up to the cabinet and started to sort the morning mail.

"Look, Sheila," Dolores said, watching Claudine inspect. "I just can't hold up the line like this. Okay?" Dolores tilted her head to watch Claudine even closer. She wanted to tell her to get her gritty paws off the mail, but she couldn't. She had no right to. They were supposedly on equal ground. Only they were both coming up for renewal and the way things looked maybe Claudine wouldn't ask to be manager. No such luck. They would both ask. Only she had more experience now at running the business, and she had made the move to hire Barbita. Someone had to take charge. "Okay. Bye-bye now."

"Not a pretty story," Claudine smiled. "Right, babe?"

"Sheila was never a pretty story," Dolores sighed. "But she'll be happier than the rest of us all rolled together in the long run. She's simple. She's an ugly duckling."

33

Dolores bit down on her hamburger, the frozen kind from 7-11 that they slip into the microwave. "What did it do?" she asked Claudine's customer, "just lift?"

"I went to the toity," the customer answered, "and it caught on my pantyhose and I couldn't get it unhooked. And my husband was looking for me everywhere. I mean," the customer continued, "alllll night," she laughed, "I was in the toity alllll night."

"With your finger up your ass?" Claudine giggled.

"Oh, it was ridiculous," the customer laughed. "Allllll night, and I didn't know how to explain it to the hostess. And, you know, she was real uptown and she'd admired my nails earlier and I'd neglected to tell her they were fake."

"You know," Dolores said from her table next to Claudine's, "I think they put rat meat into these hamburgers. They just taste like they've got everything in the world in them but hamburger."

"My daughter says that one of the girls in her dorm at college found a worm in a fried egg sandwich out of one of those frozen food machines," the customer said.

"Gee," Claudine smiled, "I'm glad I never went to college."

The phone rang and Dolores put down her hamburger

and went to answer. The rest of the girls on the floor continued to cut and pin and curl and chatter, everyone styling the same way they had been for years, only longer or shorter, with a flip or without a flip. It would have been different if Caresse had held new styling classes, but they didn't. As long as a following held together, it didn't matter.

"That was a funny call," Dolores said, sitting back down at her manicurist table and picking up the hard outside edges of the hamburger roll.

"You need two tips and I'm gonna file this one down," Claudine told her customer. "You wanta pay me now before your nails get wet so you won't smear them up later?"

"It was a man," Dolores said, sipping her Tab. She watched Claudine run the portable buffer over the woman's acrylics. The white powder frosting reminded her of the cookies she had promised Rosemary she would teach her how to make. That was something a mother should do with a daughter. Teach her how to bake cookies. Lately, with Rod around, she hadn't taught Rosemary much of anything. But there was no getting rid of Rod; he had his mind made up and, frankly, she liked the fuss.

"What'd he want?" Claudine asked.

"Nails done."

"When?"

"Today."

"Well," Claudine said, still buffing her lady's nails, "I can't do it today, Dolores. Look at my hands. They're blood raw. The polish remover is just getting to me." She breathed heavily. "You know, you could do a few too. I don't know what you're living on these days."

"I told him I would do it, Claudine."

"You told him you'd do it?" Claudine asked, stopping her work. She looked at Dolores questioningly. "Why'd you do that? You and Rod aren't gettin' it together?" she ques-

95

tioned, smiled broadly. "You and Rod havin' problems?"

"It's like you said, I need the money. I can't keep on letting Rod buy everything."

"What'd this guy sound like? This guy who wants a manicure?"

"A man. That's all."

"I don't understand," Claudine questioned, "I thought you'd decided it was your job to do all the book work and you weren't gonna work on anyone but your regulars. You're having big problems with Rod, aren't you?" Claudine smiled.

"What you got against me and Rod," Dolores grinned back. "I was gonna do you a favor. I saw that you were booked."

Claudine turned on her buffer again and continued working.

"Besides," Dolores said, "this guy sounds interesting. Cute, you know?"

"He's probably a fag."

"I don't think so," Dolores studied the glamorous Cherée, her one shoulder facing the camera. "It sounded like he was making a pass at me, you know? It was kinda cute. I don't know."

"What'd he say?" Claudine asked.

"Oh, nothing," Dolores smiled.

"It had to be somethin'," Claudine's customer said. "C'mon. Spill."

"Well," Dolores smiled. "He said that he was sure we were all going to be a little put off when he walked in the store, but that his nails were in really bad shape because he used his hands in everything he did."

"A carpenter," Claudine said.

"What then?" the woman asked. Claudine worked on the right index finger, spreading the nail outward and then around the foil where the tip had broken off.

"Well, then he said that he didn't want the girls to be

too shocked and that he'd appreciate it if I was the one who worked on him. He said it would be easier that way since he had already talked to me on the telephone and everything and knew my name."

"So that's making a pass at you?" Claudine giggled. "Jesus, babe. Rod's in trouble."

"Anyway, he'll be in at two-fifteen. Ernest Wells," she said, finishing the last of her hamburger and crumpling the waxed paper into a small ball. "Ernest Wells. Mrs. Dolores Wells."

"Dream on," Claudine filed, "the guy probably weighs five hundred pounds and's got a wife and six kids," she laughed. "Poor Rod. Poor fuckin' Rod," Claudine grinned. "When is he goin' to get a fuckin' break?"

34

"Where did you learn how to play the piano like that?" Dolores asked.

"My mother gave me lessons when I was a kid," Phil answered. "I've always loved the piano. Well, I've always been nuts about music. That's all."

"Really?" Dolores asked, sitting on the edge of the mahogany stool next to him.

"Yeah. I remember when I was real little, getting up early in the morning before my parents got up, and watching Liberace on TV . . . I don't know," Phil grinned that large smile, every tooth exposed to the dampness of the church late at night, "I suppose that there was just always something inside," he placed his hand to his thin chest, "that made me love music. You know?" He placed his slim fingers back on the yellow ivory of the keyboard. "They say that if your mother listens to the radio a lot when she's pregnant that you'll be influenced by the kind of stuff she's listening to.

Like, for instance," he said, lifting his hands to the black keys, "if your mother listened to opera all the time you'd probably turn out to be some kind of loud creative freak. But," he played an augmentive chord, "if your mother listened to, say, Sinatra all the time, you'd turn out real cool and sophisticated. You know?"

"What do you think my mother listened to?" Dolores asked.

"Let's see," he said, playing a chord in cadence, "probably Doris Day," he laughed. "What do you think my mother listened to?"

"Doris Day?" she argued. "What kind of wisecrack is that?"

"I love you, you know?" Phil grinned.

"I know," she breathed heavily, "you tell me enough."

The church, the colored glass in high arches, stood just a highway across from the bay in the darkness. Dolores and Phil sat together on a bench in the rear of the building and sang very softly, listening to the seepings of wind through cracks at the tops of the painted glass. They could only be seen in the dark; small cracks at the tips of Mary Magdalene's fingers, at the crown of the baby lord Jesus Christ, and then again, at the very top of the moon that loomed above the head of the third wise man. And the cracks were not disturbing; except in the cold breeze they let in. They were just cracks, as if the windows were meant to be a sign of imperfection.

Phil had jimmied open the lock at the rear of the church. Stupid, Dolores had thought, that the church people had not invested in a lock any better than that one. But there had been nothing inside that a thief would have been inclined to take: a few prayer books, the rostrum, some threadbare red cloth. Sliding her hand along the altar rails Dolores had felt tiny pieces of wood slip underneath her skin. But she could not complain. Being with Phil she felt no pain. Her grandfather's scoldings had not even made her feel guilty. This was what real love was about, she convinced herself.

She knew the basics. But she had never known anyone to whom she could give herself, every thought that she had ever had, like she could to Phil. He listened. He was tender with her. He could make her feel like a child who was loved. Floating in a warm cloud above the beach holding Phil in her arms, looking down at the empty waters, and knowing she would never be touched, that she was good, that was heaven.

"You cold?" Phil asked, feeling her shiver next to him in just an orange halter top.

"Not really," she said. "I don't want you to stop. I want you to keep on playing forever."

"Hah!" Phil laughed. Again, for memorization. Always for memorization. To capture every second. To be able to return to every second, as if flipping back to a still life. The wide smile. "That wouldn't be too hot," he said. "I've got plans, you know?"

"I know," she smiled. "And you're gonna be the best DJ ever."

He groaned. "I told you, I don't want to be the best. I just want to get by without too much notice. I just don't want to have to take orders."

"What do you mean?" she asked, feeling the dampness of the church around her. The damp air was making the wood of the church smell harsh, like in its wetness it could be rearranged, like she could go down the aisles whittling floor benches into soft woodcuts. I am the carpenter. I can make hardness soft, she thought. I have made up my mind that I am in love, and I will engrave the words into my soul.

"I mean, I just want to go someplace where I can get my FCC license cheap and then get a job on a radio station where I can play what I want. That's all."

"That's all?" Dolores asked. Wind whisped through the eye of the small white lamb of the colored window.

"That's enough," Phil answered. "Enough for me." He was careful to push the bar back into the lock in case they ever *wanted to go back inside the church again. Somehow, Dolores knew they wouldn't. East Ocean View was growing colder and damper as her green-horn sincerity to love began to play the savage tricks that children of nature will play on themselves.*

35

Ernest Wells pushed the front door of La Boudoir open himself. His arms were so developed from pushing himself along the floor that nothing stood as a barrier except height. The beauty parlor, he explained to Dolores over the phone, was not his favorite place. She had laughed, sounded like a nice girl, said that most men didn't find it too pleasing. Then she'd added that most men were fools. "No meaning to imply that you're a fool," she had said, "I've never even met you." "Well, you will," he'd answered.

"The reason I don't like beauty parlors," he said when he entered La Boudoir, "is that no matter how well you girls sweep there are always little pieces of hair that still get stuck to my palms."

Claudine smiled and studied the skateboard.

"Nothing I hate more than the hair of strangers." He stuck out his tongue, long and red. "It's a sign of living death," he said. "It's disgusting, don't you think?"

"I agree," Dolores answered. The man was nothing below the waist, but he did have a good head of hair and a lovely beard, red, that would be nice to touch. "Do you need help getting into the chair?"

"I can manage, thanks," Ernest Wells answered and pulled himself into the pink chair by the strength of his arms. "This happened in Nam, case you're wondering," he said. "It's always a shocker when people see me rolling

around on the board. It's hard for a lot of people to stomach, you know."

"You should see my baby," Claudine said, leaning across
her manicurist table and smiling. She pointed to the picture of Michelle and Johnnie taped to her wall. "He's ten
and she's eight, but he only comes up to her waist. Was
supposed to be dead seven years, almost eight years ago
now. Can you believe it? I'm writing a book," she said. "But
I can't write it until he dies. Ain't that a shame? His was
natural, of course."

36

"**G**od, Rod," Dolores had said, watching the stars
float through the black skies over Ocean View, the Chesapeake Bay sloshing in steady currents against the restaurant window pane, "maybe I shouldn't have even accepted
this invitation."

"Why don't you just calm down, Dolores," Rod had said,
offering a hand across the table. She'd watched their reflection superimposed on the picture of the waves in the
window. There was a slender girl playing with a small silver shrimp fork against the black waters. Dolores had
studied the picture. It was always really a second before
the picture, she'd realized. Time was funny that way. By
the time you looked, what you saw wasn't a real presence
anymore.

"C'mon," Rod had said, "this is supposed to be a happy
occasion. Another drink?" he'd asked. "Don't start crying
just because I told you I'm in love with you."

She'd shrugged. His reflection in the window had been
taller than her own, his arms thicker, heavier, outlined by
white cuffs, the arms of a television game show host. Fluent.
He had been fluent. He had been funny. He had been pretty.

In the window reflection she'd watched his fingers curl and uncurl, creep closer to her own hand, ball up in the center of the white tablecloth next to her wineglass. The hand had connected and she had felt a buzzing coldness through her shoulders, a chill close to what she had once felt unplugging a record player by tugging at a frayed cord.

"You all right?" Rod had asked, jerking her hand slightly.

"Fine," Dolores had answered. "Fine."

"You wanna go home?" he'd offered. "I'll ask the waiter for the check."

She'd thought about picking Rosemary up at Claudine's, having to look at that small face questioning the outcome of the date. For Rosemary. "I'll be fine," she'd smiled pleasantly and squeezed Rod's hand. "It's just been a damned long time since I've felt anything for anybody."

She'd watched his face. There was no real face. Lines in angles straight and hard, meeting at the chin in a kind of point that formed a protruding knob. His mouth, small and bird-like with thin lips, filled his face with what she felt could not possibly be real emotion. When he smiled his face seemed to be saying something other than real happiness. She was familiar with that; too familiar. Some trick pulled on the world, something that no one knew anything about, that was his *real* reason for smiling. And when his face was showing disappointment, his lips drew in all the air around him, as if to say no other living breathing object had a chance against him. Dolores had run her index finger, Flamingo Pink covering the acrylic, along the ski slope of his nose. Pig's nose, she'd thought. Looking at it from underneath, it was a pig's nose. A perfect little pig's nose. Strange for a man his age. Dolores supposed that when a man was a boy he could entice the world as a darling with lovely curly hair and a pig's nose, but, that when a man became a man, the same features became grotesque. "Honey," she'd asked, "would you mind if I picked up these critters and ate them with my fingers? I keep

102

fighting this awful desire to bend this tiny fork between my teeth," she'd smiled. Salmon lips stretching into that sweet motherly grin. Fooled you!

"Course not," Rod had laughed. "God knows I wouldn't want you to hurt your teeth." His eyes were bright blue and she'd seen from the lights dimly pointed over their table that his hair carried a tint of red. Only a slight tint of red. "I've seen it done in the finest of restaurants."

"Where?" she'd asked, trying to make conversation as she'd dipped the pink shrimp into the cocktail sauce with her fingers.

"Oh," he'd said, "up on the Eastern Shore. We'll go there sometime. With Rosie," he'd added. "What about Monday? You don't work on Mondays, do you?"

"I'm always busy on Mondays," she'd said, remembering her long drives down to Willoughby Spit, studying the scenery and listening to Rosie's pleas of freedom.

"We could take her to Busch Gardens," Rod had said. "I'll take the kid on all the rides. It'll be a blast."

"I said I'm always busy on Mondays." The Wharf Restaurant had been little different six years earlier with Phil. But everything was one place now. One place wasn't wet, and one place wasn't empty, and one place wasn't hard and gristly. They were all the same place now upon request. Like a watercolor portrait the colors blended, the light into darks, the darks into nothing. There was the end of the boat dock marked by lights, by great fluorescent candles streaking the dark night air against men's shirts she could not see, men who stood hour after hour pulling blowfish up from lines thrown under the wooden dock holds. And when the men pulled the blowfish up they would step on their faces, push the air up out of their lungs, and yank the steel hook from the thin pink lips. No color at all really, here in the dark. Blood held no color. Blue inside they said, red out, green at the bay's surface, white floating smoke-lit on the bay's floor. No real color. Blood lighted the men's shirts, shirts like lights, like darks, blending the lights into darks, the darks into nothing. One wasn't wet, and one wasn't empty, and one wasn't hard and gristly because they were all out of photographs, old and marked with sadness. The scenes weren't real because she felt nothing for them anymore, like she'd felt nothing for the man who sat across from her watching the color of her nails with his dancing eyes.

37

A. Jacks drew a half moon across Johnnie's face while the body sprawled backward in Rosemary's arms. The greasepaint slid over the skin smoothly, the purple coloring tints of rawness that flashed the puffy surface of the face. A. Jacks sat cross-legged on the green plaid couch and chose a bright red crayon from the cardboard box between his thighs. First, he tested the color on his jeans, already treated with colors of bright orange and purple against the faded blue; the orange he had used to color the boy's eyelids. Carefully, he held Johnnie's slack chin between one strong thumb and forefinger, and with the other hand he drew a bright red circle around the child's mouth.

"Noooooooo," Rosemary cried, looking down into Johnnie's face. His mouth hung limp, a bit of slobber slowly making its way through the painted lip line and the purple chin like the sticky drippings of a strawberry popsicle. "He looks too much like a clown now."

"I thought you wanted him to look like a clown," A. Jacks answered, continuing to draw.

"Nooooooooooo," Rosemary said. "I said I wanted him to look happy. You're making him look sad."

"I'm not making him look sad, Rosie, if you'll just wait a

minute," A. Jacks said. "Just wait a minute. Okay?"

"Okay," she whispered, holding Johnnie close to her chest and feeling the weight of him against her collar bone. "When will you be finished? Before Michelle comes home?"

"Before Michelle comes home," A. Jacks said.

"Will you promise you'll make him look happy?"

"Will you shut up?"

"Deeeeeeeayeeeeeeee," Johnnie said, pushing his entire chin out and then down to his throat. "Deeeeeayeeeeee," he groaned.

"He doesn't like it," Rosemary pouted. "Take it off."

"But," A. Jacks said, gritting his teeth, "we've been working on this all afternoon for Michelle. Don't you want Michelle to see it?"

"He doesn't like it," Rosemary said loudly. "I thought it would make him happy, but he doesn't like it. Take it off."

"I can't take it off now," A. Jacks said, picking up the purple grease crayon from the box and touching up the place where the drool had worn away the color. "I haven't finished. Just let me finish, will ya?"

"What color next?" Rosemary asked, looking into the box.

"I don't know," A. Jacks said, staring into the box after carefully replacing the purple crayon. "What do you think?"

"Deeeeeeeayeeeeeee," Johnnie struggled. "Deeeeayeeeeee."

"A. Jacks," Rosemary said, "he's heavy."

"It won't be much longer," he said, still looking into the box of colors.

"Michelle gets home soon?" Rosemary asked.

"Ummmmmmhmmmmmmmm."

"So he'll be finished soon?" she asked.

"Ummmmmmhmmmmmmmm."

"When?" she asked.

"Soon."

"Deeeeeeeeeayeeeeeeeeee."

"Soon," Rosemary told Johnnie. "Soon now."

105

There was no picture clock at Claudine's. No children holding hands in a wheat field, no movement of wire arms to clue Rosemary on how much longer she had to go. She couldn't tell how much longer it would be before Michelle came home from school carrying her old crumpled brown bag with whatever was left over from her lunch.

"How soon is soon?" Rosemary asked. She felt one of her legs falling asleep.

"Soon," A. Jacks said, coloring in Johnnie's mouth with a soft lavender.

"I think he looks sad," Rosemary said. Her hair was getting into the grease paint. "I hope Claud kills you when she gets home. I bet she will."

"Hmmmmmmm," he said, continuing to color.

"I hope she takes you by your long curly hair and swings you around the room."

"Hmmmmmmm," he said.

"I hope she swings you so hard you go flying out of the window!" Rosemary giggled. "I hope you go flying out of the window and there's no one there on the ground to catch you, catch you in one of those flat round fireman things." She laughed hard and her bones bounced against the back of Johnnie's head.

"Deeeeeayeeeeeeeeee."

"And I hope an elephant lands on top of you and the firemen don't do anything about it! And you squish to death," she laughed. "And your guts go all over the place," she giggled harder.

"Deeeeeeeeayeeeeeeeeeee."

"Hold the kid still, will ya?" A. Jacks ordered, squinching his thick dark eyebrows together.

"How would you like that?"

"Ummmmmmmmmm," A. Jacks said, replacing the lavender and choosing the orange again, "I'd love that." He painted the circles of the perfect nostrils. The kid was mishapen in every way humanly possible, and still, per-

106

fect nostrils and a perfect chest. And as long as he could breathe, what the nostrils went to—the heart, the lungs—were in perfect order, the kid could live. The kid could live.

"How soon now?" Rosemary asked.

"Sooner than before," he answered.

"How sooner was before?" she asked.

A. Jacks pointed the orange crayon at her. "I'm doing this out of the goodness of my heart," he said. "You know, I don't have to watch you, Rosemary, and if you don't shut up I'm gonna tell Dolores that I don't want any part of you from now on."

Johnnie's weight was even heavier than before, the mid-section of his body giving no aid to the tumbling arms, legs, and head that rested against Rosemary. She wrapped her arms around him and felt him breathe, felt the hate racing from Johnnie's underbelly. She had always known about the underbelly, the soft spot below Johnnie's navel that twitched whenever something bad happened. And she had shown it to Michelle who had stared at it in bewilderment, and they had tested it out together making Johnnie mad by throwing a whole can of peas at him and then feeling the underbelly; and then calling him ugly and slobbering into his eyes while they held the lids open and then feeling the underbelly; and by turning the lights and the TV set off and leaving him in the dark alone for hours and hours and then feeling the underbelly; and then, lastly, and meanest of all, Rosemary thought, by cag-ing him in his playpen, wrapping the sides in tin foil so he couldn't see out but only up, and burying him under every doll she and Michelle could find. And he had screamed in a hoarse voice, ugly and raw, like something that would come out of a dragon's mouth, and tried to toss, but he had trapped himself against the wooden poles of the crib until finally they saw the blood that was dribbling onto the white pad at the bottom of the cage from his throat, and they had felt so rotten that they had lifted him out together, and then Michelle had placed her hand in the soft fleshy part of the underbelly and felt it wiggle.

"Shhhhhhhhhhhhhhhhhh," Rosemary whispered into Johnnie's small ears. "Shhhhhhhhhhhhhhhhhh. Shhhhhhhhhhhhhhhhhhhh."

"Ahhhhhhh," A. Jacks breathed, "a work of art alfresco."

"Shhhhhhhhhhhhhhh." Rosemary rocked the boy back and forth, keeping her hand on the fleshy part below his belly button. "Shhhhhhhhhhhhhhhhhh."

A. Jacks covered the box of paints with the piece of shiny foil that they had originally been wrapped in up in Claudine's closet. Then he disappeared in Claud's room and came back with her large silver hand mirror.

"Take a look," he said, holding the mirror in front of the boy's face. "You like?" And then he pushed the heavy mirror flat up to the boy's nose and said, "A perfect grisaille all the same. Just what I thought."

"He doesn't like," Rosemary said, watching Johnnie's reflection, "he doesn't like that whatever."

"You like?" A. Jacks asked Johnnie again. He waited for a reply. Something. A groan, a movement, some show of like or hate. "You like?"

"How much sooner?" she asked.

There was nothing; no nucleus, no core, no storm center. Nada. Day in and day out A. Jacks sat and watched and worked on and tortured and still, no nothing. It had become a sickness with him. Of course, there was Claudine. Claudine in her beautiful body, her soft whiteness. Claudine in her powders and perfumes and paints; but more than Claudine, he wanted what was inside of *this*. He wanted that the most.

"Don't give me that blankness," A. Jacks screamed at the boy. "I'm tired of it," he said, thrusting the cold glass of the mirror into the boy's face with pressure. "I want an answer."

"I hate you!" Rosemary screamed, holding her hand to

108

Johnnie's underbelly. "I hate you! I hate you! I hate you!"

"I hate you too," A. Jacks screamed. "I hate your stupid little guts and I wish your mother would take care of you like she's spose to instead of leaving you here with me."

"Deeeeeeeeayeeeeeeeeeee."

"Now, see what you've done?" Rosemary said, holding Johnnie tightly and staring A. Jacks down. The room was very quiet and dusty, and the afternoon sunlight had faded what seemed like a long long time ago. Rosemary waited silently for the door to open, and A. Jacks watched as Johnnie's eyes strained toward the dark crack between the door and the painted green paneling surrounding the entrance.

"To hell with you both," he said, clicking on the TV.

Rosemary let her hand close around the underbelly.

38

"**T**aurus," Rod read to Dolores over the breakfast table from the beach newspaper. "Although your social life is full of interesting companions and acquaintances, you seem restrained in following through with any kind of meaningful commitment. You will soon realize that there is good reason for you to stay uninvolved." He looked at her and winked over his scrambled eggs. "Hold on now," he said, "let's not throw everything out the window yet. Ah hah! Signs indicate an unexpected romantic adventure. Saturday and Thursday look like your best days for rewarding love activities with a passionate partner. And we proved Saturday right," he added.

"We sure did," she smiled.

She was the kind of woman who was so pale that she had to apply blush to her white skin first thing in the morning. He didn't know if he liked that. Why, he wondered, did she always hide her face? In bed that night, somewhere between the hours of three and six, a new woman had appeared. Maybe not even a woman at all, but some kind of beautiful wild animal that he had doubted even existed. "Does this mean that you find me *only* an interesting companion?" Rod asked.

"No, not *only*," Dolores smiled and shook her head. "Let's see what yours says now," she said, grabbing the thin paper and holding it over her orange juice.

"Scorpio," Rod told her.

"Although you may be having some serious thoughts about a loving companion," Dolores paused, "it's best to lay back and maintain a casual relationship for a while. Intellectual powers are enhanced, and your influence over others will increase. Sunday and Monday look like your best bets for unexpected romantic opportunities with a dynamic partner."

"Interesting," he smiled. "And it's Sunday."

"But I've got a baby I've got to go over to Claudine's and get," she said, putting her orange juice glass in the sink, "before she comes skipping home on her own. Kids do that, you know."

"Dolores," Rod said, standing up and putting his arms around her waist. He could feel very comfortable there, like he wanted to lay his head in the curve of her hip and fall asleep forever, never have to face anything again. "Dolores," he said, "I told you this before, but I have to tell you again. I love you."

"Thanks," she answered, looked at the clock.

He kissed what he thought was sleep away from her eyes and then could feel it sticking to his bottom lip. He was nearing forty. By the age of forty practice should have made perfect, he thought. He would ignore it. Maybe if he ignored it, she would ignore it.

"You've got something on your lip," she giggled.

He wiped it away with his hand. "Dolores, baby," he said,

"can't you feel it between us? There's something really special here." Sometimes, when he said it, he began to actually believe it himself. Power of suggestion, he guessed. He put his hand against her face. He looked at the clock. Two children holding hands in a wheat field. Nine-fifteen. "Call Claudine's and tell them to keep the kid a little longer. I want to make love to you."

"You're a sweet guy, Rod," Dolores said, "and I, I don't want to hurt you."

"You're not gonna hurt me," he said. He was glad he still had his hair. Thank God he still had his hair. And his chest wasn't bad either. He knew that. They all loved his chest.

"I can't make *love* to you," Dolores said. "I can't *love* you. There are just too many memories. Rosemary, for one."

He couldn't figure her out. It was as if she used the kid to block anything that could dull a memory. He was tired of her stories already. He tried to tell her that memories weren't real, that they were cnly pictures developed by time. But she wouldn't listen. She accused him of not being interested in her, of not listening. Well, that just wasn't true. He *was* interested, but in her, not in her past. Damn, it was time he married and she was the sort. He was tired of living alone, tired of looking at the dishes that had piled up in the sink over the week. How could one man use so many dishes? And he didn't even eat at home most of the time. But, hell, he hated eating off paper plates. There was nothing lonelier than eating off a paper plate. He had begun to feel his whole world was nothing more than a disposable piece of dirty paper.

"Don't be silly," he said, kissing her neck, kissing her throat. He led her back into her bedroom, her head hanging, the tears welling in her eyes. He wondered if she could make the water well up on request. "Just lie still and let me love you. Lie still and just feel how much I really love you. You don't have to do anything. I just want you to feel how much I can love you."

111

"I won't promise love, Rod," she said, lying very still with her eyes closed. "I don't believe in love anymore."

"Neither do I," he said. "But just try to believe in being held."

39

"I'm home," Jeff called from the doorway. "Sheil, I'm home."

From the direction of the bathroom he heard her crying, soft and low, like bait waiting for him to come running into the steel trap. He checked the oven for a reheated apple pie, then the refrigerator.

"Sheila," Jeff yelled into the bathroom, "how come you didn't buy no Mrs. Jones' Apple Pie? Sheila?"

She didn't answer, the low moaning and sniffles continuing.

"Sheila?" he said, standing in front of the bathroom, "can I come in? Are you okay?"

"I'm okay," she said. "I'm fine."

"What's wrong?" he asked. "What're you crying for?"

"I don't know," she answered. "I just don't know."

She sat on the toilet seat, one leg crossed over the other, her neck bent, her thin frosted hair falling into her face, the frosting growing out and the dull roots exposed. In her hand she held a tweezer, and one by one she continued to pluck the hairs that were growing in fine strands from her inner thighs, too small to be seen easily, but sharp to the touch.

"Sheil, can I come in?" he spoke against the door, his mouth tasting paint.

"Jeff, just go away and leave me alone, will ya?" she sniffled.

"I want to know what you're doing in there?" he ordered.

"None of your business."

She pulled continuously from the left leg, the skin bleeding from the small pores, growing puffy and swelling.

"You have any alcohol?" she asked.

"Sheila, if you don't let me in right now," he said. "Let me in."

"You got any?"

"Sheila," he asked, growing worried, "is it the kid? Answer me, goddamnit. Is it the kid? Do you need a drink cause you're losing the kid?"

She bit her lip and continued to tweeze. The pain felt good. Before she touched Jeff again she was going to be beautiful. Her thighs were going to be cream to his fingertips. Why, in god's name, had she let Jeff talk her into leaving La Boudoir? She had been happy there. God help her, Dixie Pointer's postcard had lied. There were no ivory towers. Women were never happy locked up with men. "Nonsense," Jude had said. "You just go by that old let-me-put-my-head-on-your-shoulder-routine and you'll be fine," she'd said. But she wasn't. She wasn't happy. Her thigh bled more from the mutilation as she dug the tweezer's deeper into the opening. She wondered if it would scar. If only she could get to the electrolysis machine again. Claudine or Dolores would work on her.

"If you don't let me in," he said.

"I don't want you in here."

"It's my apartment and I want in," he ordered, "or I'll take my foot and break this door down."

"Oh," she caught herself from giggling, "go on kung fu. And," she added, "I don't want drinking alcohol. I want rubbing alcohol."

"Sheila, don't push me," he said, edging his shoulder up

to the bathroom door. "Sheila, " Jeff said, "I've gotta take a dump. C'mon now. It's *not* funny."

"Jeff, I'll be out in a minute. Please leave me alone." And she pulled up her jeans and washed the tweezers off and put them away in the medicine cabinet. In the mirror she caught sight of the puffiness under her eyes and her thoughts went back to Dolores. "If you want the child, grab every piece of the memory you can," she'd said on the phone. "Don't settle for just half the memory."

"I'm coming out now," she said as she unlocked the door and blew her nose in a piece of blue toilet paper. He was sitting in the living room looking at the evening paper. A newly opened can of beer was resting at his foot.

"Why ain't there any apple pie?" he asked.

"Louise Sweate called me today," she answered.

40

The psychedelic Jesus in the living room turned on the mantle. It was never unplugged even with the rising cost of electricity, and Jeff had warned them, he had told them both as they sat on the couch in the living room sharing a joint and drinking ice cold beer cause Loretta kept her refrigerator on freeze all the time that they were just plain throwing away electricity on that thing. "It don't pay," he'd said, "to throw away electricity on a thing like that." But Loretta had answered him, she had told him that some people got their pleasures out of watching television and listening to the radio and that, even though they liked those things, they heard enough music on the nights they were working and during their long afternoons of making up routines. They didn't want to listen to music any more than they had to. They liked to watch things in silence. It was their own little rebellion, she giggled, her heavy makeup

114

seeming to crack in points along her mouth and beside her dark circled eyes. The psychedelic Jesus turned, the blazes of deep purples and oranges and reds shooting from one end of the metal disk behind Jesus on the cross to the other. They toked and they watched, smiling contently to themselves. It was so peaceful, and against the window they could hear the rush of air and water from the Bay.

Louise walked softly toward him and took his hand, led him into her sanitary bedroom, pulled back the white textured blanket, and exposed the blood-streaked sheets. "Feel at home here?" she asked. At first he thought Loretta had been the cause of the girl's sterilized existence. In her room there were no girlish knickknacks. Like in Sheila's apartment there was all kinds of junk: fishbowls filled with swizzle sticks and matchbook covers, napkins from restaurants he had taken her to magnetized on the refrigerator door with little green and blue plastic frogs and yellow smiley-faces, pictures of people she had known in high school taped everywhere. But Louise was totally different. Louise had no existence outside of Loretta's footsteps. Louise's bedroom was naked except for the white bedspread and matching nondescript curtain hanging in the one window. There were no stuffed animals like Sheila had thrown all over the room; no empty beer bottles on the windowsill; no fluffy comforters and pillows covering the bed; no bottles of red and brown and gold and clear with pinky highlights fingernail polishes; nothing. And Louise had never changed the sheets. From the first time they had made love, she had never changed the sheets. And that had been months ago. The first time they had made it she had had her period and it had stained the white cotton, and the stain was still there, dried and muddy-colored, like rotated Virginia cornfields in the rain. And she had said that there was no reason to change the sheets because she would just make love with her period again and again and again, she liked it that way, like wading through a murky dream and being able to wake up and smell the dirt, and the stain would never really wash out anyway. And he had sort of understood, sort of thought it made sense. Except that he was sure he wasn't the only one she was rolling in them and the idea of another man's guck sticking to the hair on his back wasn't too appealing.

"More than I've ever felt anywhere," he grinned, the cleft in his chin disappearing again. He reached for her slender waist. She fell on top of him and they both giggled. Loretta's bath water was running. The psychedelic Jesus continued to turn in the living room; they both listened. "You know," he whispered against Louise's hair, soft against his lips, like silk against a baby's pudgy raw face, "I can't stay the night. I've gotta get home. She'll stay up worrying. You don't know how it is," he grimaced. "It's like living with your mother." They both laughed at that one, fell down, down, down into the darkness together, their bodies sending signals of reverberating passions, their groans eerie in the night, and they forgot about their lives and concentrated on the good feelings in their dreams. She saw herself sitting on the boat docks reaching into the Bay; she was wearing a flowing white dress made of lace and it tickled her ankles, reached down past her ankles and into the green slime below the surface of the water; her head was covered in the same white lace, shadowing the darkness of her hair, and she was smiling to herself, her lips painted in the deepest shade of salmon pink, like blood upon a virgin's belly; in her arms she held a brown wicker basket full of apples, black apples, and she slowly, delicately, turned the apples loose in the green of the water, swan water, because as soon as the apples touched the surface the water turned to a great wave and opened its arms to her, pulled her deep down below anything she had ever known before, and she felt so marvelous, like all of life and death had been given to her in one sweeping motion.

In the dark he dressed and left, and she stayed sprawled on the bloody bed of her empty room, feeling left, feeling pointless and silly. It had all been a hoax, a repeated hoax, and she could hear her mother snoring heavily as the front door shut. Just shut. The motor of the psychedelic Jesus turned in the dark; it was never unplugged.

41

September rains fell on the brown and yellow leaves, crisp and collected at the corners of small dunes, soon soggy and ground into the sand, small particles to blow away and stick to cheap apartment siding. Dolores and Phil held fingers, entwined like those of little children playing here is the church, here is the steeple . . . open the doors and see all the people. He shivered in his T-shirt, the gray cotton fabric split at the seams under his arms, the freckled arms without their summer burn glaring white skin from beneath the dots, the darkened hairs taking on a slick glow like some wet body risen from the deep, sick and weary.

"Fuck," he mumbled, "I can't help it." Dolores let her eyes rest on the Spit. For the moment, she knew, nothing could really change without her reaction; if she made a deal with herself not to focus on him, not to let that beak and those thick lips, those cockeyed perverted lips and those eyes mesmerize her, then she could easily stand on her own. She wouldn't move. She wouldn't be the energy he needed to freeze himself in time; if she didn't watch him, the movie would not continue to roll. If she could only keep her eyes on the Spit everything would be normal; time would pass normally; moments would not be caught out of sequence.

"You can help it," Dolores answered. The wind had turned cold, blowing from both directions, from the Spit, from the Bay. Even the sand had turned to freezing pellets. "Don't

give me your bullshit double-talk," she said calmly, still trying
not to see him. "You can't be this selfish, I know. How can
you leave something that's this goddamned wonderful, Phil?"
she asked, still feeling the warmth of their fingers stuck together, held in that childhood grasp. "I can't believe you
would be so goddamned selfish," she breathed, the cold air
stinging the bottoms of her wet nostrils and the corners of
her mouth. She felt his fingers slacken on the hold, and she
had to look at him again, to glare, to catch the moment.

42

"If you could only," Dolores said, leaning against
the bar, "listen to what I'm telling you."

"I'm listening," Rod answered. "But I've had plenty of love
affairs myself, you know. I'm not exactly a virgin. Another
drink?"

"Okay," she said. "But . . ." she paused.

"Listen," he answered in a low voice. She wondered what
it was about him that kept her interested at all. He was
too pretty. All the women who sat at the bar stared at him,
and he knew it. He enjoyed it. And he was always hanging
on, as if he had made up his mind that she was his prop-
erty and she was chained to him. Ever since they had first
gone out to dinner together, no one in the bar had tried
to pick her up. And if they had considered it, he had
somehow known things were about to happen and had
butted in, or had Jeff butt in. "Everyone has been deeply
in love at least once in their life, but you can't go on
dreaming. You have to make a life for yourself now," Rod
said. "I've had love affairs, too," he shrugged.

"You never think about that one great love of yours
anymore?" Dolores asked.

"I think of her, sure," he said, placing his hand on Dolores'. "But I never think of Claud the way I think of you."

"Claud?" Dolores asked. "I don't understand. My Claud?"

"Don't tell her I told you," Rod explained. "It doesn't matter anymore. Tomorrow belongs to us. You and me," he smiled. "I don't believe in going backwards."

"Tomorrow belongs to us, huh?" Twenty-three was too old. At seventeen she would have swallowed it hook and all. At seventeen her eyes would have grown wide and her stomach would have swelled from excitement. But not now. Now, she only laughed. "I don't believe as far as tomorrow," she said. "And I believe in going backwards as long as it takes to get it right."

"Don't fight me, Dolores," he said. "I love you. Believe that."

"Uh uh," Dolores assured him. "I have a hard time believing in anything anymore."

"Believe this," Rod answered. "Believe this."

"Tell me about Claudine," she said. "What's the angle?"

43

"And I could never find those love letters again, Claudine. I mean, they just disappeared out of the trash. Weird?"

Claudine arranged the new nail polishes on her tray. "I'll look around my place for them. If Michelle has them though, there's no telling where she might have hidden them."

"Well," Dolores said, "why don't you just ask her for me? You know, she's old enough to know that I wouldn't want things that were that personal to be just thrown around."

"I'll ask her," Claudine smiled. "But I don't know. Those kids are pretty loyal to each other. And, if she's got them then she's already read them to Rosemary anyway."

"I know," Dolores said. "That really gets me down."

Jude brought two cups of coffee out of the back room and set them on the white manicurist tables. Dolores let the coffee sit even though there was no steam rising into the air.

"It wouldn't be so bad if I really believed he was never coming back," she said, "but he's got his FCC license now, and he might come back here someday. I know I'm dreaming, but he's got no reason *not* to come back here. And I'd hate for Rosie to get the wrong impression."

"I understand," Claudine said, "but I think you're wasting your time worrying about nothing."

"Do you really?" Dolores asked. She looked up at the photograph of Cherée, then down at the picture she had taken of Rosemary. "I can't figure you out, Claudine . . ."

Claudine sipped her coffee and turned her polish color caddy. "Why?"

"I mean, I just don't understand why you've been keeping the whole thing about Rod a secret like you have."

"Dolores," Claudine answered, "we've all got love stories. It's just that some people sing while others whisper."

"Well," Dolores said, "I just wish you'd tell me these things instead of my having to find out the hard way. I mean, do you ever want him back? Is there a chance that you might want him back?"

"No."

"What kind of friends are we, anyway?" Dolores asked. "What with you not tellin' me a damn thing?"

"The best," Claudine answered, and began to file down her acrylics. "The very best."

44

Claudine mashed banana and fed it to Johnnie by inserting her fingers in his small mouth. His tongue wrapped around some of it and took it in, the rest dribbling down his chin.

"I don't like the fact that you just sit around here morning, noon, and night. That's all," she told A. Jacks. "I mean, I just think you ought to get out and see some of your own friends. If you have any," she added.

"How can I," he protested, "when I have to stay here with the kid until after two every day? You answer me that?"

"A. Jacks," Claudine said, continuing to mash banana between her fingers and push the slimy yellowness into Johnnie's mouth, "so you've got from two until whenever every day. You don't have to make this apartment your permanent hideaway. I'm getting sick of your just standing around all the time with nothing to do and complaining about it. And besides," she said, "did you ever stop to think that I might want a little privacy myself?"

"No," he said, sitting back on the hard dinette chair, "I hadn't. I thought you were happy."

"I am," Claudine smiled. "I'm happier now than I've ever been in my life."

"Sure?" he questioned.

"I am," Claudine laughed. "What else do I need? I've got a handsome man and two beautiful children."

A. Jacks watched Johnnie as his head rolled from side to side, the banana dripping from the edges of his face. Beautiful? Johnnie's weirdness did make him strangely beautiful. Yeah, A. Jacks was attracted to the way the kid got on with it all. And they had managed as a family perfectly fine before him. What made him think he could cause any change? Or would want to? All he wanted to do was fit in. But Claudine never even looked at him. He was just a convenience. She wanted him there to fill space, but she was ready to accept a vacancy. His mother had been right. What did a grown woman with two children want with the likes of him. "What do you want with me?" A. Jacks asked calmly, his head hung in depression, his neck broken-out from the length of his greasy curls.

"Don't sulk," Claudine answered. "I didn't mean to hurt your feelings or anything. You know that." She watched him as he crossed his arms uncomfortably in the hard-backed aqua chair. Everytime he took his place at her dinette set she waited for the metal framing to give way. "Have you talked to your mother lately?"

"Sunday," he answered.

"Well . . ."

"Well, what?"

"Just well," she said.

"Claudine," he shook his head, "I don't understand what's happening. We were happy enough before. What's happened in the last few weeks to us?"

She hated to listen to anyone begging. Why did men always get down on their knees when things weren't going right. She remembered Frank saying "Baby, get rid of it. Don't pick the freak over me." But she had. Frank, all he had wanted was to be free to do as he pleased and live a normal life with her, and she had wanted that too, but the kids had made him feel uncomfortable, guilty as if people thought he was the father. But that was fine. Fine. "Not a pretty story," Claudine smiled, her lips very Brick.

"How can you smile?" A. Jacks whined. "At a time like this," he whimpered.

"It's not over," Claudine said, resting her long acrylic nails on the front of Johnnie's bib. "You're talking like you're planning a move. Are you?" she asked.

"No," he said. "I *love* you."

She smiled and crossed her leg under Johnnie. The heaviness of the child's weight made it difficult. He was growing larger through the middle. "Good," she said, "you've just added a little ray of sunshine to my life."

"Claud," A. Jacks said, his voice growing louder. He was losing his temper. "I said I *love* you. Doesn't that mean a damn thing?"

"Course it does," she said, wiping Johnnie's chin with her thumbnail.

"Then why don't you give me some sort of real goddamned reaction?" he yelled and sat up straight in his chair, his feet planted firmly on her wooden floor. Between his toes she could see small puffs of dust collecting. "You're worse than him," he shook his head at Johnnie. "You can't even give me a goddamned honest reaction."

"Deeeeeeeeayeeeeeeeee."

"You could cry or scream or throw something at me," he said, watching Johnnie squirming in her arms. "Something. Anything. He's got an excuse. What's yours?"

She could see him as he should have been, like the picture book he had checked out of the public library and never returned. He never planned on returning it, liked that feeling of guilt, of getting punished, everytime he studied a picture. It made him feel more a part of the picture, he had told her one night while they were drinking beer and smoking cigarettes in bed over the book, like his suffering could make him a real artist, like the fine from the overdue book was a bounty on his head. There had been one picture, one very bright picture by the man who had cut off his ear that they had both felt close to, that she had especially somehow felt akin. And now she recognized it. It was A. Jacks with his hands clenched over his worn face, his ears exposed to the grittiness of a country room like the back of Rod's bar, feet toed-in between scraping metal chair legs, staring into the solid blueness of his own skin. And then the picture moved and A. Jacks' feet were covered in heavy black leather lace-up shoes and he was stretching backward, catching sight of himself in a mirror, listening to the bones of his neck crackle, taking off his belt, and hanging himself. Claudine stood, three steps into the back room of the Blue Garter, with her head cocked, amazed at the sight of a man stretched dead, hanging just so fatigued, the back door slowly opening against gray cinder blocks leading out to empty fields, the undeveloped land of Ocean View.

Claudine kept her eyes on A. Jacks as he sat silently at her dinette table, and then the vision continued: A. Jacks hanging limply from an exposed center beam. She thought of his weight making a gigantic hole through the floorboards, his face a crushing imprint on the ground beneath. And she didn't view the sight with pity or remorse, but only a fright that there was dripping from his mouth, his ears, his nostrils; and in the dark she could just make out the stickiness against the elongated frame, a head twisted, broken, and fallen to one side, arms limp, a body tender, rawly gentle, tongue and eyeballs swollen, ballooning, bursting.

"A. Jacks," she said. And she could feel the suicide. It was a beat of urgency, quick movement through long hours of spoken nothing, and then, all of a sudden, a more constant nothing, as if boredom had taken over, and all that had gone before was more useless than it had been. "Please believe that I do love you," she said.

"Look, Claud," he said. His feet didn't move and he sat, stuck. She wished something would crash, something would fall. "I'm not getting out. I won't leave you."

"I wish you would," she said, biting her lower lip. She could feel the inside of her mouth twitching. She could taste her lip-liner. "I think you'd be a lot happier."

"Hell, Claud," he said. "Goddamnit, why can't you understand that I *am* happy. *I AM HAPPY,*" he screamed, *"AND I DON'T WANT ANYTHING ELSE. EVER."*

124

She rolled Johnnie off of her lap and let him sprawl on the floor, some frightening little baby bugbear used to warm the floors. "If you're so happy, why are we fighting?" she asked, her arms akimbo. Get out, get out, get out, she wanted to say. His presence was frightening her, making her feel sick.

"I don't know," A. Jacks said, finally rising from the chair. "I wish I hadn't told you all there was to know about myself. I keep feeling like you're holding that thing that happened when I was seventeen against me."

"I never even think about that."

"Well, I do," he said, wiping his thick yellowed brows. "I think about it a lot."

"Not a pretty story," Claudine spoke from the corner of her mouth. "If you think that's the root of your problem, I don't want to hear about it."

"I didn't say that," A. Jacks argued. "I think *you* think that's the root of my problem. I don't think I *have* a problem." He'd been only seventeen when he'd blown off Larry Caligass and he was sorry enough for that. He had lost a friend. Larry couldn't even look at him anymore, and he couldn't look at Larry. Maybe it had been wrong, but it hadn't felt wrong then. It had felt right. It had felt more than right. He had loved Larry. And he didn't hesitate to say it out loud, but he probably shouldn't have told Claudine, he thought. That had been his big mistake, telling Claudine. Watching Larry come had been more pleasing than a successful foot lock. But somehow, just knowing that Claudine deep inside herself held it against him made things simpler, easier; he had given her an example of the role he enjoyed playing. "I don't know," he had told her, "in a way, it's the same thing as an organized contest. My first love is wrestling. I enjoy making love the same way."

"I just don't want you moping around here anymore," Claudine argued. "I won't allow you to make everyone else miserable. You hear? I don't enjoy fightin' with you."

A. Jacks looked at his foot and wondered if he could get away with kicking the sprawling Johnnie hard, breaking his ribs. God, if he could do exactly what he wanted to do, say what he wanted to say all the time without anything being held against him. And God knows, he *would* do what he wanted to do, and what he wanted to do was stay.

45

The old brown dog followed Dolores and Phil up the beach, his paw prints crossing their own prints left in the sand, the waves erasing the path only slightly each time the water rushed and swirled in the animal indentations. Dolores held Phil's hand, the warmth of the blood beating through his palm in synchronization with the beating of her own chest. The moon was too round, too beautiful; the scene like something out of a True Love comic book or a cheap detective magazine where the spectacle of perfection must come to a sordid and bitter end.

"Is there a lighthouse around here?" Phil asked.

Again, that smile flashed in odd dimensions, the too-large teeth and overextended lips there for Dolores to memorize. She felt from somewhere inside her pounding chest that what she was experiencing was not real. It was a dream. It was a dime store novel. How deeply could a dime store novel penetrate the soul?

"I knew you were going to say that," she giggled. "I knew it."

"Oh, really," Phil laughed. That laugh, almost a snicker. That was something that probably would not have come out on a tape recorder, she thought. It was something no one else would ever be able to hear, something she would never be able to describe.

"Really," Dolores said, "I knew you would ask something

uncontrollably romantic. You know? Lighthouses are un-
controllably romantic. Such desolate, cold, stone places with
only one yellow light to prove that there is a warmth
searching."

Phil touched her lips, lightly kissing her, and as he did
she opened her eyes and caught sight of the moon. Magic.
Around the moon was total darkness, and Dolores looked
for the mangy dog that had tracked the two of them, but
he, of course, had disappeared when he had no longer added
that certain twist of balance.

46

From the window of the Mustang Dolores
watched the water, too cold to touch, spread its way to
shore making ice-lace at the edges. The cold wind snatched
the frozen edges and threw them over the matted sand,
the delicate particles of sea webbings disappearing within
seconds, and then the same episode continued in instant
rerun.

"When will the ice-lace stop?" Rosie asked.

There was no consciousness to it, no broken thread, no
lull in the order. The uniformed sequence continued in
parade. Dolores wondered if it was really fair to make Rosie
such a part of it, to make her witness what could not be
explained with regularity, but that which would change
with illusional snatches of season. .

"When, Mom?" she asked.

"When it starts to be spring," Dolores answered.

"When's that?"

"When the groundhog sees his shadow," she answered.

"What's a groundhog? Why the groundhog?"

Like the smallest creature at the bottom of the sea, the
one who crawled and scavenged through watercolor mess

not knowing exactly why or how, her baby lived. It was as though the water had given life, as if that day she and Phil had made love and she had taken her hot bath, God had sent a message to the water saying, Make this seed grow. At least, that was the only explanation she could give.

"I don't know why the groundhog?" Dolores answered. "I don't know. I don't know what it is. It's just something that tells you when it's spring."

"Mom," Rosie asked, "can we get out of the car today? Please?"

"It's too cold, Rosemary," Dolores answered. "You don't want to get out of the car. It's freezing out there."

"Isn't it almost spring?"

"Not today," Dolores answered. "No groundhog today."

"But," Rosie said, "Michelle told me that Claudine and A. Jacks took her and Johnnie to the beach and they all went running around in the water and made footprints with her shoes and everything. How come we can't?"

"Rosemary," Dolores answered, "would you just sit still and watch the pretty picture?"

"They even dug a hole for Johnnie and buried him in the sand," she said.

"That's nice."

"They bundled up real real good and they were real warm, Mom. Can't we do it?"

"Rosie," Dolores said. She swallowed hard. It was difficult to explain. "Look at it out there," she said. "Look at the sand. Look at the water. Watch how it all blends together so you almost can't tell where one starts and one ends."

The child pulled herself up to the windshield by grasping the bottom of the glove compartment with tiny brown fingers. She pressed her nose to the glass, and the hotness of her breath made a cloud.

"Look what I did, Mom," she said pointing.

"Can you see very well?" Dolores asked.

"See what?" Rosemary answered.

Dolores turned the key in the ignition and started the car radio.

"See what?" Rosie asked again. Her head hung to one side; the radio blared country music, WCMS, "I Can't Stop Loving You," and Rosemary kicked it with her foot.

"Behave," Dolores slapped her leg, "and don't kick at the car."

"I didn't kick at the car," Rosemary argued, her wide lips blowing up into a pout.

It was always the same on Monday mornings; they'd sit and listen to the radio, song after song after song, and Dolores would sing. She knew most of the words, even to the new hit singles. And the words that she didn't know she picked up quickly, like a high school kid who sat at the end of the soda fountain stuffing herself with French fries, waiting to be discovered. Only she was in Ocean View, Virginia, and would never be discovered. She could dream, but she'd never be discovered.

"I wanta go out and play," Rosemary said. "I've got my tennis shoes on. Michelle said that was all she wore, her tennis shoes."

"You're not going out in it," Dolores said. "Not this week or next week, you hear? You understand?"

"I'm going out," Rosemary argued reaching for the door handle.

Dolores reached behind her and pushed down the lock. "I said you're not going out in it."

"I am."

"We don't come here to play, Rosemary," Dolores said, her hand still on the lock. "We come here to remember, okay?"

"No."

Dolores watched the spot on Willoughby Spit, where she had first encountered Phil holding the black box of cheap jewelry. At least she thought that was the spot. "Don't fight with me," Dolores pleaded. "Be a good girl now." It was all like cheap jewelry. Dolores pictured herself flinging the box with all of its sparkling contents into the bay, watching the glittering rings swim out, float out, and sink in the rolling gunk of Ocean View. What was it that had seemed so much like magic? Jellyfish and slime. She longed to step on the rings. Step on the rings. Feel the metal cut into the flesh of the foot. Feel the hot sand seep into the cut. All the pretty colors. Step on the rings.

"I can't stop loving you, for the rest of my life," the radio blared. Quickly, Rosemary slid the lock up and pulled the metal door handle open. She was free. *"I can't stop loving you . . ."* She ran across the edge of the parking lot and tumbled down a small grassy slope full of rusty beer cans. The beach was only a crunch under the soft rubber of her P-F Flyers. She ran down to the water without looking back, but she knew her mother was after her, running faster than she could run, looming larger than a hairy sea monster. *"I can't stop loving you . . ."*

"Please, God, make her stop, make her stop," Rosemary prayed. But close to the shoreline she was caught around the middle, two huge arms grabbing her stomach and squeezing the breath out of her. Together they fell into the sand, hard against their mouths and hair, getting into their clothes and scraping against their skin. Rosemary sprawled out flat, played dead; Dolores' body relaxed on top of her.

"I can't stop loving you," played on, echoed in the emptiness. Dolores felt her baby underneath her and watched the Mustang from the spot of sand where she had the child pinned. The doors were open, the radio playing, everything garbled in a high pitch. Nothing had worked. The child kept her cheek to the grainy earth as her mother sobbed against her neck. And even in the sunlight they were freezing. Dolores welcomed the warmth of her own tears.

47

"**O**kay," Dolores said, knocking on Claudine's door at the top of the stairwell, "I'm here." She pushed her dark hair behind her ears, letting go of Rosie's hand. "Claud, we're here."

Johnnie sat on the floor, leaning against the green plaid couch, his jaw hanging to his chest. He looked like he was trying to move his mouth, but only the gullet quivered and Dolores looked away. "Claud," she yelled as Rosemary disappeared into Michelle's bedroom, "you're ruining my Sunday. Rod's waiting for us. What d'ya want?"

The blender whirred from the kitchen where Claudine leaned against the counter wearing a pair of bright orange shorts. "Three cups of milk, four eggs, three bananas, two packets of Fleischmann's Yeast."

"What *are* you talking about?" Dolores laughed. Laughter was one easy way to make a friend. And even though Claudine was her best friend at work, out of La Boudoir she found her hard to talk to. They weren't on equal terms. Dolores could tell that they thought in different ways, and she found it hard to understand Claudine. She figured it had something to do with the six-year age difference. Claudine must be tired, she had thought.

Claudine had covered the kitchen, the same kitchen Dolores had in her East Ocean View apartment, in contact paper full of bright bunches of carrots and broccoli with names in print underneath. She had even covered her light switch and had cut the little vegetables away from the paper and stuck them on the refrigerator door. "To get rid of our teenage skin problems once and for all," Claudine giggled, cutting off the blender, "and to give us more energy."

"Aren't you cold?" Dolores asked Claudine, making no-

131

tice of the shorts and the suntanned stockings underneath. "It's still winter, you know."

"As busy as I am around here, I haven't got time to be cold. Are you kidding?"

The yellow goo foamed into the center of the green blender cap.

"Where's A. Jacks this morning?" Dolores asked. In Claudine's kitchen especially she always felt stiff, awkward, as if she was going to be photographed without her makeup.

"Oh," Claudine laughed as she poured the mixture, "I forced A. Jacks out of here for a few hours. God, I can't stand it. He just stands around here and sulks, drives me crazy," she giggled. "Maybe I'll be lucky and he won't come back."

"Don't talk like that, Claudine," Dolores said. "What if God heard you and made what you said come true?"

"I really wouldn't care," Claudine smiled. "In fact, I'd thank him. I'd get down on my knees and tell him what he had done was a real good thing for me and the kids."

"Look, Claud," Dolores said, holding the glass of yellow foam and inspecting Claudine's engraved powdered smile lines, "I really don't see what difference having Barbita in the shop makes, you know? If that's what you wanted to talk to me about." She took a big swallow. It tasted awful, but she didn't say so. "If it helps business, what difference does it make if she's black?"

"Deeeeeeeeayeeeeeeeee."

Claudine carried her own glass into the living room, her stockings catching and snagging on the floor as she walked. "Well," Claudine answered, "you know how Jude feels about niggers. And I can't honestly say that I blame her, and Sheila had to quit because of it."

"Deeeeeeeeayeeeeeeeee," Johnnie groaned, his jaw opened wide and then clamped shut with much effort.

132

Claudine pulled him against her lap and fell backward on the plaid couch with his weight.

"And I don't think it was exactly fair that you just went ahead on your own and hired a nigger knowing how everyone feels. Not that I feel that way about it," she said. "I mean, they live all around here. You and me, we can't hardly afford to be prejudiced living in the middle of them. I mean, with me, holy cow," Claudine smiled, "prejudice is a four letter word, you know that."

Dolores sat down on the couch and took a sip of her drink. She wondered what Rosie and Michelle were getting into.

"But don't you think you could've asked before you went on ahead and hired Barbita?" she said.

"Claud," Dolores answered, "does this have anything to do with Rod?"

"Oh, Dolores," Claudine said, "that was ages ago. I'm just talkin' about our nigger problem now . . . and how you took matters into your own hands without askin'."

"I didn't have a choice," Dolores answered.

"Well, do you think it was fair givin' Sheila's chair to Barbita?" Claudine asked. "Don't you think that if we weren't gonna save that chair for Dixie Pointer we shoulda given it to Sheila?"

"Deeeeeeeeeayeeeeeeeee."

"Fair or not, Bita is qualified and she came with her own following. And we needed a black woman in there."

"Nobody needs a nigger," Claudine said. She ran a slim hand over Johnnie's loose face.

"Look, Claud," Dolores said, sitting her drink on the floor, "the neighborhood is mostly black now. Whether you want one in there or not doesn't matter. What matters is if we get enough business for Caresse to keep us going. And that's *all* that matters. And another thing," Dolores said, "I made the decision because I think I'm just a little bit smarter than the rest of you. That's why. And if you don't like it you can take it up with Caresse."

Claudine held the drink up to Johnnie's mouth and poured some in, then caught it from the sides of his lips with her Red As They Go nail. "I could pull the ropes out from under you right now, Dolores," she said. "If I were you, I wouldn't push my luck. How smart you think you are and how smart you really are just might be two different things. Understand?"

"Rosemary?" Dolores called. "Rosemary!"

"You're not going anywheres just yet," Claudine said, rolling Johnnie off her lap against the arm of the couch. "You're gonna stay right here and we're gonna talk."

"Rosemary," Dolores stood and yelled into the back hallway. "C'mon, now. We're leaving. Come on now."

"Dolores," Claudine said, "we'll let this one slide cause I consider you my friend, and I ain't got very many. But you make another decision like this on your own and I tell you it'll be professional suicide. Okay?"

48

The ache found itself on the right side below Sheila's stomach. The pain and the sleep, the pain and the sleep.

"Jeff," she said, closing her eyes and trying to make the small of her back touch the mattress. "Jeff. Jeffffff?" The sound spilled in an unheard rush of air. Big balloons. Both of them. He screwed and ate and slept and went to work, stood in bars, and tried to be a big deal. While she lay in bed and suffered, no women friends anymore even, he was standing around in The Blue Garter making love to the topless dancer. She wouldn't put up with that after the marriage. The only thing to do was to go ahead and pick a date, pick a date soon. Of course, there were only thirty days in June, she guessed, and that *was* the month in which to get married. But that was four months away, and she'd be showing by then. But that *was* the month in which you were *supposed* to get married. She tossed. "Jeff?" Soon she would be married like Dixie Pointer with her own little baby and a real brick house, not standing on her feet eight hours every day trying to make other women look like something out of magazines. And Jeff had promised her a real brick house, not one of those little houses with siding that blew away in a bad storm, but a *real* brick house. She was gonna get that. And the wedding would be beautiful. She knew it. She'd go and get a dress with a real full bodice so no one could tell, and she wouldn't be embarrassed.

Every night Sheila lay awake looking at him, looking at Jeff and making sure he was asleep, and then looking up to the ceiling, that swirling ceiling, watching the plaster eddy and asking Him in silent prayers if He knew, if He really knew what she had done. And she would try to explain how it had been, that it just wasn't any good to be what her mother had called "nice" anymore. That to get a guy to take you for a few beers and stand by your side when you needed help to the ladies' room, to give you quarters to put in the jukebox, take you to the movies, you had to spread your legs. And after a while the urge felt good, you wanted it as badly as they did, and it became second nature.

"And please, God," Sheila prayed, "don't let those blisters pop up. Please, Lord," she prayed, "keep them away. And keep all of my friends, even those who have forgotten me, safe, because they don't know what they're doing to themselves, God. Please."

And Sheila figured she was a good Christian for the night, watching her husband-to-be resting, his fleshy round face distorted on one side by the pillow and his lips blubbering with snores. And she would save him from the evils of sinful life. She would keep him clean and pure by giving him a child. "And keep me from sufferin' too much," she added carefully at the end, "especially after the Priest blesses me. For the child's sake, Lord, keep me from sufferin' too much."

49

*"A*nd his momma cried, 'cause if there's one thing she don't need it's another baby child in the ghetto," A. Jacks sang along with Elvis on the radio.

"Jesus, A. Jacks," Claudine said, pulling the sheets up over her shoulders and positioning herself against him, her left leg over his right, "I can tell from *here* that your feet stink."

" . . . "

"A. Jacks?"

"In the ghettooooo . . ."

"A. Jacks," Claudine continued, "get up and take a shower, will you?"

" . . . "

"A. Jacks, before we go to sleep, *go take a shower.*" She moved away from him and sat up against the carved wooden headboard. "Well, are you gonna go take a shower like I told you or are you just gonna lay there?" Claudine asked.

"Another little baby child is born in the ghettoooo. . . ."

"I can't stand it anymore," she said, clicking off the radio. "Are you going to do what I tell you or are you gonna stink?"

"Would you still love me if I stank?" he asked.

" 'Course, I would," she answered, grimacing, "but I would rather you go take a shower."

"Turn the fan on them for a few seconds and they'll stop smelling."

"A. Jacks," she said, pushing him in his firm side, "get up and go take a shower. Now."

He faced her in the half dark; she was without makeup, and she was still beautiful. Her skin was so soft, so white, like you could take the back of your hand and run it over her cheek and touch a latticework of sweet petals. "You know something, Claud," he said, "you might be the most demanding woman I've ever dated, but you're still the best-looking. I love you."

"I love you too," she said, wishing he'd either get up and take a shower or go home to his mother where he belonged.

50

But let him ask in
faith, nothing wavering,
for he that wavereth is
like a wave of the sea
driven with the wind and tossed.

JAMES 1:6

Sheila sat in the church, her eyes devoted to the book of prayer, her frosted hair covered with a thin piece of fishnet cut from a discarded stocking. It was their first Sunday living together, and she had persuaded Jeff to take his place next to her in the pew so that after the service they could walk up to the priest and set the wedding date. Sheila reached for Jeff's hand without looking to her side, but his hand was not there. He had slipped both hands into the pockets of his trousers and his book lay balanced on his knees, the black cover shut.

"Jeff," she whispered. "You should read this."

He nodded. She nodded back in agreement.

"I'm listening to him read it to me," he answered.

"It's not the same as reading it yourself," she said.

He took his hands out of his pockets and opened the book, glancing at her page number and turning to the proper passage. She slid her finger onto his page and followed the scripture with a stubby pink nail as the priest read, and there was not a trace of smile along the lines of her lips. Jeff watched her face intently. He looked to her waistline to see if she bulged.

"Sheila," he whispered into the softness of her hair. The frosted streaks of blond had grown down in a ring around the very top of her head. "Sheila?"

"Hmmmmmmmmmmmmmmm?" she answered, still tracing the lines of his prayer book with her index finger.

The preacher ordered the congregation to kneel. Jeff struggled to lower his entire weight onto the low wooden knee bench.

"I think we oughta get married before June," he said.

Sheila continued to pray, her voice a low tone blending in a chant, but there were slight wrinkles along the sides of her eyes that gave away her happiness.

"Beginning of next month," Jeff said. "As soon as you can get out the invites and buy a wedding dress. A pretty white frilly one with lots of lace."

Sheila turned to face him and smiled, nodded in acceptance.

"We'll ask the priest for the first Sunday in April," she whispered. "That okay?"

51

Rod put his beer down on the table and looked up at the ceiling. "I gotta tell her. It's just gotten too involved not to."

"That's too bad," Claudine said, pushing a cigarette butt around in the black plastic ashtray, the plastic sliding across the wood. "Not a pretty story."

Rod looked at his watch; two forty-five. Help didn't come into The Garter until four.

"Quarter to three and no one in the bar but you and me?" Claudine laughed.

He noticed the whiteness of her eyes around the blue, and it made him feel a little more comfortable. "You know how I remember you?" Rod asked.

"How?"

"You're not gonna like it," he said. "I mean, it's not the way you'd like to be remembered."

"Go on," Claudine answered.

"I remember you," Rod said, "without any makeup on; nothing. And you're in the shower, pregnant, with your hair all wet, more of a yellowy color than now, and hanging in your eyes, and you're so big and round," he motioned outward with his hands, "and your cheeks are very full and very very red," he laughed. "You were the most beautiful woman I'd ever seen in my life."

"Ummmmmmmmmmmmmmm," Claudine smiled, her hand disappearing in her white teasing. "That was a long time ago," she said. "More than ten years ago."

"And we were never found out," Rod said.

"Until now," she raised her bleached eyebrows. "We've had it good up until now."

"Until now," he apologized.

"You know," Claudine said, "if I'd ever thought that you'd go and tell her everything, I'd a-never fixed you two up." She shook her head. She could feel a throbbing tension building. It made her mad that Rod could so easily give her away. "I thought what we had was sacred," she said, watching her nails claw the tabletop. "I never thought that you'd just throw it all away for the sake of honesty. Jesus Christ. You were never so goddamned honest before."

"Look, kid," he said, "I've just fallen in love again. That's all."

"Does anybody really say kid anymore?" She bit the inside of her cheek. "Damn Dolores," she said.

Until now it hadn't mattered to her; not really. So, she had had an affair. So, she'd had lots of affairs. Lots of affairs. But there had been a time, right before *this* affair, *the first affair*, when she had really been happy. Things had fallen into place in her life with Mike Downings. He had given her all that she had ever wanted, and all he had asked was that there be beer in the refrigerator when he came home from work, and that she'd wash out his socks every night and hang them on the radiator so they'd be dry and warm in the morning. Mike had been happy as a mechanic, and she had been happy in her apartment, had had free time. That was what was important. She had had free time; time to walk into the drugstore and cash enough in her pocket to buy anything she wanted: hair color, nail polish, bath soaps, anything in the world she wanted. And sometimes Mike would even bring her home a present from the Avon Lady—a box of colored bath crystals or some beautiful smelly green oil. Looking back on it, she couldn't complain about the time with Mike Downings; besides, it was supposed to be a man's privilege to get a drunk-on whenever he felt like it. And Mike had said that Vietnam had put the fear of God into him, that there was no sense in staying sober because thinking clearly just made everything look all the more stupid. Everything was just a mirage anyway. Damn him; nothing had meant anything. And that had been okay. She could have lived with that. It wouldn't have insulted her in the least. But then, for some stupid reason, she had taken offense at being called dumb and being slapped around. Of course, that had been her fault.

"Don't look so depressed," Rod said. "The two of us, it was a long long time ago. Everything is different now. That's what you always tell me."

If only she hadn't played for attention from Mike Downings by saying, "Don't hit me, don't hit me," and sobbing in her corner under the bathroom sink when she knew damn well that he had no intentions of laying a hand on her in the first place. If she had only told him that it was her gimmick; not for real. But she had kept it up, night after night hiding under the sink like some mental midget, and he had played the game with her, beating her to a pulp, her behind raw and pumping, until she screamed, "Daddy, Daddy, don't hit me anymore, Daddy. Daddy, I promise to be a good girl from now on, Daddy." And then she'd had to make up stories, so many stories that she would sit on the couch all day dreading the evening, preparing the fairy tale. And Mike had looked forward to the beatings and the stories every night, every night, until she had just gotten too scared to tell him that the game was over, that there would be no more make-believe.

Rod said, "I waited, Claudine. I waited. And the next thing I knew, instead of waiting for him to come back like you said, you were shacked up with some new guy."

"I fell in love," she said. "Any sin in falling in love?"

"Well, that's it, isn't it?" Rod answered her, looking at his watch again. Three ten. He thought it was much later. "I thought *we* were in love."

"Well," she smiled, "we were."

141

And she *had* been. She had sat in The Blue Garter day in and day out, buying every two-time loser that walked in the place their first drink of the afternoon. Even pregnant she had sat up at the bar and kept Rod company. And then they had just fallen in love. It had been natural. God, if you stared at someone for that long everyday, loaded, you were bound to fall in love. And she told him everything, confided every little bit of her life to the bartender. And he had enjoyed it. He had helped her make up stories for Mike, even helped her prepare dinner a few times when she was too blitzed to put a frozen pizza in the oven herself. They had played and made love; soft, tender love. Yeah, she had been crazy mad in love.

"Claud," Rod said, "I just gotta tell her. I gotta tell her that this thing started out to just be a dirty joke, just a way of gettin' back at her for hiring a nigger. That I wasn't *really* sposed to fall in love with her."

"She don't suspect nothin' like that," Claudine answered. "Why don't you just go ahead with it the way it is if you think you love her?" Claudine asked. "Why don't you just forget all about me?"

"Jesus Christ, Claudine," Rod said. "Don't back me in a corner like this."

"I'm not," she answered, and the tears began to make wet streaks through her pancaked makeup, "only I don't see where this love affair is necessary, and I got a reputation and a couple of friendships at stake here. Can't you just keep your mouth shut about all this? It ain't funny no more."

Rod stretched backward in the upright chair, running his hands along the rough wooden arms; they needed sanding, and he was afraid he had gotten splinters in his palms; he checked in the dim light, but it was hard.

"You know," he said, "some crazy fuckers were out in the parking lot last night head-butting. They were out there knocking each other in the brain waiting for one of their heads to crack open. We had to send one of them to Norfolk General."

"Rod," Claudine breathed heavily, "do you really have to put me through all this?"

"Sure am glad he was outside instead of in," Rod grinned, his small bird-mouth puckering. "Crazy goddamned fuckers trying to head-butt," he laughed.

"Rod?" she stretched her hand out for him to hold. The long acrylic nails looked glittering and seductive. The dark light of the empty bar was right.

"I loved you, Claudine," he said.

"What difference could that make?" she answered, pressing his hand.

"Jesus, Claudine," Rod said. "You gotta give me a chance. Everytime I turn around you got someone else living with you. What about me? Don't I deserve it?"

"Dolores was just sposed to be a joke," she said, smiling. She hoped her lipstick hadn't worn off. Things were always so much easier when you were sure of the way you looked. Thank God for the light. "You know that I've always loved you. It's just that," she paused for effect, "after Mike, I needed time to be the boss, you know," she said, squeezing his hand. "If we lived together I'd just become a little pussycat waiting for directions. I don't want to be like that again. Not yet, anyway. But that doesn't mean that I've stopped loving you."

"Well, what about that guy, Frank?" he asked. "You wouldn't give me the time of day when he was around."

"Frank," she said, "just swept me off my feet. It wasn't real love like I had with you. I mean, maybe I have a streak of self-destruction or something. You know, I couldn't even talk to Frank. I was terrible around him. I was awestruck." Claudine pulled her hand away and placed it carefully in her lap. This had to be done tactfully. She had to make him feel sorry for her, not envious. She had to make him feel like she needed someone to protect her. Poor, dumb, wild, crazy Claudine, he had to think. "I don't know," she said, "He took advantage of me. I guess I was just too open and he saw right through me, you know. He looked right down deep in my soul and he saw an empty well. I don't know how to explain it. He wanted to change me completely. He wanted to give away the kids. I couldn't give away the kids. You know that, Rod."

"Sure. Sure," he said.

"I was scared. That's all. I was scared, and I wasn't thinking. I wasn't thinking. If it helps anything, I'm sorry."

"It helps," he said. "Everytime you say it, it helps."

"I'm so sorry," she said, shaking her candy white hair.

"Does this thing with Dolores really bother you that much?" he asked.

"Oh, Rod," she said, listening to the afternoon traffic whiz by on Shore Drive. "If we could just carry it off like we planned, I promise you, I promise you, everything will be just like you want it to be."

52

Dolores ran a cotton swab of alcohol over the electrolysis needles. "They mean a lot to me, Claudine," she said. "Please ask her. I keep reminding you and you keep forgetting," Dolores said. "And they mean a lot to me."

"You were throwing them out anyway," Claudine answered, inspecting her own nails under the large heat lamp on her desk.

"But I wasn't throwing them out for anybody else to read."

"I haven't seen her read anything, and I didn't see them when I cleaned out her room."

"But you didn't ask her."

"No, I didn't ask her."

"Well, would you ask her?"

"I told you I would," Claudine snapped, the Valentine Pink blush standing out from her cheeks more than usual.

Barbita stood on high heels, heels that made Claudine's look infantile. Her long black legs, muscular through the calves, curved into slim ankles small enough for even the girls to place their fingers around. She stood with her derriere out, straight out, as if to show off how perfectly round and sensual a woman's rear could be.

"Her ass looks like a black melon to me," Jude said under her breath as she sat down facing Claudine at the manicurist table. "You know, these little pickaninnies keep waltzing in here like they own the place and giving us snide looks, and I don't like it," she said.

"Me neither," Claudine said in a low voice, "and if I was to run the place it'd be another story."

Jude looked over to Dolores at her table and then up to the picture of Rosemary and the cold shoulder photograph of Cherée above it.

Dolores threw a cotton wad into the trash can and closed the box of needles. "You know, Jude," she said, "that electrolysis machine in there?" she pointed to the back room. "We don't own it, you know."

"I know that," Jude answered, her eyes averted.

"Well, the people who own it are coming to pick it up this afternoon. And you know why?" Dolores asked.

"I know why," Jude said, picking at her own nails.

"Because we haven't had enough customers to warrant having it, that's why."

"I know," Jude said.

"With all the newspaper specials we've run and everything else, we still don't have enough customers to warrant having it."

"I said I know," Jude answered.

145

"Well," Dolores answered, "doesn't that tell you anything? Anything at all?"

"No," Jude said, getting out of her chair.

Claudine stared at Dolores and sucked on a piece of gum. The flavor was gone.

"That doesn't tell *me* a damn thing, and I don't know who you think you are for it to be telling *you* anything. Maybe if you'd just left things be we'd still have the equipment."

"You will look for them for me, won't you, Claud?" Dolores asked.

"Sure. Sure enough," Claudine answered.

53

Dolores climbed the steps of the Robbin Hood apartment with her eyes closed, one hand sliding up the peeling banister, the other gripping Phil's hand. She dreaded opening her eyes, knowing that the apartment was so cheap and in such a poor section. But it had been all they could afford, even together. Phil budgeted her money well, taking her paycheck each week and marking off what went for groceries and what went for rent and what went for entertainment. Of course, she was just out of vocational school and the money wasn't very good yet, but there would be more coming once her following was set up. In the meantime, she just had to learn how to be friendly, concerned, full of interesting conversation. She had to read the papers, read the funnies, read the editorials. She had to ask Phil questions about things she didn't understand, questions about things like highways being built across Virginia, to Virginia Beach from Norfolk, to Richmond from Norfolk, questions about buildings being torn down downtown, why the Monticello

Hotel wasn't saved, why the streets were being gutted,
questions about Mount Trashmore, questions.

"I know it's not much," he said, "but it's all we can afford
and, hell, you can fix the place up. Right?"

"For sure," Dolores said. To her the apartment was
adorable, not some overstuffed house in which she had no
freedom, not some outfitted barn in which every move was
a trap. It was her own place and the sun streaked through
the dark screened windows and made bright stripes across
the dusty wood floors. "I love it, Phil," she smiled, "I really
love it."

"And I love you," Phil winked. She noticed that his eyes
picked up the light from the sprinkling of sun, that that sea-
green color was again different from anything she'd ever
seen, like some God come to give her a peek at heaven. An-
other moment frozen.

She listened, her shoes making a fast click-clack against
the hardwood floors as she moved across the living room
into the bedroom. It was as if she had never heard her own
footsteps before, as if each solitary footstep was being made
in cement. And there was no erasing the echo. And there
was no backtracking. And Dolores was scared, and thrilled
by the excitement of the fright.

"I love it," Dolores said. "It's perfect for the two of us.
Think of all the things that are going to happen here," she
grinned, but only his grin was caught in time.

54

Jude bent over the low table in the back room
to pour a blue rinse mixture into a plastic bottle, her flabby
arms shaking as the contents seeped from one container
to another like strained mud. She wiped the counter top

with a pink Handywipe and was careful to place it in the dirty towel holder.

"Do you think Sheila ever really dated a black man?" Claudine asked, unwrapping a raisin Granola bar. "Or do you think she was making it up?"

"I don't know," Jude answered, screwing the plastic spurt top on the blue rinse formula. "You never know with her. She might have been telling that story just for attention."

"That's what I thought," Claudine smiled. She took another bite of her cookie. "I can't imagine Miss Nobility getting even close enough to hold hands with a nigger."

Jude looked around suspiciously. There was no one in sight as far as the back room.

"Don't worry," Claudine said. "You don't think I'd be stupid enough to say the word 'nigger' in front of her, do you?"

Jude shrugged. "I wouldn't care if you did, only, I wouldn't want to be the one caught sayin' it, you know?" She went to the sink and washed her hands, minding not to get the solution on her lavender polyester pantsuit. "I've been real careful not to say anything around her. Has it been noticeable?" she asked.

"I've noticed," Claudine answered. "The only one who hasn't noticed how damn fuckin' uncomfortable it is is fuckin' Dolores."

"Becoming manager is so important to her," Jude agreed.

"For a while, anyway," Claudine smiled and balled up her cellophane cookie wrapper, throwing it into the wastebasket, the one Sheila had woven out of straw and painted white with a little pink velvet ribbon drawn around the top.

"I don't understand," Jude said, settling down on top of a box marked ProCurl.

"Well," Claudine smiled, pouring herself a cup of coffee. She held the Styrofoam cup so tightly that the edges began to crack. "Seems to me that if the way to a woman's brain is from her pussy to her heart to her head, we gotta follow the logical rules to get what we want."

"I still don't understand," Jude smiled.

"May I?" Claudine asked, reaching for one of Jude's cigarettes.

55

"I don't know what it is, Claudine," Dolores said while Claudine clipped back the acrylic on her nails for her, "but Rod makes me feel like, well, it's like I can almost forget about Phil for a while, you know? He sort of makes me feel like it's okay to remember as long as I can plan a future too."

"Ummmmmmmmmmmm," Claudine answered, not looking up from the hand on her white towel. She hadn't spit out her spearmint gum, and the taste of polish remover had gotten in it.

"I don't know. I feel loved again," Dolores grinned. Claudine had noticed that Dolores' face wasn't broken out at all, not a pimple anywhere, even around the chin area where she almost always had one or two little ones. "I mean, I believe the guy. He's so, well, easy to believe," Dolores smiled. "Even Rosie likes him, I think. Did you ever feel that way with him?"

"He works in a bar, Dolores," Claudine answered with little expression in her voice. "Take it from one who knows him; I mean *really* knows him," she smiled. "He gives the same line to a million women every week."

Dolores shook her head. "I know I'm just lonely and, maybe, I'm reaching out for someone to hold me. I don't know."

"Well, do me a favor," Claudine said, running the electric buffer over the rough acrylic.

"What's that?" Dolores asked.

"Stay away from A. Jacks. He's too young to be molested," she joked.

Dolores took a sip of a Tab and placed the bottle quickly back on the table as Claudine grabbed her hand to continue working. "I wouldn't anyway," Dolores said, "Rosie hates him."

56

"I'm telling you, Louise," Jeff said, stifling a burp, "Sheila and me, we're getting married the beginning of next month. You understand what I'm telling you?" He looked down into the large eyes of the young girl. "We can't be with each other anymore like we're used to doing. That's all. We can still be with each other, but we gotta be discreet about it."

She turned away from Jeff's hold, his pudgy hands still sliding along her wire-strung shoulders. Her shoulders were like something he'd seen in a picture at La Boudoir, the girl over Dolores' table with the black dress that only covered one shoulder, that incredible girl.

"Louise," he said, "it's the only right thing I can do."

He could already see the happy family huddled together under the Christmas tree, the babies with their little pug noses pressed against the cold windows waiting for Santa Claus, listening for sleigh bells, sleek wooden runners sliding over crisp Virginia air. There would be special presents for sweet special people, a tiny white cat with pink ears and blue eyes that would sit on the nursery ledge. He could see all that there for the taking if he just obeyed the law of the Lord. It was the Lord who divided good from evil and pointed you in the direction of both.

"It's just that," he said, not able to squelch the outburst of air any longer, the long belch of regurgitated beer intruding upon his words. He'd wanted to do this gracefully, not leave any mark on the girl. He'd wanted to leave something unspoiled for her. He'd wanted to do justice to his uniform, even out of it. "It's just that she's having a kid." He burped again. "And I'd kinda like to be there when it comes out. Sorta be there to help, you know? Sorta help things along."

The hairs in her nose were like little matches, each one alight, the fire hissing from her upturned nose, from the extreme whiteness around the blue of her eyes, from the light blue veins running along the skin of her temples. He could see everything beating, and he could feel it in his own chest. It was Louise's special brand of punishment, the horsehair blanket that only someone born into sin could wrap around a lover.

"Louise, darlin'," he said, still reaching for those shoulders, "it's not the end. Far from the end."

"I thought," she whimpered, the words coming out strangly, the voice of a child in the body of a boy/woman parading as an innocent the worldliness handed down through five hundred years of whoredom, "you were a more decent man than this. I thought," she cried, "you were good."

"I am good," he laughed. GOD, I AM GOOD, he beat his chest to the heavens. "Good as they come, anyways."

"I, I thought you'd protect me," she sniffled. "I thought you loved me. You told me that you loved me. What kind of decency's in that?" she cried.

He finally had a grasp on those shoulders, those smooth shoulders, the love of those shoulders, the picture-book love of those shoulders. "I do love you, Louise," he said, pulling her close to his chest. "I love you with all my heart, all my heart."

"Then how can you marry someone else? Is it because

151

of what I do? You told me it didn't matter. You said that it didn't matter."

"It doesn't," he lied. "It's just that . . ." He couldn't think. "I feel that." She looked so damn innocent. It wasn't his fault that things had turned out the way they were. It wasn't his fault. It was Loretta's fault. "It's just that," Jeff said, "I care about Sheila too, and I can't leave her out in the cold, can I? Don't you think this is the decent thing for a man in my circumstances to do? Don't you think I'd rather be with you? You're so beautiful," he crooned. A romantic Joe singin' a love song. Strummin' a guitar. Words written in a foreign language came naturally, like a sailor shipwrecked on a desert isle just long enough to pick up the lingo. He held her shoulders tightly. "But I am a decent man. I gotta do what's decent. Marry the woman what's having my baby."

"I guess so," Louise whimpered. "Only she could get an abortion. Why can't she get an abortion?" she looked at Jeff with watering eyes. "I'd get one if it was me."

"Well, you see," he smiled and touched the tip of her wet nose with his index finger. The flames had died; her anger had turned to sobbing snivel, the thin film of stinking waste-pipe dribble caught in a vortex. "That's because you've got a heart of gold, darlin'," he smiled. "A heart of solid fourteen-carat gold, darlin'."

57

"*P*hil," Dolores said, grabbing him around the neckline of his T-shirt, the white kind men who dress up for work wear under their starched button-collared shirts, "you act so strange. You act as if nothing is for real. This is for real, do you understand? This is my body and this is your baby inside here," she hollered, the veins along her temple lines throbbing. "This isn't playtime."

"I'm not saying that," Phil answered.

"You're acting that way," she cried. "God knows you're acting that way."

He wrapped his hand around her wrist and pushed her away. She was never to grab at him again; she was never to reach out to him like that again in anger. She understood that. The message was a still, written in silent letters in the air between them. "Acting," he spoke slowly. "Just acting."

"You're scaring me," Dolores whined. He closed those greenish-blue eyes to her. "You're gonna leave me here alone." The moment was caught in time. It would play over and over again.

"I never told you I'd stay here with you forever," he said. The black case of jewelry was on the floor near the couch. It held the magic of nothing. She'd been through all that was inside, and he had been right. It was junk.

"Why can't you just get your FCC license here?" she moaned. She had ironed her hair and it was very straight to her shoulders, a shade of reddish-brown. "My following is building, Phil. I can support the three of us fine until you get your license. I can even pay for you to get the schooling. Come on, Phil," she pleaded. "We're going to need you around here," she cried. "You can't leave."

"But don't you see," he said, "I don't need to be around here anymore. I need to leave. I want to leave. Half the reason for living is in leaving."

She breathed in concise, brief measures, as if her entire life was linking itself to a short-circuited support system. There was that feeling of the gripped frayed cord.

"You can't leave me," she said, reaching. "I won't let you go."

"Dolores," Phil answered, those eyes glistening with something she knew nothing about, some enigma that had

153

her bewitched, "I won't be held down like this. It just isn't me. You see? Me?" he pointed to himself. "Remember me?"

"I don't know you anymore," she cried, her eyes puffy and almost Japanese-looking in their slant. She had tried to cover the puffiness with a lot of black eyeliner, too black and too thick. "You're acting like some kind of hippie or something. That kind of thing went out with the Sixties," she sniffled. "You're way behind times. Why don't you grow up and realize that?"

"I can't listen to you when you're like this," Phil said. "You're making no sense. Can't you see that I have to do what I want to do? I'm not behind times, I'm out of times."

"Can't you see that you have a responsibility to me and our baby?" she whined.

"I have no baby," he said and paraded his fist through the air. "If you want a baby, then you've got a baby. But I have no baby. I will not be linked to you by your insane devotion to your own fertility. Do you understand?"

"NO," Dolores screamed. "You're a selfish bastard."

"If I planted a seed in the ground," he said, "and the soil burst with an ear of corn . . ."

"Yes . . ."

"Would I be responsible for tending that ear of corn? Or would I be free to walk away from the field, and on to the highway?"

"This is not an ear of corn," Dolores pointed to her stomach, "and I'll be damned if I let you get away with calling me dirt."

Phil laughed, that wide smile again with those huge teeth, the lips curling upward; Dolores could see all the way down his reddish throat, the muscles reverberating, the tiny dingles jumping like broken nerve endings. "One day," he laughed, "we may be on the same frequency, but I doubt it." Phil placed his hand on her tense shoulder. "We've worn out this band watt." And there was no speaking to him anymore, no laughing with him anymore. Dolores stood with

154

her belly out past her feet, her body aching from way deep inside; deeper than anything he had ever felt, she was sure. How could he be so unfeeling? This could not be real, she thought. And even as he closed the front door of the apartment behind him, his worn brown leather suitcase strapped and buckled and filled with T-shirts and sandals and tattered jeans, his black jewelry case tucked up under his armpit, Dolores was sure she was only dreaming, that the father of the ear of corn would return to plow and refertilize the fields.

58

"And all along, don't you see," Rod said, looking down to the front of his white shirt. He had a dozen white shirts, all the same. "She was just using me. I don't think she really meant to do it. I really don't. I just think she was too young, too pretty, and not too good at handling herself," he said.

Dolores leaned back, his arm around her neck. "Seems she's gotten pretty damn good at handling herself," she smiled, "lately."

"Seems so."

"You still love her?"

"Naw," he breathed. He stretched his feet out to the floor in front of him, his tennis shoes making a slight skid mark on the wood. "But I can't help thinking about the process of events. I mean," he said, wrinkling his forehead, running his hand through his full head of hair, finding comfort in that. "I don't know what I did wrong. I mean, maybe I wasn't there at just the right moment. I don't know. I would have given anything to have been there," he swallowed hard, "at just the right time. Only, she told me she needed time alone. Hell, what she had with Mike Downings wasn't any kind of life. Besides," he paused. He could feel Dolores growing stiff against his arm. He ran his hand through her dark hair. It felt like spun silk, a spider web left vacant for a long time. "I'm not so sure both of those kids aren't mine." He looked directly into her face, that wide pale face spattered with freckles that needed to be tinted to show life still existed somewhere inside. "Are you shocked?" he asked.

"Shouldn't I be?" she answered. Her bottom lip hurt. She'd broken the skin.

"Yeah. I guess," he said. "I guess you should be. I am," Rod said with little expression. Only his forehead stayed wrinkled, like the wrinkles of a lonely castaway. "I am, for sure."

"Rod?" Dolores asked. He didn't look back down at her, afraid to look back down at her. She would open her mouth and snatch off his head. He would lick blood off paper plates forever, silently have to pay for what had been said in fantasy. There would be no life for him beyond this mess, this tangled mess of his own building.

"I didn't really mean that," he said. "I don't know why I said it. She was pregnant with the fuck-up when I met her. The other one could be mine though."

"Have you asked her? Have you asked her if Michelle is yours?"

"She's not. I know she's not."

"So why did you say that?" Dolores asked. She liked to move in close under his arm, pull herself close into his side.

"I don't know," he answered, then pulled her tighter. "I really don't know."

"And now she's using you to keep me in my place at the store." Dolores smiled. "But she's really backed herself into a corner this time. It's not gonna work. It's just not gonna work."

"I loved her once," he said. "But I don't think love is what

156

I feel for her anymore. I think I feel," he said and pulled his arm from behind Dolores' head, "like I owe her." Then he slammed a fist into an open hand in front of Dolores' face. "I owe her good."

"Like you owe her what?" Dolores asked. "What?"

"I don't know," he bent over, buried his head in his knees. "I don't know." His voice was muffled in the thick fabric of his trousers. There was a chill from the open window, Rosemary's fan still in its metal cabinet. Dolores put her arm around him, held him close. "I don't know," he muttered, pressing his damp face against her. "I don't know."

Dolores nuzzled her head onto his shoulder, the cotton of his shirt cold against her face. "You don't owe her anything," she tried to convince him. "You don't owe her a thing."

59

Sheila's itching began the day the white lace was wrapped around her waist, the back buttoned in fifty-four rayon-covered hooks of white. It was a high empire, high enough for her barely showing stomach to show at all. Her secret was a secret to all who saw her in the dress, but she knew that her secrets were not to be secrets for long. He would know soon enough, and life would start then.

Jude had treated her to lunch saying, "Jeff has invested enough in you already." There is nothing worse than feeling unworthy of an unworthy man.

"What's wrong with you?" Jude asked. "Your eyes are all reddy and you've got horrible dark circles. Maybe you're coming down with a case of the flu?"

"No," Sheila answered, sitting at the table, taking a sip of her cool coffee, "just a case of the nervous jitters." She'd be damned if she told Jude the truth, that it hurt to pee, that she was in terrible pain because the blisters had popped back up. She hoped she didn't get any on her lips or her fingertips. It would all be over if she was found out. She'd have to pretend that she did have the flu when Jeff got home, and then hope that he would be kind enough to let her alone for a couple of nights. She'd tell him she was contagious. He wouldn't know how close to the truth she was. Course, sooner or later he was bound to find out. Sooner or later he was bound to get it. If God was good to her, it would be later.

She was really going to need God. Sharing a bed with the enemy. God would say that you shouldn't have an enemy. You shouldn't hate anyone. Okay, Sheila thought, I don't hate anyone. I don't *hate* anyone. The damn blisters ached. She could feel the thing inside her belly crying. Lemme outa here, lemme outa here, it stinks in here. She was rotting away like an onion left for weeks split in the bottom of the refrigerator. There was nothing but brown goo inside her. She had seen it with her own eyes. She had slipped off her underpants in the bathroom and there had been brown goo all in the cotton crotch. Well, she had taken a real hot bath, so hot that the water had scalded her legs, the little hairs lying down flat like they had been ironed. And then she had gone to bed, and he had crawled on top of her, entering her while she lay there scared, holding her breath, and he had grunted and his breadbasket had shook, quivered and shook, and he had squealed, "Fuck me, fuck me, fuck me," and she had, and he had finished and rolled over on his side and fallen asleep with his heavy jowls against the pillow. And in the middle of the night, after she had fallen asleep herself for what seemed like a long time, and she was sure he was in a sound stupor by the way the snores went all the way down inside his gullet, and her eyes were adjusted to the darkness of the night, she pulled back the soft blankets and snuck a look at his penis and there it was, covered in dried brown goo. And she felt as if she was going to die, had to catch her breath in the back of her throat to keep from making a noise of horror, and crept out of the foot of the bed without waking him up. Please God, she had prayed, let him sleep, and he had slept, and she had taken a nice warm washcloth and wiped him down, taken the flaccid thing in her hands, and wiped it down ever so carefully. And in the morning he told her he had had a very sexy dream about her and held her tight and promised that he would be a good father for the baby and that he would never leave her, no matter what.

"You and Dolores," Jude said, pulling a gray sweater about her shoulders, "you two just don't have the pizazz it takes to hook a man like Dixie had. I suppose," she giggled and looked out the coffee-shop window from their booth, "you've got to have a bit of the prostitute in you."

"I think we all got a bit of that in us," Sheila answered.

"You?" Jude asked and shook her head negatively.

60

"*It's a little too late for a love song,*" Rod sang as he wiped down the bar, "*though I'm lookin' all over the world. It's a little too late for a love song,*" his voice rose and lowered and the little girl on the barstool giggled, "*for this kind of girl,*" he closed his eyes and held his Handy-wipe tightly in his fist. "*I know you're gone and never comin' back, but your heart within me stays,*" he looked into Rosemary's caramel-colored eyes, "*'cause I know you really loved me, Darlin',*" he listened to Rosemary breathe heavily, "*even though it doesn't look that way.*"

"Rod?" she asked, elbows on the bar, her mouth puckered over a straw stuck in a Pepsi Cola.

"Don't talk with that straw in your mouth," he said. "You'll choke and your mother'll blame me."

Rosemary moved away from the cola, her legs wrapped around the metal pole of the stool, the leather of the seat sticking to her thighs. "Then I wouldn't have to look at the water," she answered.

He smiled. "You just don't understand."

"What?" she asked. "I don't understand what?" She positioned her tiny lips back over the straw and began to sip. "I'm almost this many," she held up one small full hand and a thumb.

"Oh," he laughed at her, leaning closer to her face. "You think you know everything, don't you?"

The cola in the glass was almost gone, the child not taking the time to breathe so that the straw was full of bubbles. She slurped hurriedly showing her anger, and she looked into the ice and not into Rod's face.

"No, I don't," she pouted. "I know," she grinned coyly through the puffed lips, "some things I don't know. Some things I don't know," she repeated.

"Don't talk with the straw in your mouth," Rod scolded, "or I'm not gonna bring you here anymore."

"Okay," she said, releasing the plastic tube, a wisp of honey-colored hair stuck in the side of her mouth.

"You shouldn't be so smart about going down there and looking at the water every Monday," Rod continued, wiping down the counter. "It doesn't hurt you to go out there and sit."

"I hate it." she said, gritting her teeth.

"Don't you grit your teeth at me," he said, shaking a finger at her. "I'll tell your mom."

"You're like A. Jacks," she said. "I thought you'd be more fun than A. Jacks, but you're not. I hate A. Jacks."

"Thanks," he smiled. "I do your mom a favor and you stab me in the back. Where's your loyalty, kid?"

"I don't like A. Jacks," Rosemary said. "I don't like his hair. He needs a haircut."

"Yeah," Rod said, throwing the rag under the back of the bar into the bin, "he sure does need a haircut."

"I like your hair," Rosemary smiled.

"I like your hair too, kid," Rod said, touching the soft curls that had fallen into her face. "You're beautiful, just like your mom."

"Thanks," she smiled.

61

"**W**hat made the monkey fall out of the tree?" Jeff asked Louise as he held her in his arms, making his biceps flex so that she could feel his strength against her back.

"What?" she asked, those eyes so round, like she was looking through a quarter peek hole for the first time. "What? Tell me what?"

Jeff held her tighter, her flat chest hard against his extra flab, and he said in a deep voice, a voice low and unnatural for him, "Death."

"Huh?" she asked. "I don't understand."

"Death," Jeff repeated rascally, the lawless voice of a pirate. "Death made the monkey fall out of the tree," he smiled, his chin forming a knavish dimple.

"You're scaring me," Louise Little Feet said. "Jeff," she said, trying to push him away, but he was too heavy, "lemme go. Lemme go."

"If I open my arms," he breathed into long hair that lay across her white shoulders like melting licorice sticks against china plates of frozen sugar, "you're out of the tree."

"Huh?" Louise asked. "Jeff, I don't understand you at all," she said. "Please, Jeff." She looked for his eyes, but there

161

were no eyes, only cold blue-veined lids closed against her cheek. "Are you drunk or something? I've never seen you like this. This isn't like you."

"I need you, Louise," he said in that low voice. "I need you," and he grabbed her even tighter, her rib cage feeling crushed.

"I know. I know," she smiled, and watched her ceiling. White. White. Everything was white and untouched, unmarked. And daily she'd go through her room with a bucket of Spic And Span and wash the floors, the windowsills, only she wouldn't touch the bed. No use. "I know," she said, running her thin hand across the bald spot at the back of his head. "I know. You've explained it all and I understand. Really, I do," she said.

"I don't love you anymore," he groaned. "Do you understand that?"

Louise lay very still, not moving under him. She dared not swallow.

"Did you hear me?" he asked. "I said I don't love you anymore."

"I don't believe you," Louise answered. "I can't believe that you don't love me. Why are you always trying to trick me?"

He ran his thick hands down from the crown of her head, across her clear face, and let them rest against her neck. "You don't call my apartment anymore, you understand?" he spoke very slowly. She was frightened of the eyes she saw, so white around the centers, like they had been wiped clean, could not be smudged by the muddy circles of the centers, pools of filth. She was not included in his eyes. She felt her mouth curl back against her teeth and shake, like the nerves attaching the thin fleshy pink of her mouth to the rest of her face had been cut clean with wire clippers. "I can't control myself when I'm around you, Louise," he said. "You know that. And one of us has to be responsible for not spoiling my marriage. I WON'T LET YOU SPOIL

162

MY MARRIAGE!" he yelled. She grasped the edges of her sheets in her palms, his weight still heavy on top of her, his hands still loosely positioned around her throat.

"I didn't even know she'd be there when I called, Jeff," she whispered. "I woulda never called you if'n I'd aknown she'd be there."

"Wouldn't you have though?" he asked in that low voice, his dimpled chin scratching her face. "Wouldn't you have though?" His smile was overwhelming, the dimple stretching, disappearing.

"No," she answered. "Please believe me."

"Why should I?" he asked.

"Because I love you?" she whimpered. "And because I'd never do anything that you didn't want me to do?"

"Because," Jeff said, loosening his grip on her neck and feeling the softness of her shoulders, "if you ever do it again," he breathed as he touched her, "you're a dead monkey and you'll never have a chance to practice any of your monkey tricks again."

"I'm nothing but a girl," Louise said, burying her face in his rubbery neck, "and I love you. I'll do anything you want me to do. And, if you want me to stop thinking of you as mine, then I will. But I'll always love you."

Those shoulders.

"Louise," Jeff said, stroking her hair, "you ever think of getting outa here really? I mean," he said, "not just play getting outa here, but real just picking up and getting outa here?"

"Where?" she asked, her forehead wrinkled. "Every place would be the same as here."

He took his hand and ran it over the wrinkled skin above her eyes. "Don't do that," he said. "I don't like to see you wrinkling your face like that." He smiled. That pretty face, that pretty chest. Not spoiled by growth, by natural process of aging. Not spoiled by life, by things that happen along the way when you're not bothering anyone but the whole world is bothering you. Louise had no scars, not yet, but he could see them coming and he would be the cause.

"I make good money here," she said. "You know what kind of deal I got here. Besides, no one else would be fool enough to let a girl my age dance like Rod does."

"But you could still dance," he said. "You just couldn't strip."

"I like to strip," she stretched and yawned. "There's nothing wrong with strippin'." She looked to the ceiling. "What kind of work can you think of that you get to lay around all day with your boyfriend?" She watched him grit his teeth, those tiny little teeth all in a row behind his salted lips, lips that looked raw and distorted in her room's afternoon sunlight. "Sorry," she said, "it's hard not to call someone you love and screw your boyfriend."

The motor of the psychedelic Jesus turned.

"Do you have to use that word?" he asked, his teeth still on edge.

"Does *she* use that word?" Louise asked. "Does she?"

Jeff pulled her close. Her rib cage ached.

"She does, doesn't she?" she asked. "She says 'screw me, Jeff, screw me' and you do it, don't you?"

The motor of the psychedelic Jesus turned.

"Come on," he whispered. "I didn't mean to get you upset. Come on."

"And you never tell her that she can't love you, do you? You never tell her to keep her distance. You beg her, don't you? You beg her to move in with you, to share your bed with you. You son of a bitch," Louise cried.

"Shhhhhhhhhhhhhhhh," Jeff murmured in her ear. "Shhhhhhhhhh. Don't do this to yourself."

"You son of a bitch."

The motor of the psychedelic Jesus turned.

"I love you, darlin'," he said. "With all my heart. I don't want to see you hurt like this. Please," he said softly, "don't do this to yourself."

"I'm not doing anything to myself," she cried. "I'm not doing anything to myself."

"Please, darlin'. Louise," he shook her.

"I love you, Jeff," she whispered. She could hear the motor from the living room. "Isn't that more important than whatever you have with her?"

He stroked her hair, the long coils of silken thread, the butterfly nets, the seawater's weed. "I can't not do what I've said I was gonna do. Now, I gotta do what's right and I told you, I told you, Louise, that you can't try to sway me from this. Now, it would be easier for the both of us if you just picked up and moved, took your mother with you on out of this city. But, if you won't do that . . ."

"I won't," she cried softly into his chest, his hair soft against her mouth, the odor of his sweat sweet. "I'm gonna stay here and wait around for you. I know you'll be back."

"Louise," he begged.

"I know you love me like I love you, and I know you won't be able to resist it. I know it," she smiled. "I won't have to call you or anything." She wiped her nose with the back of her hand and then wiped her hand against the bloodied stain on the sheet. "You'll come twitchin' for me like a snake with his head cut off. You'll be back. I know it."

"Louise, you can't do this," Jeff said. "Don't make me hurt you. I want you outa this city. I want you," he watched her run her tongue over her lower lip and then give him a flash of her underarms. She was her stage show; she was Loretta's daughter. You couldn't separate one from the other. My mother and I are the same person she had once said. He hadn't believed her then. Impossible. Loretta was a slut, born and bred. "I want you," he swallowed hard and closed his eyes to her face, "outa this town by the time I'm hitched. You understand?"

"I don't understand nothin'," she said, shaking her head.

62

"In here," Rosemary whispered to Michelle. She held one small brown finger over her mouth. "And don't say a word. If Mommy hears us, we're in for it," she said, leading Michelle into Dolores' closet. Rosemary shut the door, pulling it from the side and then quickly snatching her fingers away before it slammed shut.

"It's dark," Michelle whispered.

"There's a light up there," Rosemary pointed. The exposed bulb hung from its socket, an exposed root planted firmly in the darkness. "Can you reach the string?"

"I'm not tall enough," Michelle whispered, stretching on her tiptoes, her arms pulling the muscles of her waist. "I can't get it."

"Stand against the wall," Rosemary ordered.

"Huh?"

"Stand against the wall, and I'll climb up to it by climbing on top of you."

"I don't think so," Michelle answered. "It's not gonna work."

"It's gotta work, Michelle," Rosemary pleaded. "You'll see why. It'll be worth it."

"Tell me what it is first," Michelle said. "Tell me what it is and then I'll give you a boost."

"Love letters," Rosemary whispered into her ear.

"How'd you get them?" Michelle asked, her eyes wide. "My Mom went over my whole room looking for them."

"Outa the trash can."

"You're gonna get the beating of your life."

Rosemary studied Michelle's face, so perfect, the skin so even like milk in a bowl. "Don't tell on me, Michelle," she leaned forward, a little bendable doll.

Michelle sighed and looked at the string hanging from the light bulb. "Dolores is gonna kill us both."

"She threw them out," Rosemary argued quietly. "She didn't want them anymore. She was getting ready for Rod to come."

"Mom'll get A. Jacks after me if she finds out," Michelle whispered. "If'n you weren't so dumb and could read yourself, you wouldn't even need me."

". . ."

"Okay," Michelle said and carefully laced her hands together, "but don't get your tennis shoes on the front of my pants. I don't wanta wear dirty pants to school tomorrow."

"Thanks, Michelle," Rosemary said as she climbed into the girl's hands and caught the string, pulled it hard, and then tried to hit the floor softly. "Don't worry. She'd never think to look in the pocket of her own raincoat for them."

"You better hope not," Michelle said, opening a long envelope. "Dolores," the letter began, "time can never erase . . ."

63

"How come the trees grow funny like that?" Rosemary asked, watching the trees that bent away from the bay, their green branches opening from brown wood looking ages old. "How come they're crippled like that?"

"What makes you think they're crippled?" Rod asked, handing her a peanut butter and jelly sandwich he had made especially for this picnic. "Wrap your sweater around yourself and button it," he said. "I don't want you catching cold out here."

"I won't."

167

"They're not crippled," he said, taking a bite of his sandwich and feeling his tongue sticking to roof of his mouth. "That's the way they grow. They're old, that's all."

"Old makes you crippled?" she asked, crawling to the space between his crossed knees and staring up into the branches.

"Uh uh," he said, feeling the warmth of her small body against his chest. "They grow away from the wind and the wind comes off the water. That's all. They don't have any choice about whether to grow straight up and down or to the side. They have to grow any way they can and they're pushed; the wind pushes them."

"Do they have to grow?" Rosemary asked, still looking into the green sprouting branches against the blue sky.

"Sure," Rod answered. "Everything has to grow, or it's dead."

"What if I don't grow?" she asked, looking at him over her shoulder, her hair caught in the electricity against his shirt. "Will I be dead?"

"You'll grow," he assured her and smiled, wrapping his arms around the front of her to keep her warm.

"I know," she giggled. "Michelle says I have to, too. We made a pact, but I know we can't keep it. Even Johnnie won't be able to keep it. I know."

"What kind of a pact?" he asked, thinking about Dolores. Dolores with her sweet smile; she'd do anything for him, he knew. Dolores, innocent Dolores who had been too sweet, too naïve, to give up her child. Sweet Dolores who worked day in and day out just to give this child a home.

"Oh," Rosemary giggled, "I asked Michelle if we could stay little forever so we could hug and kiss. Mommy always hugs and kisses me before I go to sleep."

"So do I," Rod said, looking down at the top of Rosemary's head, her light hair waving in the slight wind.

"I know," she said. "But when you first came and I had

to stay with Michelle nobody came to kiss me goodnight."

"But you knew your Mommy still loved you, didn't you? You knew that, didn't you?" Rod asked. He reached for a tangerine from the brown bag in front of her.

"Sure, but," she gasped, "my Mommy's loved a lot of people. I'm not special." She shook her head in a long twisting no.

"What's that mean?" Rod asked, peeling the tangerine. "Want some?" he asked, placing a slice on her tongue. "Course you're special. You're a very special little girl. Your Mommy's gone through a lot of trouble to have you and keep you and love you. You're very very special to a lot of people."

"No," Rosemary said, opening her mouth and sticking out her pink tongue for another slice of tangerine.

"What do you mean no? Course you are," Rod said, placing the fruit in the warm breath of the child's mouth. "Course you are."

"No."

"Look, kid," Rod said, twisting her around by the shoulders of her soft scarlet sweater to face him.

"Don't call me kid," she said, her lips turning down in a frown, the corners of her mouth jerking like cut nerves. "My name is Rosemary. Not kid," she cried, the tears jetting around the small rims of her eyes.

"I didn't mean nothing by it," he said, his eyebrows bunching together. He held the little girl tightly in his arms. "Rosemary," he whispered, "kid," he said, "shhhhhhhhhhhhhh, baby. Shhhhhhhhhhhhhh."

"And I'm not a baby either," she whimpered softly.

"You gotta know you're special, don't you?" he asked, smiling into the small face. "You know you are, don't you?"

"That's not what it said in the letters," she cried, the tears streaming down her cheeks. He rocked her back and forth, his face close to the top of her head.

169

"What letters? What're you talking about?" he asked. "You can't even read."

"Michelle read them to me," she said. "I made her. I made her read them to me 'cause I took them outa the garbage and then Mommy was looking for them and I was too ascared to tell her I'd tooken 'em."

"Looking for what?" Rod asked, pulling her away from his chest and waiting for an answer.

"For the letters."

"What letters?"

"There were bunches," she said. "But we only read a few. We was ascared we'd get caught doin' it."

"Go on," he said. "Talk to me."

"I was ascared I'd have to grow up if you came," she sniffled.

"Never," he said. "You never have to grow up."

"Michelle did," she said, "when A. Jacks came. They shut the door and never let her inside again."

"But you're not afraid of that, are you?" he asked.

Rosemary didn't answer. She let the tears run down her face and then licked the salty water with her tongue. "The letters said Mommy was selfish for having me."

"What letters?" Rod asked slowly.

"The letters from Father Phil. Claudine told Michelle Mommy was looking for the letters from my father. I didn't know who they were from when I took them outa the trash can, but I just kinda guessed from the way they smelled special. Really," she cried. "I didn't know. I don't even know why I took them excepten' I thought they were secrets."

"It's okay," Rod said.

"The letters said that I was going to be the one to pay."

"Nawwwwwww," Rod grinned and handed her a handkerchief. "That's silly."

"That's what Michelle said it said," she sniffled.

"She read things wrong," Rod said. "Besides, I'm here now. You don't have to be afraid. Those letters were probably written before you were born," he smiled to himself, letting his hand slide along the softness of her hair. "You don't have to be afraid. Father Phil won't ever be back, and I'll always be here with you. I'll take care of you," he said. "I promise."

64

A. Jacks lowered Johnnie's head back in the niche of his arm, the shock of brown hair resting against the deep creases of the joint, and he felt the tickle. The boy squinted at him, the coal blue eyes emerging from the slats of flesh pulled tautly, like some great seabird rising from out of the deep after hours of not being able to breathe. A. Jacks slid his hand up under the boy's shirt, a new one Claudine had bought at a bargain basement store because no one of any importance ever saw Johnnie but she wanted him to have clean clothes all the same, and A. Jacks felt it . . . the underbelly. It thumped, thumped, thumped, hard like it would burst and A. Jacks kept his hand still, watching the boy's eyes distort in unmalleable terror. Johnnie's legs kicked, the baby-like leverage hardly even felt by the overgrown wrestler holding him. His tiny heels struck A. Jacks' thigh like rubber pebbles, the muscles of his arms not strong enough to pull away and scratch. And A. Jacks kept his heavy hand at rest on the underbelly. Thumpety, thumpety, thump.

"You never thought we'd ever be alone together, did you, little fellow?" A. Jacks asked, his knitted eyebrows close to Johnnie's face.

Johnnie's lips fell open; his chin dropped down to his gullet. He tried so hard. "Deeeeeeeeayeeeeeeeeeeee."

"No need to feel frightened, little fellow," A. Jacks said, feeling the underbelly thump, thump, thump. There was a twitching of the fleshy stomach. "I want to be as close to you as any friend can be. You know, little fellow," he said, "we got a lot in common, you and me."

"Deeeeeeeeeeeeayeeeeeeeeeeee."

"Oh, shit," A. Jacks said, feeling the wet trickle onto his legs, the boy's diaper seeping with moisture through the rubber panties. "Now, why'd you have to go and do that?" he said, picking Johnnie up from under the armpits. "You've gone and made us both a mess, you dumb little shit."

"Deeeeeeeeeeeeayeeeeeeeeeee," Johnnie croaked, the whites around the coal blue showing wide as the boy pulled the granular-looking skin of his lids back into his skull. "Deeeeeeeeeeeeayeeeeeeeeeee."

"Jesus Christ," A. Jacks moaned, standing in the middle of Claudine's living room with the boy's urine running down his legs, across and in and out of his many curly hairs. "Don't try to move," he pointed at the boy who lay sprawled on the sofa, his pants sopping. "You wait here while I go and wash myself off and I'll be back in a minute to take care of you. Now, you wait here," he ordered. "you understand?"

"Deeeeeeeeeeeeayeeeeeeeeeee."

"Yeah, deeeeeeeeeayeeeeeee yourself," A. Jacks answered, walking stiff-legged into the bathroom, wetting a washrag, and rubbing down his own legs. The friction of the washcloth against his legs caused the smell to stink up the whole room; it was the smell of something he had sniffed once years ago in an atomizer hidden in the back of a garage. And there had been sand around and crumbled wood, gritty powder between his toes and under his fingernails. And he had found the atomizer in a corner under three boards, yellowed with brown spots of decay, and it had been buried under a pile of sawdust and had been made of salmon mesh, with black dust in every hole of the mesh, and the sprayer had been golden and thin and he had pushed the top of it down with his thumb and had gotten that smell out, and it had infiltrated his hair and gotten into his mouth and he had tasted in on his tongue for weeks and weeks. "Okay, I'm coming to get you," he yelled into the living room. "And I'm gonna clean that mess you made off you. And believe me, it's not one of my favorite things to do in the afternoon," he said, approaching the boy whose face was red and swollen with anger. "Now, you could have gotten yourself up and to the bathroom. Ain't no reason why I gotta clean you up like this."

"Deeeeeeeayeeeeeeeee. Deeeeeeeeeeeayeeeeeeee," Johnnie screamed, the saliva catching in a huge glob at the back of his throat.

"Don't you scream at me, boy," A. Jacks ordered, his long yellow hair falling to the front of his shoulders.

"Deeeeeeeeeeeeeeayeeeeeeeeeeee."

"Or I'll take you and you'll have something to scream about," he said, picking the boy up from under the pits and carrying him into the bathroom. A. Jacks set Johnnie in the sink, his small legs crushed to the sides of the white porcelain, the metal faucet in the boy's back. He pulled off the rubber underpants and Johnnie's head fell backward with a slam against the tiled wall. "Oh shit," A. Jacks moaned, "now there's no reason for a big ten year old to do this," he said, unhooking the sides of the diaper and pulling it out from underneath the boy's body. He shook the feces into Johnnie's lap.

"Deeeeeeeeeayeeeeeeeeeee," Johnnie squirmed, not able to lift himself out of the sink. "DEEEEEEEEEEEEEEAY-EEEEEEEEEEE," he yelled, the muscles at the sides of his head bulging through the discolored skin. "DEEEEEEEEEAYEEEEEEEEEEEEEEEEEEEEEEEE."

"Oh, shut up," A. Jacks said, opening the lid of the toilet, placing the diaper in the latrine water for soaking, and closing the lid on the stained material. "Just shut the fuck up." He could smell that atomizer, the discharge of noxious odor misting into his face; hell of a thing to leave festering in a corner; why couldn't they have just done it in the dirt instead of using the atomizer as a substitute septic tank? Jesus. The smell of it made him want to puke and he could conjure it up in a moment, even smelled it on himself at a whim. "Just shut the fuck up," he ordered and watched the little demon struggle in the bowl. "Shut the fuck up," A. Jacks grinned. "Daddy's gonna give you a bath now," he said and turned the hot water spigot to full.

"DEEEEEEEEEEEEAYEEEEEEEEEEE."

The hot water steamed up around the boy, the skin on the normal portion of his body red and angry from the heat. A. Jacks cut off the water and took the washcloth he had used on his own legs in his hand, dipped it into the scalding water, and rubbed white soap into the textured nubbs. "Now, I'm gonna get you all clean," A. Jacks smiled into the boy's face, the boy's head sliding down the tiled walls, his body forcing itself out of the sink. "And you're not gonna shit all over yourself anymore today, are you?" A. Jacks asked. The underbelly thumped, thumped, thumped and A. Jacks scrubbed the twitching abdomen down good, reaching his washcloth-covered index finger into his belly button. "All clean," he said, washing slowly. "Won't Mommy be surprised when she comes home and finds Johnnie all clean?" he asked.

"Deeeeeeeeeeayeeeeeeeeee," Johnnie groaned slowly, his energy almost all gone, all used up. The underbelly thumped, thumped, thumped.

A. Jacks bent down to the boy's body to see if he could still smell the atomizer. Filthy dirty man doing it in a thing like that. Why, his mother had asked, would a man want to save it, and in a thing like that where someone could find it, where a child could find it? Why, his mother had asked. Wasn't it good enough just doing it in a woman, then never having to see it again? Why, she had asked, would anybody in their right mind want to save the stuff? But, she had said, taking the bottle out of his hand, I do like the shape of this. Maybe I could clean it up, she had said. No, she'd looked at it and grimaced, a horrified look on her old wrinkled face, too much wind he had thought from the bay, and she had taken it like it was the pestilence between two bony fingers and walked out the back door, hauled it into the damp air and he had always been afraid that one day by accident, he would step on it again, hear the spritzer under the crunch of a shoe, and it would go off in his face once more.

The underbelly thumped; A. Jacks put his ear to the boy's chest and heard the heartbeat. Johnnie's eyes stretched, the whites rolling back into his head. He had no muscular strength. Thumpety, thumpety, thump. "Deeeeeeeeeeay-eeeee," he whispered.

"You still stink, you little brat," he said, his face down close to the chest, the hot water seeping down the drain, Johnnie's butt caught, sucked in the tiny metal drain holes. "You still goddamn stink," A. Jacks said, pulling the boy up in his arms and running his tongue over the boy's normal-sized chest, down under the armpits, across the puffed skin and into the navel, around the hip bones and across the genitals of the ten year old.

"DEEEEEEEEEEEEEEEEEAYEEEEEEEEEEEEEEE!"

Little struggle. It was. Little. Struggle.

"DEEEEEEEEEEEEEEEEEAYEEEEEEEEEEEEEEE!"

And he felt the underbelly twitch.

65

"*Cigarette?*" *Phil asked, the humps of his nose highlighted from the flicker of the match in the dark. He held the red package out to her, the cigarettes falling forward in neat steps. "Here," he said, pulling one from the pack, "I'll light it for you."*

"Thanks," Dolores said, taking the white stem between her fingertips and holding it in front of her, smelling the burning tobacco souring the brackish air. She inhaled right the first time, and she didn't cough, the white air escaping into the picture of the Spit in front of her.

"You don't smoke, do you?" Phil asked.

"Why?"

"I don't know," he laughed, that wide mouth opening to show those hulking teeth. "It's just that you're pulling on that thing like it was a joint or something." There were those eyes glistening in the dark, some cat on the prowl waiting for her embarrassment to show before pouncing. "You ever smoked before?"

" 'Course I have," Dolores answered, stiff and proud. "All runaways smoke, and I was one of them once."

"But that was a while ago, wasn't it?" Phil asked. "You haven't smoked since, have you?"

"So smoking makes you cool, you think?" Dolores asked, taking a bigger puff than before. "Is that what you think?" She felt heavy-headed, could feel the nausea rising through her chest, had to put her head down between her knees, could feel the dampness from the cold sand underneath.

"Nawwwww, I didn't say that," Phil answered, running his hand over the top of her dyed black hair. She had had to dye it black after that terrible orange, but she planned to strip all the color when she got back to the beauty school on Monday morning. "I didn't mean to hurt your feelings," he said softly. "Dolores," Phil whispered to her, her face still between her knees, " "Dolores, I didn't mean it. Really."

"I know," she mumbled. "But I have smoked before. Honestly."

"It don't make any difference," Phil said, still running his hand through her hair, the stiffness of it causing his fingers to occasionally catch in tangles. "It don't make any difference at all."

"You sure?" she asked, her head still between her knees.

176

The nausea was going away; the sea air helped.

"Sure, I'm sure," Phil said, holding her close. "I wouldn't even care if you hadn't ever smoked. It's not good for you anyway."

"That's okay," she said, picking her head up and leaning it back against his shoulder. The night was black, quiet, the sand was cold. Phil wrapped his jean jacket around her and kissed her softly, his thick lips covering her mouth like bay pools left warm by schools of sea creatures, his body against hers as natural as the grain of the earth against her legs.

66

A. Jacks leaned his head back in Claudine's lap, the softness of her tummy and the red rayon of her shortie pajamas easing his thoughts. Lately Johnnie had been getting to him, the way the kid was always shitting in his pants, the way he'd try to walk from one room to another getting lost down the short hallway, always ending up in Michelle's or Rosemary's arms instead of his, the way the kid squinted when he tried to touch him, when he tried to run his hands over the lung area to see if things were still really ticking. Still ticking; they were always still ticking.

"What're you thinking about?" Claudine asked, running her hands through his long hair. "Come on. You can tell me."

"Naw," he smiled up into her clear white face. She didn't need that makeup she wore all the time. Her lashes were dark and naturally long. He could see the work of God in each little point, a lighter color on the very end, probably a bleaching from the sun.

"Come on," she smiled. "Tell me."

"It's just that," he smiled and nudged his head into the soft material a little further, "I wish he liked me more."

"Who?"

"The kid. I wish the kid liked me more," he said. "Johnnie, I mean. The kid."

"He's just a kid," Claudine said, running an acrylic nail down the side of his face and around his left ear. The inside of his ear was dirty, needed to be cleaned out with a Q-tip. She ran her fingertip around the curve softly and then inspected the underneath part of her nail to see how much wax had collected. "And I think he likes you fine. What makes you think he don't like you, A. Jacks?"

"He squints at me," he said.

"A. Jacks," Claudine smiled, the mother of all creation, the large titted beauty of all beasts, "you are just being oversensitive again, you know. You just need to get out of here more than you do, see your own friends, do your own thing more."

"What *is* doing my own thing," he sat up to face her. "Don't talk to me in these riddles. How the hell do I know what doing my own thing is? I know what you're thinking and it just ain't right. My own thing, hell."

"I don't understand," she said softly. "Doing your own thing is doing your own thing."

"No," he said. He pulled his hair to a ponytail behind his neck and released it, letting the thick yellow curls fall free, pushing his feet forward on the pillow behind Claudine's neck. "Don't you get it? I don't have an own thing. You're my own thing. Johnnie is my own thing. Besides you and Johnnie, I don't have an own thing."

"Course you do," she said. His eyes looked swollen; she wondered if he'd been crying again. This couldn't go on, these temper tantrums. "You got your wrestling, and you love your wrestling."

"Yeah."

"You're smart, A. Jacks," she said, her glossed lips moving carefully. No teenage temper tantrums here. She'd have to tell him that things were coming to an end, but she did need a babysitter and that cost.

"And you like to paint. You said you liked to paint. You're always reading that damn art book you stole from the library. Least you look at the pictures a lot."

"Yeah, I like to paint," he grinned. "I like the colors. They make me feel things."

"Then paint."

"Naw," he said, folding himself across her knees, smooth and white, smelling like rose lotion. "I could never really paint. I mean, I know a lot about it and all. I mean, I've studied it. I read the book and I looked at pictures, but everytime I try to draw myself, hell, it ain't no good. I mean, everything is out of proportion. I can't get the arms and legs right. You know? They look like they're on the wrong body and everything, and the head is always crooked 'cause I can't draw a round circle. And when I finally do think I've got something, I work on it and work on it and it comes out looking like a cartoon. Naw, Claud, I just don't have it there. Much as I'd like to, I just don't have it there."

"You've got it here," she said, touching him. He smiled at her adoringly. She was his baby white lamb, the only sacrament of which he would take part. He would enter her on command, taste the blood between his teeth, encircle the rosary of her nipples, pink and sweet. Take me into your arms, let me enter the mass of your placenta, crawl into your womb, and nourish myself with your discharge. Let me slide into your stomach, let me rise through the network of your nerves into your lungs, those pleuritic lungs. Let me breathe, let me taste, let me *be* your lungs.

"I love you," he said in a sweat, his hair matting on the sides of his neck catching in her crevices, comfortable in its annoyance. "I love you and I'll never leave you," he moaned.

179

67

'What kind of fruit has its seeds on the outside?"

"I saw your *girlfriend* in the audience last night," Louise said, clutching her ankle, her thin leg straddling the practice bar at the rear of the platformed stage.

"So?" Jeff sipped his beer feeling the chill of the frosted glass against his lower lip. "Her friends thought it'd be a good idea if she got outa the apartment and came down here. You know how it is," he said.

"No. I don't." She stretched her foot, so small it looked like a child's foot, the toes all up in the air, then all straight forward making a hump of the arch like a little girl playing grownup in a pair of high heel slippers from the five-and-dime, the kind with elastic across the middle to strap them on tightly. Louise had told Jeff that it was hopeless her ever becoming a ballerina anyway; there wasn't even any use in buying those posters of Baryshnikov. She refused to hang the things on her walls, refused to hang anything on her walls. Sure, she could watch movie clippings and dream, but that was about all . . . "Darn feet," she cursed herself in front of him. She'd gone over to Old Dominion University one day and she'd found a ballet instructor, at least he'd told her he was a ballet instructor and she'd believed him, and the bastard had taken his black cane and tapped her on the knees, told her to tuck her derriere in, and she didn't even know what the hell he was talking about; he'd lost control when he'd noticed the size of her feet, God, had pulled in the sides of his mouth and laughed like some wicked villain. 'No, no,' he'd laughed, his black mustache covering a great portion of his baby pink face, 'if we put girls with feet this small in toe shoes, we cripple them for life. FOR LIFE!' he had laughed, still examining the tiny bone structure, running his pink fleshy hands across her instep. 'We'll cripple you. You must still have some more growing to do, ha ha. But there may still be hope, ha ha,' the bastard had snickered, 'Come back, come back, when you have gotten bigger, ha ha.' "I saw you slobbering all over each other at the door," she said. "No decency. No decency at all. I don't know how," she stretched from the waist, "I could have judged so poorly. I should have charged you," she glared.

"Don't say that, darlin'." Jeff smiled his never ending smile for her.

"Why not?" Louise shrugged her fragile shoulders. "No one respects it when they get it for free."

"Darlin'," he gloated, the cleft in his blubbery chin stretching into a dimple with his grin, "you know she's got more than a right to kiss me."

"Fuck you," Louise said, lowering her leg from the bar. She pressed the palms of her hands to the buffed wood of the floor.

"Don't talk to me like that, darlin'," Jeff said, pulling the long dark hair up from where it swept the floor. He wrapped it around his hand like gauze. "Especially when you know how much I love you, darlin'. You know I'm suffering too. You know that, darlin'." He let the hair slide. It fell like water around her face, dripped down to the floor.

"Sure," she said, "only," she stretched her hands back between her legs, bouncing to maintain the strength in her leg muscles, "if I was the one pregnant I'm just not so sure you'd be so considerate."

"Darrrrrrrrrlin'," he whined, still grinning fiercely, "with *all* my heart, *all* my heart, since the first time I put eyes on you, from the very first minute. You know that, darlin'."

"I know that," she said, grinning in return, "for sure."

68

Michelle felt the chill of the cement steps up through her blue jeans, the coldness making her underwear feel wet. She pulled her sweater around her chest and buttoned all the buttons, all the way down below her waist, and then reached over and began to button the small pink plastics of Rosie's sweater. Rosemary bent her chin and sniffed, the cold going up through her nose and making her head ache. Inside, they could hear Johnnie screaming, his raspy voice echoing through the exit way of the apartment building and into the street, cold and dark even in the sun of late afternoon. Rosemary's ears were red around the edges; the lobes hung delicately against her small neck covered in blonde hairs. Michelle's fingers felt stiff; the skin cracked along the cuticles, places where she had taken to gnawing throughout the school day.

"Why don't he just leave him alone?" Rosemary asked her. "Why don't he just get the hell outa here and leave Johnnie alone?"

"Don't know," Michelle answered, her long dark hair pulled in a ponytail at the back of her head, falling in strands down the back of her sweater. She flipped the tail up in the air with her hands. "But I ain't going in there till Mom gets home and that's for sure."

"You think he'd hurt us?"

"Don't know."

"You gonna tell your Mom this time?"

"No."

"Why not?" Rosemary asked, sticking her finger up her crusted nose.

"Don't know," Michelle answered.

"Why?"

"Don't know," Michelle answered.

"DEEEEEEEEEEAYEEEEEEEEEEEEEEEEEEEEEEEE."

The sound knocked back and forth in the cement passageway. Michelle hung her hands between her knees and looked down the flight of steps. "Maybe Mom already knows and she wouldn't appreciate someone poking their little nose into her business. You know?" She glared at Rosemary.

Rosemary bundled her cold hands under her sweater, held them close to her body for warmth. "When's the beach gonna come?" she asked.

"Summer," Michelle answered. She thought awhile and stretched her legs down the steps. "Maybe Mom wouldn't like some little kid in her business, you know?" she asked. "Like, I don't think my Mom would be too happy with me if'n she knew I'd snitched her love letters outa the trash can and had them read to me. You know?"

Rosemary sat very still, her brown eyes blinking in the cold sunlight.

"DEEEEEEEEEEEEEEEAYEEEEEEEEEEEEEEEEEEEEEEE-
EEEEEEEEEEEEEEEEEEEEEEEE."

"You know, I could get in loads of trouble, get my ass beaten with a broom if I was ever to be found out doing something like *that*," Michelle said, raising her eyebrows in the direction of the graveled street and whistling with no sound.

"DEEEEEEEEEEEEEEEEEEEEAYEEEEEEEEEEEEEE. DEE-
EEEEEEEAYEEEEEEEEEEEEEEEEEEEE. DEEEEEEEEEE-
EEE . . ."

"Yesirreeeeeeee," Michelle grinned, exposing two rows of perfect teeth. "I'd be covered in black and blue marks before I saw the end of that one," she laughed.

"You gonna tell on me?" Rosemary asked, wiping her gooey fingers on her sweater. The sticky stuff wouldn't rub off. "You gonna tell?"

"DEEEEEEEEEAYEEEEEEEEEEEEEEEEEEEEEEEEEEEEE-

EEEEEEEEEEEEEEEEEEEEEEEEEEEEEEEEE."

"Don't know," Michelle answered. "Ain't got no reason to. Don't know."

"DEEEEEEEEAYEEEEEEEEEEEEEEEEEEEEEEEEEEEEE-EEEEEEEEEEEEEEEEEEEEEEEEEEEEEEEEEEE."

"I'll do anything for you not to tell, Michelle," Rosemary said, huddling close to the older girl. "Please don't tell."

"DEEEEEEEEEEEEEEEAYEEEEEEEEEEEEEEEEEEEEE-EEEEEEEEEEEEEEEEEEEEEEEEEEEEEEEEEEE."

Michelle remembered when she and Johnnie had both been little, had both played in the pen and shared the same toys, when Johnnie had been halfway normal, to her anyway; she hadn't seen anything weird about him except that he couldn't move around too well. He hadn't been any different than her, she thought. Why was all this happening to him now since A. Jacks? What was the difference now? It made her want to ignore him. Growing up made her ignore him, watch anything but him.

"You won't, will you?"

Michelle looked down at the girl beside her. She wrapped an arm around her and held her close, so close that she could feel Rosemary's ribs cutting into her hip bone even through their sweaters and jeans.

"I know you won't, Michelle," Rosemary said. "You're my friend. You won't," she said.

"DEEEEEEEEEEEEEEAYEEEEEEEEEEEEEEEEEEEEEE-EEEEEEEEEEEEEEEEEEEEEEEEEEEEE."

"Don't know," Michelle answered, looking down at the younger girl and frowning.

"Michelle?" Rosemary asked.

"Uh huh," Michelle answered.

"DEEEEEEEEEEEEEEAYEEEEEEEEEEEEEEEEEEEEEE-EEEEEEEEEEEEEEEEEEEEEEEEEEEEE."

"When's summer?"

184

69

"**D**olores," Rod said, leaning over her to cut off the alarm, "how's about you and me and Rosemary going down to Hatteras for a couple of days? What d'ya say?" He laid his face on the pillow next to her cheek.

"Don't look at me yet," she said, facing him. "I don't like for you to see me before I get up and wash my face and put on my blush."

He touched her face, so pale, the freckles hardly even noticeable. You had to get right up to her to even see they were there, but they were there. "Don't be silly," he said. "You think it makes any difference to me whether you've got on a face full of makeup or not?"

"Uh huh," Dolores giggled. "I sure as hell do."

"Well, you're wrong," Rod answered. "I don't care what your face looks like. I wouldn't care if you were run over by a Mack truck."

"Thanks," she said. "It's nice to know you care."

"No, I didn't mean it that way," Rod said. "You know I didn't mean it that way."

She sat on the side of the bed and pulled on her dull Quiana robe, the material feeling silky around her ankles. "I know you didn't mean it that way, but," she paused and looked into the mirror of her vanity table, smoothing the skin under her eyes with cream before she took her morning shower, "you know I can't take Saturdays off. That's our busiest day of the week, always. You know that."

"I'm talking about a Sunday and a Monday," he said, sitting up on his elbows.

"Busy," Dolores said, opening the door to the hallway. "You know that by now, I *hope*."

"Jesus Christ," Rod said, pulling the sheets around his bare shoulders. The window fan was whirring in the living room, the air freezing throughout the apartment.

"What do you mean you're always busy on Mondays?" he yelled. "That's the stupidest goddamn thing I've ever heard."

"I'm always busy on Mondays. Period," Dolores yelled back. "Will you put the hot water on for the coffee, Rod?"

He could hear the TV click on, the kid starting in on the cartoons already. It was time to move. "Put your own damn coffee on."

"Rod," Dolores whined from the bathroom. "No fights this morning, please."

"Put your own damn coffee on if you want it," he yelled from the bedroom. He lighted a cigarette and blew the smoke into the air. "I ain't no houseboy."

"Thanks a lot," she said, stomping out of the bathroom with a towel wrapped around her, her hair in a pink plastic shower cap. "You could at least help me out, you know."

He heard the water running from the tap, the kettle in place. Dolores stomped back into the bathroom.

"You know my reasons," she yelled into him. "You know I don't go out there for fun."

"I don't know about that," he said, propping himself up on a pillow and blowing smoke. "Rosie tells me that he called you selfish."

"What're you talking about?" Dolores asked, pulling on her pantyhose, snapping her bra in place, and pulling it around the front and up over her shoulders. "Rosie told you what?"

"Seems she's got her hands on some old love letters of yours," he smiled, the cigarette dangling between his fingers, burnt down to the filter and hanging like a long gray firecracker snake in the air.

"How'd you find out?" she asked.

"I'll tell you in Hatteras," he said. "Come on, the kid'll love it."

Dolores stood, her hand on one hip. "Rod, so help me, you tell me now or I've had it with you."

"Dolores," he laughed. "Dolores, kid, get a grip."

"ROSEMARY," she yelled. "ROSEMARY . . ."

"Dolores," he whispered, "why get the kid mixed up in this? She's finally started to trust me. Now you're gonna go and ruin that? Don't do it," Rod pleaded. "Not if you want things to work out beween us. Don't do it."

". . ."

"Look in your raincoat pocket," he grinned. The ash fell to the sheet; he tried to wipe it away with his hand and watched the gray mess smear.

"Oh, thank God," she said, finding the long envelopes and ripping them in halves, then in quarters, then eighths. "Thank God."

"Don't thank God," Rod smiled, outstretching his arms. "Thank me, why don't you?"

"Because I'm late already," she said, dumping the shredded letters back into her raincoat pocket. "I've gotta get dressed and outa here this morning, Rod."

"Take the day off," he said. He ran both hands through his brown curls. "Come on. How can you pass this up?" he said, pulling the white sheets back from his naked body. He propped one leg up high and cocked a hip. "You know you want it," he smiled, his bird lips puckering dead center of the grin.

"Rod," Dolores said, shutting the door, "I've got a kid in there."

"The kid loves me."

"Is that so?"

"Yeah," he answered, "ask her yourself."

"I don't care," Dolores said, sitting down to her vanity table and shaking a white liquid into the palm of her hand.

"She's a kid. What does she know anyway?"

"She could probably teach you a few things. Aren't you cold?" he asked, feeling the biting chill from the window unit against his exposed body.

"Naw, used to it."

"Soooooooooo," he grinned and settled back into his pillow, quickly covered himself with the wrinkled sheets, "how's about you and me and the kid taking off for Hatteras this Sunday?"

"I told you," she said, looking at her face in the mirror. She saw the lines that were beginning to scar around her mouth, the redness of the skin around her nostrils from too much scrubbing. The bay winds were bad for facial tissue. "I can't. I got plans."

"Jesus, Dolores," Rod moaned. "You know, I could take a hundred girls to Hatteras, but I wanta take you and the kid. Doesn't that mean anything to you?"

"Sure, sure it does," she answered, spreading a brown formula across her chin, "but you don't seem to understand, my world doesn't revolve around you."

He stared at the back of her head, caught the reflection of her half-colored face in the mirror. He was silent, his jaw set. No woman. He sat up in the bed, threw his legs over the side where his feet touched the cold floor. He pulled his underpants off the pole at the foot of the wooden headboard, slipped them up around his waist, pulled in his gut.

"Where you going?" she asked, running a thick brush full of pink-colored powder along the curve of her cheek. "I need you to take Rosemary over to A. Jacks for me if you're not gonna stay with her today."

"Take her yourself," he said. No woman.

"Come on," she whined. "There'll be other trips to Hatteras for us, won't there?"

He shook his head. "You refuse to make me a part of your life, Dolores," he said, pulling his shirt up over his arms, buttoning it along his chest. "You've got plans."

"Only on Mondays," she said, folding her hands in her lap. "I didn't mean that we could never be together, away together. I, I," she said, staring into his pretty-boy face, raising one arm, and dropping it to her side, "I guess I love you."

His eyes opened so wide, like the heavens were right there in that bright blue, like you could swim into them and be tricked by the sun, be burnt up alive by that trickery.

She watched him stand steady, his jaw set. She was inside those bright eyes, and she was looking right into his story. She had figured him out; she knew everything about him at that very moment, and it was strange because she had thought she had known nothing at all. "You've been through all this before, haven't you?" she asked, swallowing hard.

"That's right," he answered stonefaced. "I've played this game before."

She sat with her lips wide apart, unpainted. He was a sorry, pitiful sight. He slid his belt through the buckle, the metal knob entering the cut leather through the hole. "I'm sorry," Dolores said. She bit the loose skin away from her bottom lip.

"You gotta make up your mind, Dolores." he said. "You gotta make up your mind whether you want that little girl in there to feel loved and happy, or whether you want her to go on carrying your torch for you for the rest of her life. And I'll tell you, Dolores," he said, letting her study his pretty face for a good long time, "as much as I need her, she needs me more. Now, you decide. You decide for the two of us."

189

70

Jeff would be coming to her forever, Louise knew, if she didn't stop it. His arms would reach out for her in the night and she would be there, there in the dark, to take him into the comfort of her side, to hold him against the blood-stained sheets, and let him groan contently. There were no barriers to hold him apart; he would never care about the other men as long as he was always welcome. But she was not a horn of plenty. She would not be scattered, tossed as if she really never belonged in the first place, while he married another girl and set up his happily-ever-after home. He would be coming after her forever. Everyone needed a place to rest in the darkness.

"I love you, darlin'," he moaned, that fleshy cleft in the chin unfolding into morning stubble. He had come after night duty, lying to that girl who lived in his apartment again so that he could hold Louise in his arms and scream, "darlin', darlin'," and in the dark, even though she had scrubbed everything, everything in the room except the sheets, it was all black, all dirty, and there was nothing beautiful left.

"Here," she said, stretching him out on his back, "relax." And he relaxed. He could hear the motor of the psychedelic Jesus and against his own eyelids he could see the colors rising from the dark. "Relax," she said, her face close against his paunchy gut. She let her fingers run wildly over the tiny hairs covering the pubic area, and she touched the tip of her tongue to his navel and drew it down, down, down until the coldness made his organ stand upright. She lightly lifted her tongue from his body, reached to the side of the bed where she had slipped the small black tube under the sheet. The cap slid off easily, and she ran the tip of the container spout between his balls, the adhesive gleaming in the night light like the glistening of baby spittle against the pinkiness of a mother's breast. It eased into the crevices of his body and glossed over onto his thighs, dripping down to the sheets. He moaned heavily, his body urging her to spread more of the epoxy, her fingers pressing the metal tube with all her might, until the tips of her own hand felt numb and she could no longer carry on the charade. She sat up against the blood-stained sheets laughing so hard she thought she would never be able to stop.

"What is it?" he smiled, trying to sit up, inspecting his body to see what the hell she had thought was so funny, what the joke was, only the hair of his legs stuck to the sheets and he could feel the skin of his rear holding tightly together. The smile vanished from his face as she ran to the light switch and flicked on the electric overhead, a nightmare he would never forget as she held the empty tube of Goofey Glue in the air and clutched herself in a frenzy. He couldn't even hear himself think over her madness, and the sight of the shriveled penis, exhausted, caught in the clammy goo, made him clutch hurriedly, his fingers catching themselves in the mess of the balls solidifying to his thighs. The excitement made the pain more miserable, the skin raw and aching, and in her laughter her hair was thrown over her face like some sort of witch he had never known. "Call an ambulance," he groaned, his hands holding his genitals, the bloody sheet pulled from the bed as he tried to release himself from the stinging hold, "CALL THE GODDAMNED AMBULANCE NOW!" Jeff screamed, his face a reddied mass of bulging veins. "CALL THE GODDAMNED AMBULANCE ON THE GODDAMN DOUBLE! YOU SLUT! DO YOU HEAR ME?!"

Loretta woke from sleep and ran to the doorway naked, her eyes searing into her daughter's face with anger, and it was she who finally called the ambulance and had him

191

sent to Norfolk General. It was she who implored him to punish not the girl, but herself, because Louise was so young, was hurt so very easily, and could not be held responsible for her actions. And in his pain, the dirtied sheet covering the swelling flesh, he nodded in agreement. Not because he felt the least bit of passion or sympathy for the girl; for her, he felt bitter hate, confusion, betrayal. But for Loretta, he consented, because he had seen the whore without her mask, and the shock had hit him harder than any gruesome act he had ever witnessed.

71

"You've gotta history of long-term guilt feelings, don't you?" Claudine asked, holding Johnnie against her chest, his face buried in the soft fabric of her short-sleeved blouse, the spittle dribbling down into her brassiere sticky and unwelcome. "Why don't you just go home where you belong?" she argued.

"Awwwwwwwwww, fuck you," A. Jacks screamed, flipping his head to the side, the long greasy curls in motion. "What would you do around here without me anyway? No way you could survive without me anyway. You ain't no manager, you know." He sucked in the hollows of his wide face.

"Michelle," Claudine asked, looking at the child sitting silently in front of the television set, "what *would* we do around here without A. Jacks?"

"Don't know," Michelle answered, never taking her eyes from the set. The pictures of people in a strange shade of pinky red danced before her. She had fiddled with the color buttons until that tone had arrived on the tube.

"Huh?" Claudine asked. "Speak louder. A. Jacks can't hear you."

"Don't know, Mom," Michelle said louder.

"Not a pretty story," Claudine grinned. She could feel her lips cracking.

"Claudine," A. Jacks said, sitting close to her and Johnnie on the plaid couch, "you gotta know that I only hate *myself*. It's just *me* I can't stand anymore." He wrenched his face into a pathetic twisted position. "It's *me*. *I'm* not right in my head anymore," he whined. "I need your help."

"Go home to your mother," Claudine argued, patting Johnnie tenderly on his large back, the spindly backbone, each vertebra jutting into the soft cotton of his clothing. "Go home to someone who loves you, A. Jacks," she said.

He buried his head in his hands, large hairy hands, and whimpered. Johnnie opened his coal blue eyes and took it all in, smiled and gurgled as A. Jacks' head wrinkled in anguish and his body shook with pain. "Deeayeeeee." There was a lip turn, the pinky flesh reaching toward a nostril from one side of a crooked mouth, a thick tongue falling forward with pleasure like some gumball machine, and the underbelly twitched against Claudine's chest.

"Just get up and get outa here," she screamed. "I can't stand having another baby around here." Her eyes widened with disgust and hatred as she watched A. Jacks sobbing into cupped hands. "You know something, babe?" she asked. "You're a hundred times more trouble than Johnnie here. He suffers like a man. You hear that," she said proudly, gritting her evenly shaped white teeth. "My Johnnie, he suffers like a *man*. Not like some pansy-assed little boy."

A. Jacks sniffled and flipped his head backward, his neck cracking slightly, his nostrils resting in the open air as he caught his breath, breathed for his life, and dared not look at the boy who lay huddled against his mother's breast. If you were distorted enough, enough out of the normal, no one expected a damn thing from you, no one expected you to live at all. You could do anything you damn well pleased and still be. It wasn't fair to just *be* in life; you had to play the game; you had to follow orders.

"I am *not* a pansy-ass," he said.

Silence. A. Jacks wasn't crying anymore.

"And tonight, Claudine," he spoke, in a perfectly grown-up man's voice, so perfectly grown-up that Claudine took extra notice and held Johnnie that much closer, he said, "when you're all alone in your bed, when the lights are off and you want someone strong to pull you close, to breathe against your face," he opened the door, pulled on his leather jacket, and picked up a green duffle bag he'd had waiting outside on the cement landing. He slung it over one shoulder, looked like a million other guys, "want someone to fuck you till you're blue in the face, you'll be sorry that I'm gone."

The door closed, shut hard against the warped painted woodwork, and A. Jacks wasn't there anymore. Michelle never took her eyes away from the set. All was quiet, and Johnnie was half asleep.

"I'll be damned if I'll be bullied into being treated like a mother," Claudine spoke softly to Johnnie. "Let him take that wrestling scholarship and go to college where he belongs. Don't you think?" she asked. Johnnie's jaw fell limp. "I don't know. Paint. Do something with his life. He can't just mope around here forever, can he?" she asked. "That wouldn't be fair. Would it?" she asked.

"I dunno, Mom," Michelle answered from in front of the set.

"Well," Claudine said, rolling Johnnie off her lap, allowing his arms and legs to sprawl around his well-formed midsection, "I guess I better call his mother and tell her that he's left. Finally," she sighed.

72

"**H**ave you seen him?" Claudine whimpered, her face a flushed mess. Johnnie lay on the dusty floorboards howling.

"He hasn't been around *my* place," Dolores answered. "Did he take everything with him?"

"Everything," Claudine gasped. "I checked the bedroom over a hundred times and the only thing he left was an overdue art book that's been out of the library for years. I guess he forgot it was under the bed. I don't know," she sniffled, "I was so upset last night the kids cuddled up in the bed with me. I haven't had them do that in a long time. Why the hell," she slammed her fist down on the brown wood cabinet of the telephone desk, "why the hell did he have to go and upset my life like this? And with Sheila's wedding only a week away," she whined. "You know, I've really been looking forward to this wedding. Don't ask me why," she grinned through her reddied face, "I just thought it was gonna be so nice to take him to a wedding, you know, hold his hand, and feel like we was a family and everything. I guess that was stupid," she said, forgetting about acne pimples and running a wet finger across her cheek. "I guess that was really stupid, huh?"

"That's not so stupid," Dolores said, reaching for her cup of morning coffee. "I felt sort of the same way about Rod . . . I wanted it to be a little fantasy, you know?"

Claudine tried to smile. "You really think it's okay to act this way?"

"Shows we're human. That's all."

"Not a pretty story," Claudine laughed. She studied the portrait of Bettina, the girl whose yellow eyes held violet dots. "You think Bettina would carry on like this over some

195

nineteen-year-old boy who she didn t really love to begin with," Claudine joked, her throat swelling so that she could not make laughter.

Dolores watched Bettina herself. The silver blonde hair cut below the perfectly powdered lobes, the nose perfectly pugged. "I don't think so," Dolores answered. "But, then again, Bettina's only a picture. And she's coming down soon. They're sending black photographs."

"Not a pretty story," Claudine wept.

The morning turned pretty when the doors to La Boudoir were opened, the last Saturday morning of March and the sun streamed into the shop with force, customers already making their standings for the Easter weeks, the wedding right around the corner. Claudine noticed the new picture of Rosemary epoxied above Dolores' desk. Everything was set up early in anticipation for a big booking day, cutting and shaping utensils spread out all silvery on white towels exuding the odor of ammonia, and there was the new snapshot of Rosemary in her yellow-and-white dress leaning back in Rod's arms somewhere along the beach. It looked like the Spit, the boats anchored behind the two of them, his arms around her little waist like he had held her for all of her life, and Dolores had thought enough of the shot to glue it on the wall for all of her customers to study, ask questions about.

"You in love again?" Claudine asked. "With Rod?"

"No," Dolores answered. "Just tired," she said, checking her face in the sunlight against the distorted mirror at the edge of the receptionist desk. Dark spots showed through the creasing white-out she had carefully smoothed in the folds under her eyes. "I don't know," she said, "maybe floating manager is really enough for me. I don't know," she paused and looked at Claudine, Claudine's face swollen and unpowdered, "would you consider it again? I just don't think I'm cut out for full time. I'm afraid I'm gonna lose it all. Lose my mind," she laughed. "That is, whatever mind I got left, and there ain't a lot of that to lose."

"Don't make me laugh," Claudine grinned, her lips, for once, only a shade deeper than the rest of her complexion, and she drew the smoke into her lungs heavily, with power, the whole of her abundant chest rising, followed by a slight fall. She grinned, inspected her own acrylics. "Well," she sighed, "not a pretty story. Not a pretty story at all."

73

Rod and the new kid brought the pink and green and purple lights onto the bar, the new kid's muscles brown and sweating in the heat of the night's amusement. It was a bigger batch party than anyone had imagined, the word getting around the base that the undercover cop at The Blue Garter was getting married the next day and all grain alcohol was on the house with no cover charge at the door. And I.D. cards weren't even being checked. The heavy brown doors of The Garter were wide open to the public, the better part of the police force pouring liquor down their gullets in honor of Jeff's bride-to-be.

Jeff sat in an uncomfortable position, his thighs and genitals bandaged heavily. They still ached, throbbed from having to be surgically separated. He grimaced and listened to Lynn Anderson on the juke, couldn't wait for the show to begin. He wanted to point her out to the boys; none of them were to miss the show. That had been stated with a finger, a fat finger, in each and every one of his buddies' faces. They were not to miss the show.

The room was hot, even the front and back doors open to the thick Virginia air didn't help. It was just plain stale and no open doors could make a cool breeze.

Rod stood behind the bar in his shirt sleeves, his starched

white shirt looking just as casual as ever, but his hands moved steadily, never pausing to look at a young face, never leaving the spigot, never taking his eyes away from business for a moment. There were no women in the bar, except for the waitresses, all topless for this special occasion, with bottles of grain alcohol strapped around their shoulders and under their bosoms. This was strictly a batch party; no women were to intrude, made plain by the signs posted on either side of the open doors: MEN ONLY TONIGHT. OPEN BATCH PARTY. NO WOMEN, PLEASE. And women obeyed signs posted by men.

The grain alcohol poured freely from the topless waitresses' tits, the rounded metal spouts of the liquor bottles barely touching their nipples. The spectacle made the men giggle like young girls, their beards and their fists sweating in the heat, the laughter loud, blending with the many colored lights. And the show began. Jeff sat still in his wooden chair as Loretta ran to the platformed stage carrying the olympic torch high in the air, her face plastered a thick whiteness, flour paste, her lips painted Fire Engine Red as she turned to face her screaming audience, their faces directly beneath her breathing hard, harder, as she moved slowly within her black stockings and dropped the top of her costume. Jeff settled back in his chair and grinned. The animals hollered obscenities; they only drew a smile to Loretta's painted face. She took those obscenities as compliments, cherished each and every word, each and every vile action, tried to hold to them, keep them for later when she was unmasked and alone in bed.

As a special honor to Jeff, Louise was ushered out by three topless waitresses and placed in the center of the stage. The new boy spoke from the loudspeaker introducing Louise "Little Feet" Sweate and there was a round of applause. She appeared to be blushing, but Jeff knew that the color brought to her cheeks was because he had made it a point to be spotted. She had looked directly at him, and even though she had to have known that he would be present at his own bachelor's party, it appeared to be an embarrassment.

"Normally," the young boy began, "a delicious young girl jumps out of a whipped cream cake in the buff," he laughed. "But," he continued, "tonight we offer the lucky groom something a little out of the ordinary! The whipped cream," he continued, "jumps out of the girl!"

The waitresses bent her over, Louise's mouth a bright pink, her long dark hair curled very carefully and reaching to the floor. Jeff remembered times when he had loved that girl so much, when he had convinced himself that the only really right thing he could do in life was to be with the one he couldn't live without; but things had changed, and he had found out that the only right thing to do in life was to destroy whatever it was that he couldn't live without. He would have to live without.

She kept her eyes away from him, staring at the floor, remembering how once he had almost convinced her that she could make her dreams come true, that she could really dance, would be a real dancer one day, not some cheap trick with a painted face and a naked underdeveloped chest, but some beautiful swan winging her way to stardom, some fantastic dream coming true, like in the movies. She had believed. How could he have cheated her out of her dream so casually? She would never forget the way he had made it all seem so real. And she would hold it in her belly, prove him wrong after all. She would show him that what he called reality was nothing more than his own dream, and that her dreams were just as real.

The waitresses took two cans of whipped cream and sprayed them at her from her underside. She could feel the soft coldness come from between her thighs, spread across her belly, and she closed her eyes, let the whiteness take over her body, let the whiteness take hold of her senses. She could feel her mother standing beside her.

199

Nothing terrible would happen. Her mother would be beside her every step of the way, whatever was to happen next. There was no break between the two. Often she had heard herself say, "My mother and I are the same person," and she had meant it. It was a soft pain and the men had gained pleasure from it. No harm had been done and her eyes had been closed. Once, she had opened her eyes and tried to softly appeal to Rod, but he hadn't been anywhere in the bar and she was thankful for that. Even when the whistles began to blow and the sailors had begun to scatter like ants when a heavy boot appears out of nowhere, she had been calm, had known that everything would pass and that she was simply taking part in someone else's dream because her mother had been busted before, and she had been warned that this might happen. She had almost expected it, and much worse. She had seen herself growing old in a cement cage, without sunlight, her own blood on the floors . . . wasted blood. She had seen her own face wrinkled and sallow, ugly beyond belief, and she had made up her mind that if that was to be her payment, then she would just have to live with it. But the dream, that would always be there too. Instead, she was wrapped in a warm blanket and hurried into a patrol car, one like she had been given lifts in a hundred times before. And she felt comfortable, even when they inked her fingers, because everything was warm and settled, and she would dance again, she knew. It was *his* dream she worried about.

74

The book of French painters had deliberately been left open under Claudine's bed. The idea of the portrait rising through the mattress and cursing her soul had given A. Jacks instinctive pleasure. As he opened the heavy glass door of the Navy recruiting office, felt his weight push easily against anything standing in his way, he gave thought to George de La Tour cursing Claudine, causing her hair to turn black like a thousand snakes, poisonous liquid seeping into her brain. And her heart would be dead in a matter of days. He would stand outside that church, they couldn't keep him from standing outside the church, and he would watch her and the boy, and he would know that they both were poisoned, that neither one of them would function correctly. He wouldn't be the only one who would be made to pay. He wouldn't be the only one made to feel the guilt. They would all share. And he would be the winner because he would force himself to honor the rules. The penitent Magdalene had been dressed in red and white garb, a skull with empty eye holes upon her lap; she'd spend eternity repenting behind the reflection of a candle in a mirror. There had been too many for her own good, too many who had left, her soul burning in the reflection as she sat peacefully waiting, waiting, waiting for a return. But there were no returns, would never be a return, and she would clasp her own hands for the touch of comfort, for she held herself too aloof, surrounded her face in soft white powders and gold shellacked frames. A string of pearls lay in a heap, her chest so bare, so open behind the thin white gauze. There is a waiting heat, yet the air is still and frozen. She has caused him to take his own hair, to beg for the strength from his body to be sucked into the earth, to become one of the mass, like Samson walking among caged lions, and she would be made to pay, for Jesus was the son of a saint, and had knowingly given his love to the wicked and the undeserving.

75

The pink and red potted azaleas splattered the carpeted aisles of Saint Pious with a fragrance of new life, the metal pots covered in silken pink ribbons and birthday bows. The walls of the cement monstrosity swept high, the concrete tubing reaching toward eternity in what resembled organ piping. There was the smell of fresh dirt against cold cement; even though the sun was shining in midday brightness outside, the air thick with a musty warmth, the girls in their crinolines and dyed-to-match pumps, inside there was the cold potter's field sense of serenity, the true warmth, the inner warmth. This was the cold home of all that was real, the cheaply carved plastered statue of a man looming from a cross.

Sheila planned on collecting the potted plants after the ceremony, bending down upon her knees in the middle of the church and hugging each green can of dirt, her face buried in the soft brush she would use to plant up the front of her new brick home. She hoped that they would look as eloquent there as they looked this day in the church, that the rest of her life would be this peaceful, this readily accepted by her friends. No matter what happened, no matter how dirty or sordid she had been, there was always someone else bearing her cross, and she would be forgiven and tipped a new life. Jeff had promised her a surprise when both the service and the reception at the Gigantic Supermarket were over, saying that they couldn't afford a honeymoon yet, he hadn't saved enough for the perfect honeymoon just yet, but that he had someplace really special he'd bought for the two of them to live for the rest of their lives and he wanted to drive her over there the second they could manage to get away from the bunch.

She'd warned him that it might be late, that she was sure her friends would party forever and a day, but he'd said he'd already bought a mattress from the secondhand warehouse, one with real pretty flower and striped ticking, and that he wanted to try it out before the baby got too big inside her belly and ruined everything. Course, that had been before he'd gone and gotten his balls glued together, but she supposed it would be nice and memorable to spend her first night married someplace she could really call their own together . . . a real brick house, she hoped. Puerto Rico and the Baha Hotel could always come later. She could always send Jude a postcard that said, "Missing You And Loving It," be assured she'd have a place on Jude's mirror right next to Dixie Pointer. She'd make them all wish they were in her shoes.

The man in the black tuxedo played the organ softly, the tails of his coat falling over the wooden bench where he sat tucked in his niche between a statue of a woman fawning over an infant and the Lord with his fingertips outstretched to the congregation, his robes frozen in a flow around his naked feet. The organ player was the hurdy-gurdy man, his black plastered hair combed smoothly over his ears, long on his neck, the perspiration evident on his white collar. At his feet sat a candelabra, the flickering electric bulbs spreading illumination against the pale-skinned figure in black. And melodious wind music cast out.

Jeff came to Sheila's side, walking ever so stiffly, as if this were the most important moment of his life, the holding of hands in front of the altar, the bowing to their knees; they were two children in a wheat field. Sheila's white dress spread on the red carpet before her as she took the metal cup and touched it to both their lips.

There was only the shuffling of prayer book paper, new shoes and the soft lapping of damp white gloves against wooden pews. Michelle held Johnnie close to her chest, her hand nervously pressing against his soft underbelly. He didn't breathe a word, his head falling to one side, caught on her sweet smelling shoulder, his legs dangling in the darkness. It was only Michelle who could feel the wetness seep through the diapers under his navy jump-suit, bought special and cut down through the arms and legs to fit only Johnnie. And she could feel the heat of his urine against her legs and feel it slowly roll down into the hems of her white high-top socks.

The sun shattered through the tall thick panes of clear glass at the back of the church, the dark blue stained panes easing the light and sending speckles of dust into the synod. Claudine turned around in her seat, cupping her hands over her eyes, squinting, aware that A. Jacks was outside waiting, causing her to form premature wrinkles around her eyes. She had seen him when she had parked the car and walked the children around to the front of Saint Pious. He had been standing across the street from the church entranceway. She was sure it had been him; she had rec-ognized the build, those burdening wrestler's muscles seeming to throb through his shirt. It hadn't mattered what he was wearing. There he had stood in a Dixie Cup and stripes and she had recognized him, and looked directly across the street when there had been no need to. Some-times, out of habit, she looked across streets just to see if it was safe to cross, for the children's sake, even when they had no intention of crossing. But, today, she had looked straight across the street and there he had been, A. Jacks standing there like he belonged, bug-eyed and stiff; she was sure he had had his hair shaved off. All of it; it had been shaved clean. Either that or he had just wanted to throw a scare into her and let her believe he had had it shaved. Probably, he'd just had it tucked into the collar of that Navy uniform he wore. She'd have to call his mother as soon as the reception at the Gigantic was over.

Rod held Dolores tightly around the shoulders and felt

embarrassed, flushed as he watched Claudine's face, light striking.

The ring slid over Sheila's finger, and the corners of Jeff's eyes turned up. Sheila tasted the wine and held the goblet to Jeff's lips, those thick chubby lips, and she watched him drink, watched the liquid slide down his fat throat, and he gave her a grin, a full grin that made his dimple disappear, and that moment for her was frozen. She would make him wish he had never smiled. She would make him forget that he could. She felt as if she would faint, the baby kicking hard today, the air so thick with sweet fragrance she could hardly breathe. But she could tell her family was proud. She had done it all. For one day of happiness, one day of pride, she had done it all. And Jeff wouldn't find out about the blisters for a good while. He had his own excuse for not sleeping with her this week; there would be other excuses later. Once she had wanted to exchange personal vows, but, today, whatever the man in the robes said was okay with her.

76

The double doors at the rear of the church spread open, a heavy ray of sunshine at his back, his arms out to either side. A. Jacks stood in silence as the congregation turned and watched. Claudine's eyes grew wide with fear, and Michelle clutched Johnnie even tighter to her chest.

Sheila and Jeff turned from where they kneeled, his arm around her, Sheila feeling sick in her belly, Jeff waiting for the next step, waiting to see what would happen.

"You fucking bitch," A. Jacks cried in a loud high voice. "You fucking, fucking bitch . ."

Dolores watched Rod close his eyes, breathe deeply.

Claudine looked as though she might speak, but didn't dare.

"You fucking bitch," he moaned softer, his chin falling to his chest, the Dixie Cup sliding forward. He caught it with one hand, turned his back to his audience, and walked away, the doors to the church closing behind him, a loud gasp coming from nowhere, like an echo.

It was then that they could feel the heat of the house of prayer. Claudine cried softly, her mascara running down the powdered whiteness of her cheeks, and Rod clutched Dolores' hand as if he would never let go, as if he were frightened, a child before God.

77

It was done.

The flashbulbs snapped, brightness striking light in the church for an instant and then, once again, the delicately cool darkness of the cement, the slick-headed man in tails playing soft organ music. They stood and made their way into the sunshine.

It was done.

Outside, handfuls of white rice splashed in front of their eyes and caught in the fine strands of their hair; they crowded into corners of glistening pavement, Sheila smiling happily beneath the trails of white organza she wore draped over her head. Sheila's hair was no longer streaked, but short and twigged against her face; she had told Jude to take it all off, to scalp her. Jeff stood at her side, not daring to look away, the heat attacking his black patent shoes causing his ankles to swell beneath woollen socks.

It was done.

Claudine held Johnnie in her arms, his heaviness causing her to find a place on the steps outside the church.

There was no sense going straight over to the Gigantic supermarket before the bride and groom. There would be no party before their arrival. "I know you peed in your new pants," she whispered. Johnnie let his tongue fall to the side of his mouth, the drool slipping over his pink gums and down his chin. She caught it in the thumbnail acrylic. "You're just a mess," she grinned and allowed her eyes to wander across the street. A. Jacks was still there in his Dixie Cup and Stripes and she couldn't believe it. It was true. He wasn't just dressed up for play. He had gone and joined the service, gone and enlisted like a common fool. He had thrown it all away. He'd have been better off going to school, going to school on his wrestling scholarship and learning how to paint, she thought, and she juggled Johnnie on her lap. That had been A. Jacks' dream. Claudine didn't understand. He had done this for spite, she knew, and she wasn't going to walk across the street and make a spectacle of herself and her children. He could stand there and stare back at her for the rest of his life for all she cared. She wasn't going to move off her step. If he couldn't come back to her as a man, if he had to hide behind a uniform, then he could never come back to her at all.

"Deeeeeeeeeeeeeayeeeeeeeeeee."

And she looked up from her child's reddened face in time to see the closely clipped sailor put one foot forward and make his way across the street, in the opposite direction.

78

"*C*ould you ever love me like I love you?" he had asked. Dolores sat on the small strip of beach and held her knees tightly together. She didn't care about her dress. It would get wet, get dirty. She didn't care. They had walked through the grocery store and found the staircase up to the reception room. They had held hands and Rosemary had been so happy, she had been glowing with happiness, hanging on to Rod's pants legs and smiling into his pretty face. She had been like a little princess who had finally found heaven. And they had even danced together, the three of them to an old tune, one that was so old they never even played it on the piped-in stereo in the shop. And all three of them had such a good time. Then he had turned to her and said, *"Could you ever love me like I love you?"* and she'd looked down into Rosemary's face and the child was waiting, waiting for her to answer, and she couldn't do it. Dolores sat and hugged her knees the way she used to when *he* was with her, when *he* had convinced her that love was real, as real as the person next to you. *"This love shit's for the birds,"* she had said. She remembered saying it. She had never believed in love, still it had haunted her like a witch's curse. She'd never be tricked into that again. And the child had stared up into her face waiting for her to be tricked. Well, she thought, leaning back against a soft grassy mound growing at the slope of the beach, she couldn't blame the kid for believing; it wasn't the kid's fault she believed.

Dolores pulled a patch of small wild strawberries from the grass, held them in the lap of her dress as she made her way to the shore. Her stockinged feet felt the coldness of the sand, felt the grainy pebbles seep into her skin and scratch, and she didn't care. The muddied water darkened her hose and stuck between the soft spots of her toes, and she watched the ships sit silently, never moving, never moving, she thought, from one day till the next. Still, the old ships were gone and the new ships were anchored. And the Spit would always be the same. The winds blew from the Bay against her shoulders, and she let the lap of her cotton dress drop, the wild strawberries sink into the muddy green goo of the water. They were gone forever. They would not rise. They sank. And they made no sound.

There was stillness and at her feet she noticed a French tobacco tin had washed to shore, the edges newly bent, not even rusted. The sailors dumped and they dumped and they dumped, and you never knew what they dumped, but you had a pretty good idea when you immersed yourself in the water and came up covered with filth. Claudine was right, it wasn't a pretty story. Not a pretty story at all.

79

The smell of the fresh dirt in the potted azaleas was delightful, and Sheila settled back against the slick plastic upholstery of the patrol car, the back seat full of the plants she and Jeff had stopped by the church and collected. She was a little drunk, and the baby kicking in an uproar didn't seem to matter anymore. The baby would be okay. The air was turning cool even though she was burning up under her wedding dress, and she couldn't wait until Jeff pulled into the driveway of their new brick home to break open the gown, tear it apart without undoing the fifty-two rayon buttons up the back. She would never wear this gown again anyway. It would go in a box in the back of her closet along with her Valentines and stuffed animals and she would begin her new life sophisticated. Jude had said that with this Mia Farrow haircut she couldn't be anything but seductive and sophisticated. And she would stock her closet with hundreds of pairs of high-heeled shoes, spiked and black. And she'd been glad Barbita had been at the wedding. It had showed everyone that she wasn't prejudiced at all. It had showed everyone that she had an open mind to things like that and that dating a black boy in high school hadn't been all that bad. She hadn't been bad. And Jeff and the baby and the new brick home would prove that.

"Jeff," she yawned sleepily, "tell me about the house. Where is it? Where are you taking me?" she giggled.

He grinned at her, that wide fleshy smile that made the dimple disappear. "I ain't telling you nothing," he said. "It wouldn't be no surprise then, would it now, darlin'?"

"Come on," she begged. "You can tell me. Come on. I don't wanta be surprised."

"Look, darlin'," he said. He sat very straight. She knew he had it all bandaged and propped up between his legs in just the right position. He hadn't even been able to dance with her at the reception. He'd just sat there with Rod and his copper buddies and put away one hell of a lot of champagne, but that was okay, she guessed. Every man had the privilege of tying one on whenever he wanted. That was what Claudine had told her. Don't worry about it, she'd said. And Sheila had felt very sophisticated and answered, "Believe me, he can do whatever his little heart pleases," and she had meant every word of it. She had danced with her father, and her mother had taken pictures of the two of them, Sheila with little cousins she had hardly ever seen before, cousins and aunts and uncles and girlfriends from the vocational school who were cutting and blow-drying around town who told her that anytime she wanted a job, now that she was married and all, to come into their shop and they'd be sure she could have a chair. It all seemed so easy now. So easy. She could have a chair. "Look, darlin'," he said. "I don't want you to be disappointed now. I done the best I could picking out a place for the three of us to live. It's got one bedroom, and I figured we could make the living room into a combination living room/ nursery, you know? But I don't want you to go and get all your hopes up."

"Sweetheart," she glowed. All that champagne and the Gigantic supermarket had done such a beautiful job of the cake. It had been fourteen layers, one layer sweeter than the next, all covered in frothy white and pink sugar. She had loved it. And even though he'd felt too poorly to get up off the chair and walk over and help her cut the damn thing, she'd cut it fine by herself, done a swell job, and they'd all snapped her picture while she was doing it. "Sweetheart," she smiled and touched his hand, the one on the steering wheel. He looked at her and grinned that grin. A moment frozen again. She would never forget that moment on the way to the new place. "Tell me," she begged.

"Well, okay," he said. "We'll have plenty of space to plant those pots back there cause there's lots of ground around the place. Enough if you even wanted to plant a little vegetable garden or something," he grinned. Frozen. "You know," he said, "so's we could save a little money, maybe have our next kid real soon."

"Gracious," she said. That was a sophisticated expression, and she being a cop's wife now she'd have to get used to saying gracious and my word, and Lordy be, although that last one she'd have to remember to use sparingly. "We haven't even had this little sucker yet." She felt for a kick through the white ruffles of her gown, but there wasn't one.

"Okay," he said. "And, all the guys chipped in and their wives went out and bought you a bedspread and matching curtains from Sears and Roebuck so's you don't have to go out and buy any of that."

"Oh," she said, closing her eyes for a second, "I wanted to buy all that stuff myself. I wanted everything to be perfect."

"Well," he grinned that grin. Frozen. "It will be, darlin'. I knew that from the first time we were together." He slapped her on the thigh. Through the rayon lace it stung. "Everything will be just perfect."

"Are we almost there?" she asked, looking anxiously out the windows. He had the doors locked again, that special device of his. "Is it around here?"

"Almost," he grinned. She refused to look at him anymore. She kept her eyes on the passing scenery and let the smell of fresh azalea plants comfort her. And she was silent.

He pulled the patrol car into a dirt pathway and she grit the backs of her teeth, let her tongue catch on the chipped part of that tooth in the front of her mouth. She held her breath as he pulled up and parked, took the key out of the ignition. "Wanta get out and take a closer look at it?" he asked. He reached under his seat, pushed the electric button to unlock the doors. "Go ahead," he punched her in the arm.

"You're kidding me, aren't you?" she smiled. She could taste that she was wearing no lipstick. It must have worn off, and she hadn't reapplied it the whole day. All the wedding pictures of herself were probably going to come out terrible. She should have remembered to excuse herself and check her face. "This is a joke, isn't it?" she smiled. She could feel the tears welling, the lump in her throat. She couldn't take this. "If this is your idea of a joke, I don't think it's funny."

"What funny?" he asked, his face drooping, the cleft sagging with weight. "I thought you'd like it. I thought you'd get a kick out of it."

"It's a trailer," she whined.

"I know what the hell it is," he answered.

"But," she swallowed, "it ain't even *brick*. I told you I wanted *brick*. We didn't get no Baha Hotel in Puerto Rico and now we don't even get no *brick*?" Her mouth fell open and she pressed her hand to her chest. "Not even *brick*?" she asked.

"It's got *brick* on the inside," he said. "Get out and go see it. You'll like it. It's got this nice baseboard heating job, and it's like brick all up and down one wall, only it's better than brick cause it's made of plastic and you can peel it off anytime you feel like it. Understand?"

"Sure," she said, looking at the trailer. A pink stripe ran

around the white aluminum body. "Sure, I understand."

Jeff sat behind the wheel, his arm over the front seat around her shoulders. "Darlin'," he said, nudging her with one thumb, "believe me, I only wanted to make you happy. Really, from the first time I set eyes on you, darlin'," he moaned, "I only wanted to make it good for us. You'll like it, darlin'," he said. "You'll see. You'll be crazy about it in no time," he said, and he touched the top of her cropped head. "You'll see, darlin'," he said. "Darlin', believe me," he said, "I love you."

She felt the baby kick, hard; she looked Jeff in the face, pulled open the metal door handle with the acrylic nails Dolores had built on her hands as a wedding present, made clicking noises with the tips, the acrylic feeling heavy against the bones of her fingertips as she made her way up the dirt path and pulled wide the door of her new trailer home. And it was prettier than anything she'd ever seen, all spanking brand new with unused kitchen appliances and a wall that could pass for real brick any day as long as you didn't walk up and touch it. And he'd said that he'd loved her from the first time, from the very first time, and that had made all that had gone before meaningless. She turned on her heels in a whirl, one hand against the aluminum door jamb as she leaned her whole body forward over the cinderblock steps. "Jeffrey, Jeff, honey," she yelled hoarsely, her knuckles turning white from the pressure of her weight practically held by the metal door framing. Jeff stuck his head out the window of the black and white Virginia patrol car, swallowed hard, and tried to smile, his dimple disappearing. "Jeffrey, Jeff, honey," she screamed wildly, her thin lips tremulous against her freckled face, "I love you, darlin'," she grinned. "I love you forever, darlin'," she said, shaking her head whimsically.

80

The evening light was still and soft, the sun and the moon on opposite sides of the skyline, the interstate crossing the smooth sea line of the Spit. Dolores somehow knew that when she turned, that when she lifted one sopping sand-filled stocking from the dirty water and glanced backward, Rod would be standing on the grassy knoll waiting for her smile. She watched the automobiles in motion, their many colors slurring into the pinks and blues and oranges of the almost summer sky. Did the colors take the passing strangers, she wondered, anywheres different from where they had been, or did the same place just look different all the time?

She turned and he was there, the wet hem of her dress clinging to her ankles. He had followed her from the wedding, knew exactly where she would go, and he held his bird mouth very tightly in a stifled grin, the small girl clutching his large hand between both of her own. For Rosemary, Dolores realized, there was only the dream. There had never been any before. For Rosie, anyway, there was still magic.

She studied his face as she made her way across the narrow patch of cold sand, the pain of her toes half frozen from the cold made her appear to smile at the two of them; the man was intent on comfort, the child intent on love. A million pictures flashed through her mind, things that really were and yet had never been felt. Too much champagne and romance had caused her to think ahead too much, to interpret things that had never happened, and she realized that the thinking had caused the pain and not what had gone before. She could let the pain pass, her pastel-powdered lids drooping in before unrealized ease. Dolores lifted her hands forward and the child's face relaxed into a feverish mask as her fingertips met their free hands. And she knew she had given up the hardest and most desirable part of her life because she would never have to feel that much pain again; she would cease to have that freedom.

There was the sunset and the man and the child and all that was good. Frozen. Cold. Still.

81

The newspaper article read:

PROSTITUTE AGREES TO LEAVE VIRGINIA

Ocean View, Virginia—Saying that he could understand prosecutor's frustration in dealing with her, a judge agreed Friday to place often-arrested prostitute Loretta Sweate on probation, with the understanding that she is to leave the state.

Circuit Judge Elliot S. Mummery, Jr. noted that Miss Sweate has been arrested for prostitution-related offenses 16 times in the Norfolk, Ocean View area since the early 1970s, and twice has been sent to prison. Upon release from confinement, she would return to her old business each time.

Martin E. Espritte, Miss Sweate's lawyer, and prosecutor William T. Arnold last month worked out an agreement under which Arnold would not oppose probation if Miss Sweate would leave the area.

"To be perfectly candid, Loretta's been to a prison and has had the training to be a beautician, but apparently it didn't take in her case," Arnold said Friday.

"We could see no alternative," he added.

Miss Sweate told Judge Mummery from the witness stand that she and her daughter, a minor, plan to move in with her sister in Utah.

Asked after the hearing if she is satisfied with the arrangement, Miss Sweate said, "We don't want to leave, but we feel like under the circumstances we have to."

She was a secretary with the Federal government before she turned to prostitution to make more money. She said in the interview that she will try to rejoin the government. "I don't know if I can because of my record, but I'm going to look into it," she said. "If not the government, maybe something in the way of the church."

The 39-year-old woman's latest brush with the law came the morning of April 1, when she agreed to have sex with an undercover policeman at her East Ocean View apartment. In return, the policeman, who was posing as a doorman at a local bar, was to give her a garden tiller.

The officer testified in General District Court that he and Miss Sweate went into a bedroom and stripped, and that he arrested her before any sexual act could occur. She was convicted in General District Court of soliciting for immoral purposes, maintaining a bawdy performance, and prostitution. She also was indicted on a felony charge of attempted oral sodomy.

Arnold and Espritte worked out a plea-bargain arrangement under which the felony charge would not be prosecuted and Miss Sweate would receive a suspended one-year jail term for the three misdemeanors.

Arnold said Friday that it was "out of a sense of frustration" that he accepted the deal. Espritte, who had represented Miss Sweate for several years, said that he is frustrated, too, but for different reasons.

82

The call came in the middle of the night. Dolores picked up the phone; Rosemary dragged her blanket into the hallway sucking her thumb, waiting for the news.

"He's done it this time, Dolores," Claudine cried. "I don't understand him. Why did he have to do this?"

"Dolores," Rod called from the bedroom, "what is it?"

"It's Claud," she answered, cupping her hand over the mouthpiece. "Something about A. Jacks. I can't get it out of her, but she's pretty upset."

"He's just gone and fucked up everything," she cried. "I know it was him. It had to be him. Who else would have done it?"

"Done what?" Dolores asked, watching Rosemary sit on the floor at her feet. "Claud, will you talk to me for God's sake? You're not making any sense."

"What is it?" Rod asked, standing at Dolores' side, a towel wrapped about his waist. "What's going on?"

"I can't get it out of her," Dolores answered, swallowing, shaking her head. "I can't find out what's happened."

"Here. Give it to me," Rod said, taking the phone out of her hand and placing it in the crook of his shoulder. "Claud?" he said, turning toward the wall, away from Dolores.

Dolores reached down for Rosemary's hand.

"I can't fucking believe it," he answered in a low voice. "I can't believe that asshole."

"What? What happened?" Dolores asked.

The night was chilly and dark, and time had become disoriented by the unexpected ring.

"Of course it was him. It's gotta be him. Who else would have done it?"

217

"Done what?" Dolores asked.

"The shop," he answered. "It's all busted up."

"What happened?" Dolores asked. "What, what happened? What do you mean busted up?" she asked, her chin sticking forward. "What d'you mean?"

"You want me to come over?" Rod asked.

"I don't understand," Dolores said, grabbing Rod by one shoulder, the phone still against his ear. "How did it happen? Why did they call Claudine?"

"I'll be over in a minute," he answered. "Naw. Naw. It's okay. Shhhhhhhhhh," he whispered into the receiver. "Naw, it's gonna be okay, really," he said. "No, really."

"Rod?" Dolores asked, her fingers clutching his shoulder.

"Mom?" Rosemary questioned in a small voice. "Mom?"

"Where're you going?" she asked him as he lowered the phone back into its cradle. She bit her bottom lip, tasted that her nose was running.

"I think I have to go over there," he shook his head "She's sure it's him what's done it. All the windows of La Boudoir are busted out. She's sure it's A. Jacks. She's kinda scared."

"It coulda been the niggers," Dolores answered. "They don't like the place much. It coulda been the niggers . . ."

"I'm goin' over there, Dolores," he answered, walking into the bedroom, reaching into the closet for his white shirt on a metal hanger. "I think she needs me. I think he could come back tonight and kill her. I think I owe it to her to be there with her."

"You don't owe her nothing," Dolores answered, following him into the bedroom. "You don't owe her a damn thing. I'm the one you owe. I'm the one who opened up and let you into my damn life. Goddamnit, I'm the one you owe."

"She needs me," he answered, bending forward to catch sight of himself in the dressing table mirror. "What do you want me to do? Ignore her? What do you want me to do?"

"We'll all go." Dolores answered, reaching for her robe on the floor at the side of the bed. "Come on, Rosie," she said, "put on your bathrobe. We're going over Claud's."

"No," he said, catching her by the arm as she leaned toward the floor. "No, you don't have to. I can take care of it."

"I want to," she answered. "Rosie . . ."

". . ." he looked at her and said, "I don't want you to . . ."

". . ."

"Mom?"

"The niggers coulda done it . . . ," she answered.

"Do you understand?" he said.

"But," she answered, holding the faded robe against her chest, "it's so late. It's, it's too late. It's three o'clock in the morning."

"Dolores," he swallowed, still holding her arm, "I'm sorry. I didn't know this was gonna happen. I never thought that she would . . . I, I never thought that I would . . ."

"Just," Dolores said, looking up into his face, the moment frozen, *"just get the fuck outa here. Just get the fuck outa my life."*

"Dolores, I never meant . . ."

"Just get the FUCK outa here," she said pulling her arm out of his grasp. *"I want you outa here NOW."*

"But I never wanted it to be . . ."

"NOW," she said.

"Mom?" Rosie said, standing in the doorway.

"Now, before I have to throw you out," she answered.

83

"**B**ut I never thought it would come to that. Do you understand, Jude?" Dolores asked. "Does that make a whole hell of a lot of sense?"

"I don't know," Jude answered, stuffing a rolled army blanket, a deep shade of muddy green, into the side of the trunk.

The radio played, *"It's a little too late for a love song, though I'm lookin' all over the world. . . ."*

"Just seemed like laziness to me all along. Hell," she grunted, pulling herself out of the trunk, "I never thought you two looked right together from the beginning. I don't know why. There just always seemed to be something missing," she shrugged her heavy shoulders, the extra flab of her upper arms shaking.

"It's a little too late for a love song," the radio crooned, *"for this kind of girl."*

"You know what I mean?"

"It's been a long crazed road of passion. . . . A story too fine for my eyes. . . . It's been a second too hard forgotten. . . . It's been some nights of lonely lies."

"Yeah," Dolores answered, slamming the lid closed with both her hands. It made a loud thump, then she wiped the dirt from the car onto her jeans. "I guess I know what you mean. You can't force things, but I never thought it would end in the middle of the night," she laughed in a huff, letting her chin hang down toward the ground as she shook her head.

"It's a little too late for a love song. . . ."

"In the middle of the night, without no warning, not even an explanation," she said, in bewilderment.

Jude pulled a leather cigarette case out of her pants

pocket, selected a smoke, and placed it between her lips. "Aw, that's just Claudine," she said. "You know that. I don't have to tell you that."

Dolores watched the flame flicker from the lighter. "It wasn't her fault," Dolores answered, leaning back against the car. "Really. It wasn't," she said.

"It's a little too late for a love song. . . . Though I'm lookin' all over the world. . . . It's a little too late for a love song. . . . For this kind of girl. . . ."

"Then whose fault was it?" Jude asked, sucking in at the cigarette so that the loose edges broke off into burnt ash. "Whose fault was it?" she asked, looking up at Dolores. "Answer me that?"

"I remember your arms around me. . . . And I know you must remember it too. . . . I remember the child who found me. . . . She looks a lot like you. . . ."

"Mine," Dolores said, letting her arms fall to her side, then immediately catching them up in a cross over her chest. "Mine," she repeated.

"You're a crazy fool, Dolores," Jude answered.

"I was a fool to believe anything would ever come of him," Dolores said, studying the white sky of an early Monday morning. She sucked in the sides of her cheeks.

"It's a little too late for a love song. . . . Though I'm lookin' all over the world. . . . It's a little too late for a love song. . . ."

"I was a crazy fool to believe that anything that wasn't there to begin with could just happen 'cause I wanted it to," she said, then let out a little laugh.

"For this kind of girl. . . ."

"Who the hell did I think I was?" she asked, letting her arms fall to her sides again. "Just who the hell did I think I was?"

"Dolores," Sheila called from midway down the cement staircase, her arms full of kitchen bowls, the glass kind that fit one into another, all balanced over a tiny protruding

221

belly. "You sure you don't want these things in the kitchen? You got a lot, Dolores," she hollered. "You sure you want to leave 'em all behind?"

"Jeff," Dolores said, looking over her shoulder to where the man was stringing a wire clothesline across the backseat of the auto, "go help her," she instructed. "She's gonna fall and hurt herself."

"You keep 'em, honey," Dolores called to Sheila. "I'll collect new. I can't take everything with me," she smiled.

"You sure?" Sheila hollered, holding the bowls against her chest as if she were sure they were going to fall and shatter any second. "You got all kinds of stuff left in the cabinets."

"Keep it, honey," she said, waving her back. "I don't have room for all that junk."

"What about the shop?" Jude asked. "You just gonna let her be manager? Just like that?" she asked, exhaling a long breath of smoke.

Dolores ran her tongue over her upper lip. "Yup," she said, pursing her lips and then inverting them. "Just like that," she smiled.

"Don't it mean nothin' to you?" Jude asked. "Doesn't it mean anything?"

"I don't know, Jude," Dolores answered, uncrossing her arms and watching Sheila ascend the steps. "Does it mean anything to you?"

Jude had smoked her cigarette down to its filter. She inspected the edge, then let it fall to the ground, stomped on it. "It's just fast, that's all, Dolores," Jude answered. "I can't believe you'd just walk out on it without thinking."

"I've been thinking for years, Jude," Dolores smiled, her feet sliding out from under her as she leaned against the rear of the car. "It's just that everybody thought there was a bubble in this head cause I didn't say nothing, didn't do nothing. I never moved, Jude. I just sat here and died."

"Hey, Dolores," Jeff said, sweating even in the cold

morning air, his face reddied, "you sure you don't want all that furniture up there? You could sell it and get something for it."

"Nah," she said, slapping her own shoulder, "I don't want it. You and Sheila enjoy it. Name the kid after me," she smiled.

"What if it's a boy?" he asked.

"Shit," she grinned. "Name it after me anyway."

Jeff laughed, watched her face closely.

"You gotta contract, Dolores."

"Let 'em stuff their contract," Dolores said, standing away from the automobile. "They'll get over it just fine," she answered. "Where's Rosie?"

"I think she went over to say goodbye to Claudine's kid," Jeff answered. "I think that's what she said."

"Shit," Dolores said. "I'm ready to go."

Jude just stared at her, then put out her hand, palm up. "I'll turn the key into the landlord for you," she said, "if you want me to."

"Yeah," Dolores said, swallowed, then dug deep down in her pants pocket. "That's a good idea, Jude. Thanks."

"I'll explain things," Jeff said. "It won't be no problem. You write, send an address along, I'll send you the deposit."

"Okay," she said, looking up at her apartment, "thanks," she said.

84

She pulled out on the highway, the car so packed and weighted that she could hardly see out the rear windshield. Beside her Rosemary rested her chin on the dashboard, staring vacantly at the road ahead. "Where're we goin', Mommy?" she asked, turning to face Dolores, her cheeks resting on a small hand.

"Sit back," Dolores answered. "If I have to stop short, you go right through the windshield. I don't want you bein' no road pizza."

The siren blared in her ear. Jeff strode nearby, looking handsome in his blue uniform, but the sound was deafening. The hog burned oil and it smelled.

"Sit back," Dolores ordered. "And I don't wanta have to tell you again."

"Am I ever gonna see Michelle?" Rosemary asked, her mouth in a pucker.

"You'll never have to go to the beach on a Monday again," Dolores answered, turning to face her child.

The siren blared.

"But am I ever gonna see Michelle again?"

"Maybe when you grow up," Dolores said, "you'll come back."

"When's that?" Rosemary asked, her hands in fists beneath her ears.

Then there was sudden silence as the hog turned away, and the tunnel was dark and long and empty. The Chesapeake Bay Bridge Tunnel was a seventeen-mile stretch to another part of the world. A real manmade wonder.

Dolores reached for the radio, clicked it on, but no sound came out. They were too far under already.